# BLOOD MONEY

## Murder In Memphis

a novel by

James C. Paavola

**Follow Lieutenant Julia Todd
in the first three books in
the "Murder In Memphis" series:**

### The Chartreuse Envelope

"...an intricately plotted mystery thriller...Sleuthing is engaging...Paavola keeps the action coming and his characters consistently interesting..."—*Kirkus Discoveries* (2010)
"...well thought out...riveting...couldn't put it down."—*Colonel Lori Bullard, Memphis Police Department Precinct Commander, Union Station* (2010)

### They Gotta Sleep Sometime

"...a brisk, engaging whodunit...Todd is a well-drawn heroine...The plot sizzles as case leads and shady characters smoothly integrate themselves into the author's grand design and rousing conclusion. An assured soft-boiled sequel steeped in revenge, cold-blooded murder and contemporary calamities."—*Kirkus Discoveries* (2011)

### Which One Dies Today?

"After a flurry of explosions lights up the streets of Memphis, Lt. Julia Todd and her team of investigators have to play catch-up to stop the bombers before the next strike...but they always seem to find themselves a half step behind—too slow to stop the bomb but close enough to feel the flames... The action is electric: There's no shortage of bombs and smart, intense sleuthing. A fun, keep-you-up-at-night thrill ride"—*Kirkus Reviews* (2012)

# Acknowledgements

I want to express my sincere gratitude to my wife Marilyn, for her continued encouragement and constructive feedback...To our daughter Shannon Paavola who once again designed the book cover...To Bradley Harris who, for the fourth time, edited my work...Thanks also to Charlie Lambert for attempting to teach me something about money laundering and the role of the federal government... And to our daughter Nicole and her husband Jerry Penley for advising this technophobe about computers. To all of you—Thanks. The portrayal of the computer technology and money laundering within this book is my responsibility alone. Lord knows, they tried.

# DEDICATION

This book is dedicated to Bridgette Ann Amalfitano Correale—a **Life Force** who immersed herself in family, friends, Our Lady of Perpetual Help church, cooking, charitable causes, and life. She had the ability to take over a room with her stories, her humor, her compassion, and her signature uninhibited laugh. And, when the occasion called for it, she could teach sailors a few new words. Bridgette and her husband Vince owned and operated the Brooklyn Bridge Italian Restaurant in Memphis, Tennessee. For over 25 years, Bridgette welcomed customers into their family restaurant—a down-to-earth woman who nurtured others through laughter, hugs, and food. Bridgette died of cancer May 19, 2012 at age 72.

## Chapter 1

# Never Know What You'll Find

*Saturday, May 16, 2009...no good deed.* Julia fished in her pocket for the key as she climbed the porch steps, but stopped when she saw the door cracked open. She looked around quickly, moved to the door, and pushed it open gradually, a faint musty scent drifted out, the darkness of the living room contrasted with the sunlit porch. She listened hard—nothing. Surely no burglar's in here in broad daylight on a weekend with lots of neighbors outside, she thought. Maybe Aunt Louise asked a neighbor to check the house. But, still...

Julia moved slowly through the doorway—her steps soft, measured, trying not to let the floor's usually comforting groans and creaks announce her presence. Her eyes adjusted. The living room and the dining room looked unchanged. She continued, senses alert. Stepping guardedly into the kitchen, Julia caught a blurred movement coming down from her left. Her body instinctively swayed back like a fencer avoiding a thrusting foil, feet anchored in place. She felt a puff of air as a knife blade flashed inches from her face. Julia sprung back through the entrance, eyes wide. The assailant's hand returned, driving the point of the blade upward, directly at her midsection. Julia shot both arms straight in front of her, blocking a sweaty forearm. The blade sliced into her right arm. She held tightly with her left hand, her grip with the right insecure, only her fingernails digging into flesh. She stepped back on her right foot, and snapped a quick kick into what she hoped was a knee. A man howled. For a second, his arm relaxed. Julia grabbed his wrist with her right hand, slid her left to his armpit, twisted, and leveraged the man forward, slamming his face into the lower cabinet doors. His painful cries ceased. A switchblade spun on the floor, in slow motion. Stopped.

***

Memphis Police Sergeants Anthony Marino and Johnnie Tagger arrived minutes apart—Tagger, a tall African American, workout shorts and wick-away T-shirt showcasing his muscular build, and his Caucasian partner Marino, fresh from the public library, his stomach gently straining the buttons on his white dress shirt. Four patrol cars had already made the scene, surrounding an ambulance. They found their boss inside directing traffic.

"He's groggy, but his vitals look okay, Lieutenant." said the paramedic. "He has a few loose teeth and his nose is broken."

"You might need a cervical collar," said Julia. "He hit the cupboard pretty hard with his face."

"Good call," said the paramedic. "I'll get one."

"Oh," said Julia, "and you'll probably need something to stabilize his knee while you're at it."

"Lieutenant," said Marino, hurrying in. "You all right?"

"He got me with a knife," Julia said, holding up her bandaged arm. "Paramedic said I'll need stitches."

"What the hell happened?" Tagger asked.

"Just came over to open up the house for my aunt, and this joker takes a couple of swipes at me with a switchblade," said Julia. "I'm surprised to see you two."

"Teresa," said Marino. "She heard the officer needs assistance call to this address, and recognized it as your aunt's place."

"She at the station?" Julia said.

"I'm not sure," said Marino. "But she always seems to know what's going on."

"Hey, Lieutenant," said Tagger. "Have you taken a good look at this clown? If you straighten out his nose, he looks an awful lot like the person-of-interest sketch we put out on the guy who's been beating up and robbing senior citizens."

"The one who killed the eighty year-old woman?" said Marino.

"That's what I'm thinking," Tagger said.

"I'll be damned," said Julia. "And my aunt was supposed to be here instead of me. I don't want to think about that."

"According to his wallet, he's Wilbur Sanderson," Tagger said.

"Lieutenant," said the paramedic. "We'll take Sanderson to the MED to get checked out. Can we get someone to ride along?"

"You got it," said Julia, pointing to one of the officers. "Make sure you keep him handcuffed to the bed."

"It'll be a while before he's cleared and transported to *201* for booking," said Marino.

"Yeah," said Tagger, "I'll get cleaned up and meet y'all down there."

"Remember to go to the ER, Lieutenant," said Marino. "You don't want to be messing around with a wound like that. You don't know where that knife's been."

"Appreciate the concern, professor," said Julia. "I'll take care of it. Promise."

# Two-O-One

*201 Poplar Avenue, the Shelby County Criminal Justice Complex*...Julia, Marino, and Tagger met in the large complex known simply as *201*, and made their way to the interrogation rooms.

They looked at Sanderson through the two-way mirror. He sat in a wheelchair, his nose taped, lip cut, face and forehead bruised and swollen.

"He looks worse than I remember," said Julia.

"That's Mr. Bernquist's doing" Tagger said. "You know, the husband of the murdered woman? He heard about the arrest and went to the MED to see for himself. Told the hospital staff MPD had asked him to come down and identify a person-of-interest in his wife's murder. They led him to Sanderson's room. Bernquist grabbed a bedpan and began wailing on Sanderson's head and face. He got in five or six licks before the officer pulled him off."

"Five or six licks?" said Julia. "How incompetent is this officer that he or she couldn't stop an eighty year-old man?"

"Don't think he tried very hard," said Tagger. "But he did call for medical attention."

"Sanderson needed treatment?" Julia said.

"Not Sanderson," said Tagger. "Bernquist was sucking air, looked like he was having a heart attack. They helped him get one of his nitroglycerin pills under his tongue, and sent him home after an hour's observation."

Julia shook her head and sighed. "Let's do this thing." She and Tagger entered the interrogation room while Marino observed.

"You the bitch who did this to me?" said Sanderson.

"Depends," said Julia. "You the SOB who tried to kill me, in my own home?"

"I'll get you," Sanderson said. "I've got plenty of friends. And you'll need more than this big-ass jock to protect you."

"After looking at you, tough guy," said Tagger, "I don't think the Lieutenant needs any help."

"Some crazy old bastard beat me with a bedpan when I was handcuffed to the bed," said Sanderson. "I'll sue his ass."

"You sure you want it getting around that an eighty year-old man with a bad heart beat the crap out of you?" said Julia.

"You think this is funny, bitch?" Sanderson said. "We'll see who's gonna be laughing out the other side of her head."

"You're going away for a very long time," Julia said. "Going to a place where you can't hurt any more old folks and women."

"I want my lawyer," Sanderson said. "Now!"

***

*Friday…a plea bargain.* The officers sat around a conference table, Assistant District Attorney Robert H. Diggs at the head.

"I've got good news and bad news," said Diggs.

"Good news first," said Julia.

"You caught the man responsible for the rash of aggravated burglaries and battery targeting senior citizens, including the death of Mrs. Bernquist," said Diggs.

"And the attempted murder of a police officer," said Marino.

"Yes, Sergeant," said Diggs. "That too."

"And the bad news?" said Julia.

"I finalized a plea agreement," said Diggs. "Sanderson will plead guilty to all counts except murder."

"And in return?" said Tagger.

"He does twenty years, no parole," said Diggs. "I really don't think we could get more than second degree murder, given Mrs. Bernquist died of complications due to an existing medical condition. And even then, he could be eligible for parole. Besides, this deal saves us the hassle and expense of a trial."

"Well, at least he'll be a senior citizen himself when he gets out," said Julia.

"Lieutenant," said Diggs. "He's still worked up about the beating he took from you. His attorney couldn't keep him quiet. Says he has friends in high places and that you'll pay. He only shut up when I told him one more threat against a Memphis Police Officer and it'd be twenty-five years without parole. Watch your back, Lieutenant. Just in case."

## Chapter 3

# Hide the Dongle

*Tuesday, May 26, 2009...time to pay the piper.* Two agents escorted an attractive African-American woman into the building. Everyone around them wore a holstered gun. Security pads on each door. Long, windowless corridors. The crisp echoes of her high heels softened as the trio chewed up more of the unending hallway. The woman's posture relaxed, her eyes tracked every movement, her body reacted to the slightest sounds—electronic beeps and soft metallic clicks of doors opening, closing. The trio stopped in front of a door, 127 C stenciled above the security pad. The male agent swiped his security badge and punched in a five-digit code. When the lock clicked, he opened the door and entered. The female agent nodded to the woman to follow. Special Agent Anita Davenport sat behind a desk, pen in hand—mid-forties, short brown hair, light make-up, a dark blue long-sleeve blouse, an authoritative presence.

"Ah. Welcome to Langley, Dr. Mitchell," said Davenport, setting down her pen. "We've been waiting for you."

No response.

"Any problems?" Davenport said as she turned to the agents.

"No, ma'am," said the female agent. "Mitchell's been the perfect guest all year—obeying the rules, brushing up on her languages, learning the customs of the various countries, exercising, and keeping up with the stock markets."

"Now we'll see just how good she is," said Davenport. "And the doctor, here, will stay out of prison by providing an invaluable service to her country. If all goes according to plan over the next five days or so, you can prep your safe house for another guest of the government. Thank you."

The two agents left.

Davenport gestured for Mitchell to sit. "You and I are going to become close friends, the next few days."

"Can't say I'm looking forward to it," Mitchell said.

"Believe me, Dr. Mitchell, this is nothing anyone would look forward to. You'll want to hang on my every word. Your life will depend on it."

"Charleze," she said softly.

"What's that?"

"Charleze. Since we're going to be so chummy you can call me Charleze."

"Okay, and you can call me Special Agent. Coffee?"

Mitchell shook her head.

"Let's get started. We're on a tight schedule. I'm going to assume the agents didn't tell you much about what the US government is expecting in exchange for keeping your ass out of jail."

Mitchell smiled.

"Yup. You made a deal with the devil, and the devil wants his due. I see from your file you're a fast learner," she said, placing her hand on a thick blue hang folder. "You'd better be. This won't be any cake walk. One misstep and you lose a limb, maybe your life."

Mitchell's stomach tightened. She said nothing.

Davenport eyed her intently. "I understand you speak several languages," she said.

"Five, fluently. I can read a few others."

"And that includes Arabic? Specifically, speaking and reading literary Arabic?"

Mitchell nodded.

"Good. Very good." Davenport leafed through the blue folder. "You've got a PhD in business, rode the fast track on Wall Street. Ran your own hedge fund. Made hundreds of millions…before you went belly up. Allegations you used industrial espionage and insider trading to manipulate the stock market, not to mention the five murders in Memphis. I see the name of a colleague of mine. His office is in New York City. You remember FBI Special Agent Lawrence Masterson?"

"I've heard the name. Don't remember meeting the man."

"He worked your case. Even moved down to Memphis for a while to assist the local police. He's the kind of guy takes everything personal—the murders, the fraud. I bet, even after a year, he's still pissed your attorney got the murder charges thrown out. Probably plans to be at your trial next month, sitting in the front row."

No response.

"Okay, let's move on. Ever hear of Hakam Bin Kadar al-Ahmad?"

Mitchell shook her head.

"A powerful man in the underworld. People in the business call him, *the Judge.* He's smiling in almost every picture we have. Come to think of it, you're smiling in almost every picture I've seen of you. I asked our chief psychologist about people who smile all the time. You know what she said?"

Mitchell smiled. "I suppose they're happy?"

"Actually, she went into a lot of psychobabble about disarming defense mechanisms, poor relationships with parents…usual stuff. But the one thing she said stuck with me is that when a person I don't know smiles at me, I should count to three before making any assumptions. And during those three seconds, I should study their eyes. Like right now. You're mouth is smiling but your eyes aren't. In fact, I'd say your eyes are scared."

Mitchell lost her smile. Her eyes flashed anger.

Davenport raised her eyebrows, then smiled. "Anyway, as I was saying, the Judge has a wonderful smile. He's charming, engaging, and like a colorful snake, extremely dangerous. Makes your *alleged* crimes look like child's play. He runs an international money laundering business for drug lords, gun runners, terrorist organizations, and even a few terrorist nations. Each year he moves well over a hundred billion illicit dollars through legitimate banks. He gets a cut, banks get a cut, and the bad guys get the bulk of their money back—laundered. For kicks, he also dabbles in the markets, preferring to improve his odds with insider information."

"And this involves me how?"

"As it turns out, the Judge has just had a few vacancies in his cadre of techies. Seems they flew too close to the sun. Found the allure of money overwhelming—the allure of the Judge's money. No one's seen or heard from them since last Friday. We can only surmise."

Mitchell's breathing quickened.

"Lucky for us the vacancy leaves the Judge short of expertise in playing the markets. And thanks to you, we have someone the Judge would love to have in his circle."

"What do I have to do?"

"Pretty much what you've been doing. Except you'll need to be more careful. The Judge is not as forgiving as your Uncle Sam, and he's far more paranoid." Davenport let that sink in. "We've put the word out on you. Seems you've skipped town on your bail just days before your trial, and gone into hiding. We know the Judge will be enticed by your skills, and we're hoping he'll buy our cover story. If so, he should be pressuring all his informants to find you within a day or so. He'll want to have a little chat."

"What do I tell him?"

"Nothing. We'll take care of that. In the meantime, we have maybe five good days to prepare you."

"Prepare me?"

"So many things could go wrong. Dead wrong, you might say. It's incumbent upon us to prepare you. We've sunk lots of time and money into this project in the hopes we'd find someone just like you. Now that you're here, all systems are go." She paused. "It might be helpful for you to think of this as a game. A game with life-and-death consequences. But a game all the same."

"What kind of game?"

"Let's call it *Hide the Dongle.*"

Mitchell knitted her eyebrows, and looked away, lips pursed.

Davenport stood, motioning to Mitchell. They left through a back door, opening onto yet another windowless hallway. Davenport stopped before a door on her right, sliding her badge through the security slot and punching in her code. The lock clicked open. She waived Mitchell in ahead. An elderly Caucasian man adjusted items on a table—a high-powered computer positioned in the middle of a bank of monitors, a pencil, a single sheet of paper, one worn sandal, and a glass bowl of what appeared to be small, rectangular, black jelly beans.

"Dr. Charleze Mitchell, this is *The Amazing* Fred Preston," said Davenport.

"Pleased to meet you, Doctor," said Preston, using both hands to shake hers.

"In his day, Fred was quite a performer, specializing in prestidigitation."

"In what?" Mitchell said.

"Sleight of hand. Magic," said a smiling Preston, holding up the bracelet he'd taken off Charleze when they shook hands.

Mitchell frowned, held out her hand. He let the bracelet drop.

"Not bad, Fred," said Davenport. "I was watching and I still didn't see you take it."

"This is the game?" Mitchell said. "I'm supposed to be the shill in a pickpocket show?"

"You're certainly attractive enough to distract the audience," said Preston, still smiling.

"Pay attention, Charleze," Davenport said. "Our techies have developed an amazing virus. Or is it a Trojan horse? I forget. Anyway, they tell me this program is *smokin*. And they've created a type of paper that will stay rigid enough to upload the virus, but within days the paper will disintegrate, releasing an acid which in turn will reduce the microscopically fine wiring to powder. There'll be no obvious sign it was ever there. The program allows us to enter a computer without triggering any alerts, send every scrap of information to one of our satellites without leaving a record of the transaction, unleash this super destructive virus wiping out all the data whenever we tell it to, and then just disappear. It's all packaged in this ultra-small black paper thingy." She dropped something on the table. It bounced with a soft tapping sound, like a cheap toy from a *Crackerjack* box.

Mitchell watched intently.

"Our next step is much easier," said Davenport. "We simply need to plug the black thingy—"

"Dongle," interrupted Mitchell, her gaze fixed on the

black paper object.

"Yes…dongle," said Davenport. "We simply need to plug the dongle into the computer. But as these things go, it's not that simple. The computer is always being monitored."

"Monitored?" Mitchell said.

Preston walked to a projector and flipped a switch. A sketch appeared on the white board.

"This is what the Judge's computer room looks like. At least it's our best guess," Davenport said.

"You don't know?" said Mitchell.

"Not really," Davenport said. "But anyway, it's our best guess. Take a good look. The network consists of a large central computer in one corner of the room, kitty-corner from the doorway. Two screens sit on either side, dwarfed by the computer's monitor. The screens correspond to the four smaller satellite computers evenly spaced around the walls. One's dedicated to international smuggling operations—drugs, guns, human trafficking. One handles dirty money taken by bankers, investment organizations, mobsters, gangs, etc. Another is devoted to terrorist organizations and countries being sanctioned by free world countries, seeking to hide their wealth. And the fourth is committed to the world's stock and bond markets. This room is staffed fourteen hours a day, with cameras going twenty-four/seven."

Mitchell's skin felt tingly, as goose bumps covered her limbs and neck.

"It gets even more exciting," said Preston. "Money is no object for the Judge. Everything is state-of-the-art. In addition to the computer network and cameras, there is a sophisticated full body scanner located outside the door, just like the ones the TSA is encouraging the big US airports to install next year. Each staff member is scanned going in and coming out. If there are any questions, they are wanded with handheld metal detectors, and sometimes they're strip-searched."

"We needed a way to get the dongle into the room and into the central computer without being caught," Davenport said. "We asked Fred to help us."

"So Fred's going to do this?" asked Mitchell.

"Oh, no, love," said Preston. "You are."

"Fred's going to teach you how to play hide the dongle," said Davenport. "Think of it as a video game. You have to sneak past the monsters at the gate, outwit the vampires in the living room, find the evil king's key, enter his treasure room, avoid the poison darts, and find the button that will take you home—alive."

"I'm glad you're having a good time, Special Agent," Mitchell said. "This doesn't feel like a game to me."

"Take it easy, love," Preston said. "I'm going to make sure you come through this in one piece. I promise."

"Yes, Fred will take care of you," said Davenport. "But only if you buckle down and learn *everything* he has to teach you. You stay here for the rest of the day. I'll send food in. Just knock on the door if you need to use the facilities. An agent will escort you. I'll be back at six o'clock to see how you're coming along." The door clicked shut behind her.

Preston picked up a dongle and placed it in Mitchell's hand. "From now on you carry this with you everywhere," he said. "Get used to the feel of it. Know which end is the male end. Be able to orient the dongle so the outside end is at your fingertips, right side up, the one with the tiny nipple. Alternate left and right hands."

Charleze moved the dongle around in her left hand, using her thumb and fingers. Its small size and lack of weight made it difficult to register neurologically. She turned her hand over, palm down, squeezing where she thought the dongle would be. The dongle fell.

"Damn. I can't even feel this thing."

"Keep at it," Preston said, handing her a second dongle from the glass bowl. "Your brain will adjust and sensitize your fingers. Take this one in your right hand."

***

"I understand you know your way around computers, Dr. Mitchell. Certainly much better than I do," Preston said. "The tower on this model stands upright behind the monitor. Without looking, describe it for me."

"On this particular model, there are probably six USB ports facing away from the monitor. Each of these monitors should have a line plugged in to a port."

"So, there would be two open USB ports?"

"That depends on what other equipment is run through this computer."

"Let's assume there's at least one open port. Still not looking, orient the dongle in your left hand, reach around, and insert it."

Mitchell reached. She made several attempts, each time dropping the dongle.

"I don't have any more feeling in my fingers," Mitchell said. "I can't even tell if I'm still holding them."

"Time for a little rest," Preston said. "But don't put the dongles down—one in each hand, keep them moving. Okay, let's back up a bit. You need a way to conceal the dongle, a way to get it into the room." He handed her the sandal. She grasped it awkwardly as she continued to hold the dongles, balancing it off her chest. "This is a classic style sandal from the Middle East," he said. "Inspect it carefully."

"What am I looking for?"

"Run your fingertips over every part of it. Do you feel any lumps, cracks, any imperfections?"

"Just the stitching."

"If you were going to hide the dongle in the sandal, where could it fit?"

Mitchell rotated the sandal. "The only place I can see is the heel," she said. "But it's not here."

Preston smiled widely. "It's one of my better jobs. There is, in fact, a dongle in that sandal. Indeed, in the heel."

Mitchell pushed and scratched every part of the heel—nothing. "I give up."

Preston took the sandal, pressed his thumb into the worn big toe indentation and tapped on the inside of the heel. A spring-loaded drawer popped out, revealing a dongle.

"I'll be damned," she said.

"I certainly hope it doesn't come to that," he said, smiling. He closed the drawer, and inspected the sandal. "The wiring is too fine to be picked up by the metal detector or scanner. And I'm counting on the guards being just as successful as you when they inspect your sandal. First of all, the seal is impeccably tight. Second, it's a two-step process. You must depress your big toe and tap the inside of the heel at the same time. Try it on. I was told you are a size six, yes?"

Chapter 4

# Deliver the Dongle

*Coming into form...*They sat behind the two-way mirror peering into a rectangular area about the size of a large American living room. Not a single picture, painting, or window broke the monotony of the pale yellow walls. Soft lighting bathed the room from a ten-foot ceiling, casting no hot spots, almost no shadows. Furniture and equipment placed against all four walls in keeping with the best-guess scenario. One large, rectangular, wooden desk sat angled across a corner, supporting a twenty-five-inch monitor with a keyboard in front and a tower behind it, USB ports facing the corner. Smaller monitors flanked it, two on either side. Four smaller wooden desks were spaced around the room, one abutting each wall. Each held a single fifteen-inch monitor and a keyboard. The only allowance for comfort came in the form of modern, adjustable, steel-framed cushioned chairs, on wheels. Two cameras hung in the upper corners, one directly above the large wooden desk, the other in the opposite corner. Outside the door stood the latest full body scanner.

"How's she doing?" asked Davenport.

"Impressive. Very impressive," Preston said. "She's a quick study. If I'd had her working with me in the old days, especially with her looks and figure, I'd be famous."

"She's adjusted to the attire—the sandals, the hijab?"

"She's a natural. Probably picked up the culture and dress when she learned the language."

They heard shouts.

"American whore!"

"Yankee slut!"

"Bitch!"

"See? Not a flinch. She's adjusted to the name calling—in English and Arabic," said Preston. "And of course, the guards have been describing in great detail what they plan to do to her during their strip search."

"Everything we can do to make this more realistic is going to improve her chances," said Davenport.

"Watch her extract the dongle. She's getting quite adept at using her other foot to open the drawer. She uses distraction and misdirection when opening the drawer, and takes advantage of random events in the room to collect it."

"Well done, Fred. How about the insertion?"

"Not as good."

"Are we changing the placement of the USB cords to make it a challenge each time?"

"That we are. But coming up with an excuse to leave her satellite computer and walk to the central computer is problematic. Our man is giving her as much grief as possible to keep her in line—telling her what a moron she is, and what he's going to do to her. Charleze keeps working through it. This last time, she crashed her computer in order to seek assistance from him. Then she took her pencil and paper with her as potential distractions. But when she reached around the back of the tower, she couldn't locate the open USB port. Close, but no cigar."

"I'm afraid that kind of near miss falls in the hand grenade camp. Close, but no more Charleze."

Chapter 5

# Akilah

*Charleze, meet Akilah...*Mitchell's flight touched down ahead of schedule at a small airport, near the border between Saudi Arabia and the United Arab Emirates. Her attire matched that of a woman in a religiously moderate Arabian country—an ankle-length skirt and long sleeve blouse of dark colors, as well as a black hijab covering her head. The intense heat took her breath away as she passed through the darkly tinted glass doors. She squinted and shielded her eyes from the blazing sun. A limo squealed into the NO PARK-ING area in front of the entrance, dust plumes trailing. The driver jumped out and ran past, carrying a small cardboard sign and talking angrily, unconcerned who might hear. She recognized his curse words. The CIA had done a good job acclimating her to the language, at all levels. Mitchell guessed the driver had not been aware of the plane's early arrival and was under the gun to find his passenger.

She heard him muttering as he came back. His sign read, *Akilah al-Qasim*—the name on the passport the Judge had arranged, keeping her under the US radar. Odd, she thought, he chose the name Akilah, with more masculine connotations—intelligent, logical, one who reasons.

"I am Akilah," she said in her best Arabic.

The driver's mouth hung open. Without a word, he

frantically opened the back door, grabbed her suitcase, and in his haste practically shoved her in. Akilah wondered what kind of fear could be motivating this man. Perhaps the Judge?

The driver turned away from what appeared to be an ancient town and raced along a stretch of broken blacktop through the stark desert countryside, the large tires muffling the noise as they hit ever-present potholes and buckles. Akilah thought she was looking at a mirage when she caught a glimpse of far off buildings sprouting from the sand, shimmering and waving in the heat. Then they were gone. Ten minutes later they returned, taller, but still shimmering. Another ten minutes and she could easily make out multi-story buildings. A long, high, white wall surrounded them like a frontier fort. Guards armed with automatic weapons waited at the entrance. Her limo was waived through without slowing, and did not stop until it pulled up to a seven-story building. The driver seemed uncomfortable serving women. He awkwardly stole glances at Akilah, expecting her to carry her own bag. One of the doormen relieved her of the suitcase and escorted her into the lobby of what looked like an upscale hotel. Check-in appeared to be a formality. Clearly, she had been expected. The doorman escorted her to her room, a giant step up from her cell-like accommodations inside the CIA complex—spacious, subdued colors, silk bed-covers, both sheer and heavy window coverings, furnishings in classic Middle East style.

She had been cautioned to expect her room to be bugged for sound and video. The reality of her situation welled up in her chest, overtaking her like the cloud of dust that enveloped the abruptly stopped limo. Her heart rate increased. She felt panicky, violated.

Similar feelings had exploded in her some fifteen months earlier—a flashback, a powerful PTSD flashback. She'd held her panic at bay for over twenty-years, since having been sexually molested as a seven-year old girl. Twenty-years since her parents had prostituted her to earn their drug money. Akilah sat in a cool sweat, struggling to compose herself. She turned to the skill which had protected her for so many years—her capacity to wall off feelings, to intellectualize, to compartmentalize, to focus, to be in control. She had become adept at keeping many plates spinning simultaneously, attending to them only as they became a priority. Maybe the Judge knew her better than she knew herself? Maybe her name should be Akilah.

She felt calm returning. Her breathing slowed, her new posture reflected poise, control. She stood, walked casually to the large basket of fruit, and pulled the yellow card.

Hakam Bin Kadar al-Ahmad
will receive you at 7:00 for dinner.

Fahad will collect you at precisely 6:55.

Akilah checked her watch, 5:40. She decided to face her sense of being violated head-on. She compartmentalized her need for privacy and safety, walling them off while she played the game. She would freshen up for her dinner meeting, with the full knowledge one or more cameras would record every inch of her. This would only be an initial concession as there would surely be strip searches, and worse. The game, she thought. All for the game.

Chapter 6

# The Judge

*Tuesday evening…let the game begin.* At precisely seven o'clock her escort rang the doorbell to the second floor of the Judge's penthouse. An armed guard answered the door. No signs of surprise or interest. The escort stepped back, Akilah entered.

"This way," said the guard, leading her across stunning polished marble floors, through opulence rivaling the fanciest mansions—paintings, furnishings, vases, carpets, mirrors, window coverings.

A man waited in the adjoining room. He wore an immaculately white thawb, intricate white stitching embellishing the collar, sleeve cuffs, and bottom of the body-long tunic. His white keffiyeh fell across his shoulders, held in place by a double wrapped black agal. The Rolex was unmistakable, its brilliance enhancing his numerous gold rings. Clear polish covered his medium-length fingernails. A thin beard and moustache framed his face—short, impeccably trimmed. His dark eyes flashed. Although well under six-feet, his bearing exuded confidence and power.

"Akilah," the Judge said, smiling. "So good to finally meet you. To see you in the flesh."

"Thank you for inviting me, sidi," she said with a slight bow.

"Oh, please. We don't need to be so formal. Call me

Hakam," he said. "I approve of your dress, hijab, and the way you walk without striking the ground as it is taught in the Quran. Very respectful. And your Arabic, I can tell already… extraordinary for an American."

"Thank you, Hakam. And thank you for arranging this meeting. Your situation sounds interesting."

"And you are, how do you Americans say it? Between a rock and a tough spot?"

"A rock and a hard place."

"Yes, that's it."

"I guess I am. If I go back to the US I'll be arrested."

They walked into a large open room. Hakam nodded to a man, and a table rose from the floor.

Akilah's eyes widened. She smiled.

"Impressive, is it not? We have so many visitors from different countries. Some are accustomed to eating on the floor, some to eating while sitting on the floor with only a small table, and some accustomed to eating at a high table while seated in a chair, like you Americans. So tonight, since there are only the two of us, I raised this section of the table for you."

"I am honored."

"Please. Be seated," said Hakam, gesturing to the chair across from him.

Akilah sat. "I was surprised to hear from you. How did you find me?"

"It was difficult. But I am not easily deterred. I had this vacancy and I read about you in the Memphis papers."

"You read the Memphis papers?"

"It would be a mistake not to keep up with the news in Memphis, one of the major American transportation routes for trucks and trains, not to mention Federal Express. Many of my best customers make their living using those routes," he said, smiling. "As I was saying, I read about your little… *problem*. I was intrigued. As I understand it, the plan that got you into trouble seemed quite good, actually. Creative. Imaginative. Then with my vacancy I started to think about what I could learn from this Dr. Charleze Mitchell from Wall Street. A hedge fund manager. A person skilled in insider trading and short-selling.

"This vacancy, does it have anything to do with the stock market?"

"Indeed it does. My employee was, shall we say, exploring the profitability of insider trading."

"Why did he leave, if I may ask?"

"I helped him with that decision. I found him stealing from me."

"Oh."

"You Americans have a slang word, *chum*. Are you familiar with this word *chum*?"

"Sure. It means *friend*."

"Do you know it also is the word used when fish are cut into small pieces and used to bait sharks?"

Akilah nodded, slowly.

"Well, my employee did not act alone. So we took him and his chums, and we cut them into small pieces and fed them to the sharks. Chum for chums," he said, smiling.

Akilah counted to three.

"I'm certain you would never do anything like that to me, Akilah," he said still smiling, eyes piercing.

She did not respond, but continued to focus on Hakam's eyes. Not a hint of a smile in those eyes.

"But in case you did, I would enjoy cutting you into tiny pieces myself." With a flourish, he cut a piece of his chicken, letting his menacing smile fade, replacing it with a pleasant one. One with softer eyes. "Please. Try the chicken. Flown in especially for you. More meat than the scrawny birds being raised in Saudi Arabia. It is most delicious."

***

Men cleared the table and brought coffee. One repeatedly glanced at Akilah.

"You may have noticed," Hakam said. "My men do not approve when I dine with women, especially when it is a business dinner.

"An Arab woman's place is with other women, not discussing business with men."

"Just so. The coffee is not too strong?"

"I actually enjoy it this way," said Akilah, taking a sip from her small intricately decorated fenjan.

"Shall we talk a little business?"

"By all means."

"I want to learn from you, Akilah. I am especially interested in beating the stock and bond markets. I want to be able to do what you did from your hedge fund."

"And I would be happy to show you. It would be good to see what technology you are working with, what algorithms you are using, which markets you are playing."

"Ah, yes. I can tell I already like you, Akilah," he said. The smile faded. "But I've stayed alive in my business by being very careful. There are few people I trust. I want to be able to trust you." His smile returned.

"And I you," said Akilah.

"Good. My word is my bond, Akilah. This is my proposition. I want to see you in action, in my computer network, starting like a new employee. You'd learn all about my technology from the inside, and you'd be better able to advise me as to how to train new *employees*. As for me, I'd have the opportunity to observe you in action, and to make sure I can trust you."

"I have no interest in being an employee."
"Understood. This would be short-term. Say, four months?"
"One month."
"Two."
"Deal."

Chapter 7

# Close, As In Hand Grenades

*Prestidigitation…*The Judge's desert high-rise had two floors below ground level. SUBFLOOR 2 housed the living quarters for the employees working in the Judge's computer network—five computer operators, three guards, a repair technician, and two alternate computer operators. Individual sleeping quarters were spartan, not unlike the one Akilah had stayed in at Langley. The computer room sat above, on SUBFLOOR 1.

***

This was Akilah's third day. The CIA's best guess had been accurate as far as the network computer room layout and the body scanner. The only significant difference involved the protective film screens placed on each satellite monitor. These coverings restricted the viewing angles so the screen could only be seen by the person sitting directly in front of the monitor, eliminating prying eyes.

Akilah's mind raced as she scoured the market, searching for ways to make big money, to establish her credibility. The algorithm program she'd recommended had been installed the night before. She needed to select stocks, set automatic buy-sell points, and plug them into the program. The algorithm would monitor each of the assigned stocks and make the trade within milliseconds. No wasted time. Her job would be to continually assess the advisability of maintaining the selected buy-sell points. Akilah turned her attention to ticker MRTX, Morton Therapeutics, a name identified by one of the Judge's insiders as being prime for an unexpected pop in price. She could find no reason to anticipate a jump, but she had to buy, if only to test the accuracy of the insider's tip. She bought one million shares, at $17.24 a share. She became aware of yelling. It's that jerk Layth, she thought. What's *the lion* want now?

"You stupid pig! You bucket of camel dung!" hollered Layth from his large computer complex in the corner. "You can't buy that many shares at one time."

He's seen my purchase on his screen, she thought. And he's challenging my decision. Time to play the game.

"Come here now! You useless bitch."

Akilah positioned her feet, released the dongle. Waiting for the perfect time when eyes had been diverted, secured the dongle, and closed the tiny drawer. She pushed her chair back, grabbing her allotted pencil and single sheet of paper in the right hand, and walked calmly to the corner station. Layth continued his barrage of insults. She approached from the left, placing the paper and pencil on Layth's desk. He reacted instantly, slapping them to the floor. Akilah took advantage, bending down as if to retrieve them, using her right arm and shoulder to obscure her left hand as it shot quickly to the tower in search of an open USB port.

SMACK! Layth smashed her in the side of her face with the back of his hand, knocking her against the wall, and momentarily unconscious.

"The rules, bitch. You know the rules. Never put anything on my desk. You *will* learn."

The other satellite operators watched.

"What the hell are you looking at?" Layth bellowed. "Get

back to work. Now!"

Akilah's eyes fluttered. She closed them tightly, then opened them. The room gradually came into focus. Layth stood over her. Akilah became aware of her left hand, in a fist. Oh no, she thought. I still have the dongle. She gradually opened her fingers. Layth grabbed her left arm, trying to yank her to her feet. Akilah panicked, wide eyes locked on her hand. No dongle. She searched the floor desperately, looking for the dongle as Layth yanked on her, still screaming obscenities.

"You gambled millions of Hakam's dollars," Layth said, so close he sprayed her face with spit. "How could you make such a huge buy? You put my life in danger. I'll make sure he knows you alone made that horrible trade."

Akilah struggled to pick up her paper and pencil while searching for the dongle. Layth kicked her, and she took the opportunity to fall behind the desk. Glancing up she saw the slightest edge of the dongle, secured inside the third USB port. Her brain told her she must be in pain, but she felt none.

The game was well underway.

Chapter 8

# It Works!

*3:00 AM, Friday…I'll be a monkey's uncle.* The telephone woke her from a deep sleep.

"Davenport," she answered, using as much voice as she could force from her dry mouth.

"Special Agent, this is D.J. Wallace in IT. You told me you wanted to know the second we heard…Ma'am?"

"Yeah, Wallace. I remember. What do you have?"

"She did it. Mitchell did it. We're getting a full download from the Judge's computer. More files than we ever dreamed of. You've got to see this."

"Be there in forty. Call Fred Preston. He deserves to see this."

***

Akilah sat at her monitor, pain pounding in her head, willing herself to concentrate during this critical time. She knew the importance of monitoring the rise of the MRTX stock, and predicting the peak price in order to sell her shares, gaining the maximum from her trade. She watched the price rise in rollercoaster fashion—up, down, then up again, approaching a thirteen percent gain. Almost Zen-like, Akilah brought her instincts in sync with the stock. That sixth sense had always been her gift, an edge over other traders. She felt it in her being, and clicked on the SELL button.

Within seconds MRTX's price pulled back, never returning to its high of the day. Akilah allowed herself to relax, to savor the moment. A quick mental calculation yielded a 2.2 million dollar gain. She smiled. Voices interrupted her personal moment of celebration.

Akilah did not turn her gaze from her monitor, afraid Layth would strike her again. Facing forward, she shifted her attention to the sounds that seemed out of place in this high security room. She heard different languages—Spanish, German, an Iranian dialect, and English. Then a familiar voice—the Judge. He must be leading a tour for his customers, she thought. She followed the voices as they moved to Layth's work station. That meant they could be looking at her site. Her fingers made her monitor roil with data—scrolling, changing sites, giving them something to look at. The voices grew louder. Someone tapped her shoulder. Akilah jumped. She turned to see a smiling Judge. She smiled, although her eye was already swollen.

"And this is my latest addition to our network," said the Judge. "Akilah is a master in the stock market. In fact, according to my most recent text," he said, holding up his iPhone. "She made over two million dollars for me just minutes ago." He bowed with his head, never taking his eyes from her.

She returned the bow, her eyes lowered.

***

*5:00 AM, Friday…a gold mine.* Loud voices and laughter spilled out from the IT wing of the CIA complex.

"I can't believe our program worked so well," said Wallace. "We hit the mother lode. Not only that, but everything is already neatly organized, sorted, and packaged. We've got dollar amounts, bank codes, fees, names, addresses, emails, phone numbers—"

"Boss!" a tech interrupted. "Look at this. The dongle

program's even tapped into the cameras."

"Throw it up on the big screen," said Wallace.

A live view from one of the corner cameras appeared on the sixty-inch monitor, high on the wall.

"I'll be damned," said Preston. "Our guys really did get the layout right. And over there, on the side. That's got to be Mitchell."

"You did it, Fred," said Davenport. "We wouldn't have this if you hadn't figured out how to hide the dongle."

"Thank you," said Fred. "But none of it would have happened without that woman right there," he said, pointing.

"Whoa," said Wallace. "We even had back footage from the cameras." He exchanged the real time images on the big screen with older ones. "Here's this dude yelling at Mitchell a few hours ago."

"Right there," said Preston. "She did it. Did you see her? When the lead man turned his attention to the other operators, she secured the dongle. I think this is it. We're going to see her place the dongle in the tower."

The laughter and enthusiasm turned to anguish as they watched Layth knock Mitchell unconscious, then jerk her limp body around trying to pull her up.

"Bastard," muttered Davenport.

"That lead operator's body blocked the view of the camera," said Preston. "But that had to be the moment Mitchell inserted the dongle. No one ever saw it. What an effort."

"Really?" Davenport said. "You think she did it then?"

"Had to be," Wallace said. "It corresponds with the time the information started uploading."

"Holy Shit," said Davenport. "I didn't think she had it in her."

"I knew she did," Preston said. "That's my girl."

***

Hakam sat in front of a large computer monitor displaying images from six of the twenty-four permanent security cameras located in, around, and atop his building. He clicked on the program to sequence through all the cameras, pausing thirty-seconds on each block of six. Something caught his eye. He clicked on the camera outside the computer room. The guards had made Akilah take her clothes off. She stood naked before them. Hakam smiled, taking it all in, starting with her feet and working his way up, enjoying every curve. Then he saw her eyes, staring directly into the camera. His smile disappeared. He couldn't read her expression—fear? No. Contempt. She knows I'm watching, he thought. Hakam felt as if he'd been caught—embarrassed, guilty. Feelings he hadn't experienced since adolescence. A guard grabbed Akilah's breast. Hakam snatched up his cell and punched speed dial.

"Yes, sidi," answered Fahad.

"The guards are strip searching Akilah," barked Hakam. "Order them to stop immediately. She is not to be strip searched, nor is she to be touched. Do you understand?"

"It will be done, sidi."

Hakam tried to understand. Why did I give that order? he asked himself. Why should I care about any woman, about this American woman? Do I wish I was the one touching her? Could I be jealous? He watched as the guards backed away sharply, ordering Akilah to get dressed.

Hakam's smile did not return.

Chapter 9

# Half-Time

*Atta girl*...Fahad collected Akilah from SUBFLOOR 2. At precisely 7:00 PM he rang the doorbell. A security guard opened the door and led her to the dining room. Hakam stood on the opposite side of his raised table.

"Akilah," he said, extending his hand. "I am so glad to see you.

"Sidi," she said, taking his hand lightly with a slight bow of her head.

"Please," he said. "Call me Hakam."

Akilah looked up. "As you wish."

"Sit, sit, sit," he said. "We have much to talk about. But first, let's eat."

As if on cue, men appeared with trays of food and drink. Hakam remained motionless, his expression impenetrable, his eyes fixed on Akilah. She sensed danger, struggling to compartmentalize her fear, telling herself to play the game. The men left. Hakam picked up his knife, held it point-up for a few seconds, and then cut his lamb. Akilah breathed deeply, picked up her utensils and placed a small portion on the back of her fork.

Hakam said nothing during the meal.

***

Two men cleared the table, one returned with coffee.

"That's better," said Hakam. "I find it is always better to talk on a full stomach. Don't you?"

"Remember I am an American," said Akilah. "My country's women have a habit of talking incessantly during a meal."

"This is so," Hakam laughed. "Not unlike our women. I have seen many of your movies. But I don't remember watching American women talk business over a meal."

"You are a keen observer, Hakam. Although women have many more freedoms in America, most business is still handled by men. Perhaps we will learn the ways of men as more of us enter the world of business."

"You, too, are a keen observer," he said, smiling for the first time.

Akilah sipped her coffee.

"I must admit, I've been surprised. Pleasantly so. I did not expect you to have so much success. You have made me a great deal of money, in a very short time. And I never dreamed you'd be so courageous in your trading. You are fearless, and your timing flawless. You buy and sell like no man I have ever seen. And you shame poor Layth. He may never recover."

Akilah managed a smile, overcoming an urge to touch her face where Layth had struck her. "I am glad you are pleased."

"By the way, I apologize for his being so rough on you. He, too, had never seen such a skilled trader in action."

"I never forget when someone strikes me," she said.

Hakam bowed his head slightly.

"You came in with that group of men," she said. "They are all clients?"

"Yes. And after hearing how much money you made, several wanted to hire you away from me," he said, smiling. "It is rare such different men find themselves in the same room."

"Because they speak different languages?"

"There's that. But for the most part these are men who have no respect for anyone else's perspective. They are all about using others for their personal gain."

"That *is* sad. These men can neither trust nor be trusted. Can I assume they are dangerous men?"

Hakam looked pensive, then smiled. "Yes, I suppose we are."

Akilah said nothing as she began to count, watching his eyes.

"An interesting group. If you had looked you would have seen one very tall person and one very short person. The tall man is actually from Memphis, Tennessee—a banker. The short man, shorter than you, heads the largest cartel in Mexico."

Hakam sipped his coffee.

Akilah waited.

"The tall man uses his size to intimidate. The small man, I believe, has devoted much of his life proving himself, compensating for his size. His cartel has many men, many guns. I would be surprised if I ever saw the tall man alive again."

"That would mean fewer customers."

"Indeed," he said, studying her intently. His smile returned. "We agreed on two months. You have one month remaining."

Akilah nodded.

"I want you to train a few of my people. Teach them about your algorithm and your sense of timing, or at least the cues they should be watching for."

"I can do that."

"I'm thinking it would be better to assign women to you. I am afraid our men would have...*difficulty* taking instruction from a woman, especially a woman of such talent and courage, so intimidating in our culture."

"I'd prefer that myself."

"So, August second will be your last day. I will be sorry to see you go. Not only am I a richer man because of you, I have enjoyed your company."

"And I yours." For an instant, Akilah imagined Hakam watching the videos of her naked body, but she quickly shut it out.

"And one more thing, Akilah. I am a generous man to those who have served me well. I have already wired a sizable sum to a Venezuelan bank in your name. If you continue to perform as well, I will wire more."

She bowed slightly. "I am truly grateful."

## Chapter 10

# Son of Dongle

*Two-part harmony…*Wallace reviewed every line of code for the fifth time. He smiled broadly. *This baby's gonna work,* he thought. *We just have to upload her into the banks' computers and she'll coordinate with our original dongle.*

The lock on the door clicked open. Davenport walked in. "You wanted to see me, Wallace?"

"Yes, Special Agent. I think it's ready."

"You think?"

"I *know* it's ready."

"Okay, so how does this whatchamacallit work?"

"Let's call it Dongle II."

"You mean more of those little black things?"

"Don't need that kind of security. This program is loaded onto a thumb drive of the standard bank examiner's forms, the ones they use when interfacing with the bank's computers. The bank computers won't record the Dongle II upload and, as soon as it's uploaded, the program will be deleted from the thumb drive, leaving no trace."

"You're grinning like the Cheshire Cat. So, what does Dongle II do? Does it talk to Dongle I?"

"This is so cool," he said. "Not only will they talk, they'll harmonize. Better than Billy Joel. The crooks at the various dirty banks will click on ENTER to wire the laundered funds to Costa Rica or wherever. Records at both the sending and receiving banks will confirm a transaction. But the money itself will be wired here to Langley."

"You shitting me?"

"We'll have to construct a new building to hold all that dough."

"How much money we talking?"

"From what we've seen coming from the Judge, I'm guessing eighteen, twenty billion every month."

"Twenty *billion!*"

"No one will be the wiser until they try to withdraw money from the receiving banks. And since these guys have a boatload of money there already, I'm hoping no bells and whistles will go off for months."

"And in the meantime, we're still collecting data on everyone involved?"

"Absolumundo. You'll be able to swoop in anytime you want. We'll have up-to-date documentation on all the players, as well as huge amounts of their unlaundered money. So by law, since it'll still be dirty money, we can impound it. Use it to build me a larger lab with all the latest technology."

"Cool your jets, Wallace. There'll be lots of people in line for that confiscated money."

"A guy can dream, can't he?"

"Okay, dreamer, how long before all these programs are uploaded?"

"My understanding is the Judge's banks are already scheduled for routine examinations by the FDIC, the Comptroller of the Currency, or the Federal Reserve depending on whether they're state, national, or international banks. We just need to assign one of our folks to each of those teams. So, maybe four weeks."

"Good. Mitchell's scheduled to get cut loose by the Judge

in about ten days. She should be in the clear long before anything hits the fan."

## Chapter 11

# Political Realities of Cooperation in DC

*New York office of the FBI's Economic Crimes Unit...*Special Agent Lawrence Masterson's phone rang.

"Lawrence, this is Anita," Davenport said. "I need help."

"The FBI lives to bail out our cousins in the CIA," said Masterson. "What've you got yourself into this time, Anita?"

"For almost two years we've been tracking a guy who calls himself the Judge. He's a huge player in the international money laundering game, moving close to a quarter of a trillion in US dollars annually through his network of banks. His clients are diverse and their crimes fall under the responsibility of the majority of our alphabet agencies, including yours. But I've been unable to gain a single agency's cooperation, because it wasn't *their* idea. They want full credit or they won't participate."

"Sounds like our inefficient government at its bureaucratic worst."

"Lawrence, this is a monster operation. The amount of money they process is unimaginable. And that's just the laundered money. The Judge's clients are the dregs of humanity—terrorists, countries supporting terrorism, financially sanctioned governments, organized crime, drug suppliers, gunrunners, human traffickers, human smugglers, bootleggers, bulk cash smugglers, insider stock traders, and probably a few others that've slipped my mind. A high percentage of the smuggling and trafficking involves the US. And just as a sidebar, these clients murder tens of thousands every year."

"Congratulations," he said. "You've made a real find. As for the alphabets, off the top of my head I can think of at least eight agencies that have a puppy in this race—sometimes the same puppy."

"I counted over a dozen, when I included umbrella departments like Treasury, Homeland, and Justice."

"Lots of overlap…or should I say lots of opportunities for cooperation and coordination."

"I'm so frustrated. No one has the guts to jump on board with the CIA," she said. "Everyone's so damned afraid of losing their little brass nameplate and corner office. They're so skittish, scared of getting involved outside their defined sphere of influence, scared they're being set up, scared they won't get credit, scared when things go south they'll be left holding the bag. How do I break through to all these wimpy political appointees?"

"They need a political life-and-death reason to join in. Like, what happens when the CIA goes public with all this information and the other agencies get caught with their drawers around their ankles? They'd all be doing the beltway cha-cha when the media learns they knew about the Judge but decided he wasn't worth their time."

"So, I need to make a strong political case for joining in that'll trump the political rationale they're using to do nothing?"

"Remember the press'll be all over this, Monday morning quarterbacking every move. We alphabets don't want to be on the wrong side of that public second guessing, especially the political appointed agency heads."

"Okay, how can I make it happen?"

"You need a reasonably neutral sponsor for a meeting, preferably outside DC. The Federal Reserve Bank of New York has taken on that role in the past. Let the agencies know you'll be sharing the data you already have—a good faith gesture, something the CIA's not usually known for. Get as many alphabets in one room as you can. Make those rabbits afraid *not* to be involved. Give them a sense of a sure win, something that'll give 'em points with the President—positive points if they join in, and negative points if they don't."

"If I can get a meeting, will you back me up?"

"Only if you serve those fancy pastries. Now, how about filling me in on just what information you have…"

## Chapter 12

# Busy Weekend For the Bad Guys

*6:35 PM, Friday…one final withdrawal.* The last of the federal agents headed to the elevators, pushing carts loaded with computers and files. Terence Porter stared out the seventeenth-floor window of the Morgan Keegan Tower in downtown Memphis, searching for reality. He watched a towboat negotiate a group of barges down the Mississippi on its way to New Orleans, four barges across, five long, as usual. Above the barges, cars and trucks filled the Hernando de Soto Bridge, as usual. And behind them all, the bright sun hung over Arkansas, as usual. Looking almost straight down he saw his two bosses, handcuffed, and being manhandled into waiting cars, not usual. This can't be real, he thought. How could this have happened? It had been all so smooth. So easy. Investors so gullible. Money so plentiful. What went wrong?

Porter's stomach dropped as if the floor under him had just disappeared. My God, I'm next, he thought. No way they won't talk. And the feds have my files…they'll take my home. My cars. My life. Fear overwhelmed him—his knees weakened, forcing him to grab the window sill. He felt incredibly alone. Vulnerable.

He steadied himself and stepped away from the window. Must get out of town, he thought. He pulled his iPhone and confirmed a flight to Saudi Arabia, first leg leaving tomorrow from Nashville. There's no extradition treaty there, and I've squirreled away enough to live on. As soon as the feds leave, I'm driving to Nashville. The hell with packing. I'll buy whatever clothes I need on the way. Using his iPhone, he began transferring money from several US banks to his account in Saudi Arabia, leaving enough for necessary ATM withdrawals.

Porter looked up. Everyone had gone. His fears intensified. He haphazardly stuffed supplies into his briefcase and hurried to the elevator, pushing the G-2 button.

***

A large black car blended into the shadows, far enough around the corner to be unnoticed, close enough for the driver to see the GARAGE LEVEL 2 elevators. The distinctive ding rang out, followed shortly by the sound of doors sliding. The driver picked up the remote and pushed the button—security cameras went black.

***

The elevator doors opened to a deserted parking level. Porter stepped into an unrelenting wind coming off the river. He felt his hair blow straight up, but made no move to finger comb it. He turned automatically toward his car. The steady echoing of his heels striking the concrete floor blended with the constant hum of the wind, calming him. Porter's car sat against the far wall, isolated. His mind elsewhere, he never sensed the car approaching from behind. It picked up speed.

***

*2:00 AM, Saturday in Arkansas…the oldest profession.* Eighteen-wheeler tractor-trailers packed the lot in West Memphis, Arkansas. Diego zipped his pants. The young woman in the passenger seat straightened her blouse.

"Now you know why they call me Angel," she said. "Like you died and went to heaven. Right? I can stay the night if you'd like. I'll give you a good deal."

"No hablo ingles," he said.

"Right. You talk good English when you want something."

He smiled. "Yeah. You need to give me a real good—"

Through a sliver between his privacy curtains, Diego caught sight of a single headlight. The hair on his arms stood up. He stared as the light swayed back and forth.

"Mother of God," he whispered. "That's Ernesto."

"Friend of yours? I like parties."

"Get down, bitch," he said, shoving her off the seat.

Angel cussed, but curled up on the floor.

Diego watched the motorcycle turn onto his row. His breathing quickened. The throaty moan of the engine grew louder then stopped. The silence frightening. Diego looked around for a place to hide.

Three sharp metallic raps on the passenger door. "Diego," Ernesto whispered loudly. "Unlock the door." Diego stretched across the passenger seat and flipped the lock. Ernesto climbed in. "What's this? Diego you didn't tell me you had company." He helped Angel to her knees.

"It'll cost y'all more," she said, smiling. "More for two."

"Naturally," said Ernesto, returning the smile as he reached to hold her face. Then with a quick twist—CRACK! Her body dropped to the floor. Ernesto turned to Diego. "What the hell you doin', man? You know the rules. Nothing gets in the way of the delivery. Nothing. I should put a bullet in your ear—"

"No!" Diego interrupted. "Please. I can make up the time. The delivery will be on schedule."

"I really should just shoot your ass." He pulled his Glock 17.

"No. Please. Please," Diego said, turning his face to the

door, hiding behind his upraised hands.

"Maybe this once," Ernesto said, returning the nine-millimeter to its holster. "Get back on the road. Now! And get rid of the whore."

"Yes," Diego said, starting the engine. "I'm leaving right now, and I'll dump her after I cross the river."

"I'll be watching," Ernesto said, opening the door. "And, Diego?"

"Si, Ernesto."

"There's no second chances."

Ernesto climbed down. Diego gripped the steering wheel, trying to steady his shaking hands. He jumped when the door slammed shut. Ernesto strapped on his red helmet, started the motorcycle, and eased out of the lot. Diego's watery eyes distorted the motorcycle's red tail light, making it look like a slow dancing firefly. He wiped his eyes on his shirt sleeve and dared to look over at Angel, lying in a heap, staring up at him. A shiver ran through his body. He summoned the courage to touch her, making sure she was dead. He took a deep breath and pulled her into the passenger seat, fastening her seatbelt. He pulled down the curtains, tossing them behind their seats. Diego buckled himself into the driver's seat and dropped the gearshift into first. The big rig lurched. He fumbled with second, turning the wheel hard left.

***

Diego took the Hernando de Soto Bridge over the Mississippi, Angel bouncing like a ragdoll next to him. He passed downtown Memphis on the right and the St. Jude Children's Hospital complex on the left, then slowed for the long looping left turn that would put him on the northern leg of I-40 toward Nashville. The only car on the road passed him. He stopped the truck on the turn, stretched to open the passenger door, and shoved Angel out.

***

*Saturday, 9:15 PM…upon reflection.* Herman Traner scrolled through his spreadsheets. The numbers look good, he thought. I'll just feed some money to the earlier investors, keep them on the line. He stood to his full six-foot six inches and stretched.

CRASH! The second story window burst, glass flew.

"What the hell was that?" said Traner. "That damn neighbor kid. Throwing rocks again." Striding to the window he heard a car race off. He stared hard, but saw nothing. Turning around he discovered a full length mirror had also been cracked—two holes, side by side, surrounded by radiating cracks. Long thin shards lay on the floor. Traner dialed 911.

***

Shelby County Sherriff's Deputy Morton followed his flashlight as he searched the street in front of Traner's house.

He radioed to his partner on the second floor. "Nothing here, Frank."

"Okay," Frank said. "Come on up."

Morton glanced through the broken window. "Frank. Is there a big mirror up there?" he said.

"Yeah. A real fancy one. A good eight feet tall. This guy says it's worth three thousand bucks, and he's really pissed about it taking two rounds."

"Move to your right," said Morton. "A little more…Stop."

"What's going on, Derrick?"

"Those weren't random shots. I can see your reflection through the window. The shooter hit his target dead center. Except the target he saw happened to be the reflection in that mirror. Tell the homeowner it's the best three grand he ever spent—it saved his life."

## Chapter 13

# Saturday Chores

*Saturday morning in midtown Memphis…a homeowner's work is never done.* Julia took the turn, going back for yet another pass, when a puppy bounded across her path, yapping at the lawnmower. Julia released the handle, killing the motor. The puppy continued to challenge the lifeless machine.

"Parsley," Julia said, smiling. "Hey, Parsley. How's my lucky charm?" She bent down, scooped him up. Parsley bathed her in wet tongue kisses.

"Parsley. Parsley," called Mrs. Woozley from the other side of the new wooden fence. "Now, where did you get to?"

Julia carried Parsley to the sidewalk, and around the fence into her next door neighbor's front yard. "I have him," she said, jerking her head away from his excited tongue.

"Thank you, Julia," Woozley said. "He's just too fast for me. Can't move like I used to. And he won't mind a lick."

"You know he doesn't bother me. How can I be upset with the dog that saved my life?"

"Seems to me you saved each other. I still have flashes of the two of you flying over this fence…er, I mean the *former* fence, just as that bomb went off. It gives me chill bumps."

"Have to admit, I get a little wound up myself every now and then, thinking about it."

Julia set Parsley down, rubbing him behind the ears,

coaxing him over to his elderly owner. Woozley bent over and clipped a leash to his collar.

"He just squeaked through when I opened the door to get the mail. I guess I'll have to get the rest of the front yard fenced."

"May not be a bad idea. Least till he outgrows his puppy stage."

"The new fence looks good. And I see you're driving a new car. A convertible. Love the bright red color."

"Yeah. That pipe bomb did a number on the old Ford. Wasn't much left. This one's a Mini Cooper, and the color's chili red. Got lots of zip and it's fun to drive."

"I'm glad the neighborhood's back to normal. I like it nice and quiet."

"Me, too, Mrs. Woozley. Me, too."

Julia's phone vibrated. "Todd," she answered.

"Lieutenant, this is Marino. Got a body in the Morgan Keegan parking garage."

"Be there in twenty, professor."

***

Julia took a quick shower, dressed, and drove her Mini Cooper the four miles to downtown Memphis. She pulled into the parking garage, stopping at the crime tape on level two. Marino squatted over a body.

"I thought we all agreed you'd get an armor-plated Hummer," said Marino, looking at the Mini. "Something that'd have a better chance of surviving a bomb."

"It was a tough decision, professor," Julia said. "But taste won out. Fill me in."

"Victim's name is Terence Porter, employed for the last twelve years as an investment consultant for Morgan Keegan. Looks like a hit and run—maybe two or three times. Coroner is counting the tire tracks on his back."

"So, no accident."

"Looks more like one of those really angry wife drive-overs," he said. "Except he's not married."

"Witnesses?"

"No other cars on this level. Probably the last to leave the office, after the feds left."

"The feds?"

"Yeah. They swooped in, grabbed up all the computers and files from a few of the upper floors. Made two arrests. They think they've got a solid case of fraud, conning investors out of big bucks."

"Porter work on one of those top floors?" Julia asked.

"Yup. What I can gather, he may have been next on the feds' list."

"Maybe one of his investors chose not to wait for the feds?"

Marino nodded. "His iPhone was smashed, but I could still make out the airplane ticket he'd reserved for tomorrow, out of Nashville."

"Nashville? Where was he going?"

"Saudi Arabia."

"Saudi Arabia? That's hotter than Memphis. But like they say, it's a dry heat."

"True. But, more importantly, it doesn't have an extradition treaty with the US."

"Maybe he had money stashed in foreign banks?"

"Sounds reasonable. I wonder if he had any friends over there."

"Getting back to the car…"

"Black paint chips on the victim's clothing," he said. "Skid marks made by large tires. More Hummer than Mini Cooper."

"Got it. See if the feds'll be willing to share some of their files. We need a printout of Porter's client's."

"That was next on my list," Marino said.

Julia's phone rang. "Todd."

"Lieutenant, this is Tagger. I'm just north of the I-40/240 junction coming in from West Memphis, on that big turn to the northern leg of I-40. Near Autumn Avenue. You might want to see this."

"Be there in ten."

***

"Hey, Lieutenant," said Tagger. "Cute car. Not much bigger than one of my shoes, and about as safe as a skateboard."

"Everything looks small to you," Julia said. "And no, I'm not getting a Hummer."

"You sure, Lieutenant? Still time to turn in the Mini, before you get any scratches on it."

Julia rolled her eyes. "What do we have, Tag?"

"Dead female. Late teens, early twenties. According to an ankle bracelet her name is Angel. And according to the wad of bills and condoms in her pocket, I'd say she's a working girl."

"Any idea how she got here?"

"No signs she was dragged or carried over the fence from the neighborhood. The tall grass hasn't been disturbed, except where her body rolled. My guess is someone shoved her out of a car or a truck from the entrance ramp. Doc says she's got a broken neck. But the break is a twist fracture. She thinks Angel was dead before she hit the ground. Killed by someone who knew what they were doing. Up close and personal. Time of death between two and four this morning."

"I haven't seen any recent reports of serial killers working the truck stop hookers in this area."

"I'm with you," said Tagger. "Maybe she saw something she wasn't supposed to."

"Thoughts on the killer?" asked Julia.

"Someone who's been trained to kill. Someone who does it for a living."

Chapter 14

# Sunday Dinner

*Feeling vulnerable...*Julia walked across the Haven for Seniors Retirement Community parking lot, carrying a paper sack containing two bottles of Tavel, a popular French rosé from Buster's Liquors & Wines, and two French breadsticks from La Baguette bakery. Aunt Louise's best friends Beth and Dell would be joining them for dinner. *I hope this will be enough,* thought Julia. *The ladies do love their wine.*

The sensitive automatic doors slid open in advance of her arrival. She crossed the spacious lobby to the receptionist's desk and signed in. Minutes later she rang the doorbell to her Aunt Louise's second floor apartment.

"There you are," said Aunt Louise, exchanging a one-arm embrace and kissing Julia's cheek. "Right on time."

"With the Todd genes, how could I be late?" said Julia. She carried the sack to the kitchen counter, and turned to hug the two women. "What's new, y'all?"

"We just came from a..." Dell said, looking at Beth.

"Seminar," said Beth. "They called it a seminar."

"Really?" said Dell. "I thought you got college credits for seminars."

Beth shook her head. "Honestly, Dell. You have to get with it."

"As I was saying," Dell continued. "We just came from a

seminar on someone named *Pironzi.* Odd name. But very informative."

"Ponzi," said Beth. "Charles Ponzi from the 1920s. Remember? The man talked about Ponzi schemes *and* pyramid schemes."

"I just hate it when the names begin with the same letter," said Dell. "I can never keep them straight."

"Anyway," said Beth. "Bernie Madoff cheated folks out of billions of dollars using one of these Ponzi schemes."

"Don't forget about the banks," said Aunt Louise, matching her friends' energy. "In addition to forcing homeowners into bankruptcy, they've come up with all these hidden fees to cheat us out of even more money. It's unconscionable."

"Aunt Louise," said Julia. "I can't believe my ears. You're always the calm, rational one. You're really worked up."

"We all are, dearie," said Beth. "So many people have been hurt in this great recession. Greedy bankers and those Wall Street crooks are the main cause of it."

"Brings back too many memories of the Depression," said Dell. "We were very young, but we remember."

"Everyone out of work," Beth said. "Nothing to eat. No warm clothes."

"Who gave this seminar?" Julia asked.

"The AARP sponsored it," said Aunt Louise. "A *huge* number of seniors have been cheated out of their homes and their retirement money."

"That stupid reverse mortgage," said Beth. "They hire old actors to smile and tell us how safe they are. They're still handsome of course, but you've got to be so careful."

"The government gave the banks billions of our tax dollars," Dell said. "That money was supposed to be for the people. Banks were supposed to issue loans, help folks get back on their feet."

"But no," Beth said. "They're just sitting on that money to gain interest for themselves."

"Raising their salaries and giving themselves bonuses," Dell said.

"They get interest-free loans from some kind of government window," said Aunt Louise. "But they won't loan the people any money. They say they can't trust us to pay them back."

"Can't trust *us?*" Beth said. "We're not the ones who got the country into this mess in the first place."

Dell chimed in. "All those greedy—"

"All right, all right," Julia interrupted, holding up her hands. "Everyone breathe. What is it your generation says? Count to ten? Well, start counting. Slowly. I'm getting indigestion, and we haven't even begun dinner."

A blush grew on Dell's cheeks. She looked down.

"We're sorry, dear," Aunt Louise said.

"I'm wondering if it's safe to open the wine," said Julia.

"Don't know if it's safe, but it's absolutely the right thing to do," Beth said, picking up a glass.

Dell nodded, her eyes brightening. "Just what the doctor ordered."

***

*What about blondes?*…The women chatted while they cleared the table and washed dishes.

"So, Mark's leaving tomorrow?" said Aunt Louise.

"Yes," said Julia. "He's polishing his two presentations."

"Why do psychologists have to have conferences half-way around the world?" Aunt Louise asked.

"For starters," said Julia. "It's an international conference. Not everyone wants to come to the United States, too violent. And secondly, professional organizations are always looking for ways to get better attendance."

"Well, I'm sure he'll enjoy Sweden," said Aunt Louise.

"I hope so," said Julia. "You know Mark. He's going early for pre-conference meetings, and he'll be staying until they pack up the microphones on the last day. He'll probably be the only one attending talks every day, all day. Most will be checking out the sights in Stockholm."

"We're going to miss him," said Dell. "The Haven just won't be the same without Dr. Mark."

"I never had much use for psychologists before Mark came here," said Beth. "He's just so down to earth. Such a nice young man."

"It's only for ten days," Julia said. "I pick him up at the airport Wednesday evening."

"You know, you have a little Scandinavian blood in you, my dear," said Aunt Louise.

"This is the first time I'm hearing this," said Julia. "Which country? On whose side?"

"As I recall, someone way back on my father's side came from Finland."

"I'm a Finn?" said Julia. "Isn't that where the reindeer live? Shouldn't I be a blonde?"

"Lots of reindeer," Aunt Louise said. "But I fear you are too far removed from the original gene pool to be blonde."

"I wonder what I'd look like with blonde hair," Julia said.

"We'll be glad to have him back at the Haven," said Beth.

"But not half as much as you'll be to have him back home, dear," said Dell, smiling. "I'm sure he'll be tired of looking at all those beautiful blondes."

Chapter 15

# Tire Tracks and
# Composite Sketches

*Monday…midtown Memphis.* Julia rose early, slipped into her running clothes, and began the 4.7-mile run through her midtown neighborhood, ending at the InsideOut Gym. Her feet struck the pavement with only the lightest sounds, while the sun cast long shadows of her fluid stride. Julia kicked up the pace. Once in the gym, she began with burpees—a demanding combination of squats, push-ups, and jumps. Next were the Spiderman lunges and stretches across the floor, followed by a variety of leg lifts, and sit-ups. Julia worked the heavy bag, with sharp kicks, punches, and combinations. She toweled off and drank a bottle of water, stealing a peek at her profile in the mirror, hand on her stomach. Not bad, she thought. Julia left the gym, running the 2.4-mile direct route home. She showered and dressed, ready for the next phase of her daily routine—quality coffee and a Cup of Gold nutrition bar.

***

Julia pulled into the Deliberate Literate coffee shop, a midtown establishment on Union Avenue. The featured coffee of the day, a nutrition bar, and reading the *Commercial Appeal* helped her ease into the work day. Union Station precinct house awaited her, less than a quarter-mile down the street.

***

"Morning, Lieutenant," said Teresa Johnson, Union Station secretary. "I hear you've got a sweet ride."

"You can't keep a secret in this town," Julia said.

"Got you one of them *Italian Job* minis. Hear tell the color's awesome."

"Yeah, but mine's not filled with solid gold bars like the ones in that movie."

"Still, guys dig the car."

"I'm no Charlize Theron. Besides, she's a blonde."

"All that's true, but the car can't hurt."

Julia rolled her eyes and walked down the hall to her office. Marino and Tagger met her halfway, coffee cups in hand.

"Morning fellas," Julia said. "This a good time to discuss cases?"

"Sure, Lieutenant. We're right behind you," said Marino. The two took seats in front of her desk.

"Y'all act as if you've got new information," she said.

"I'll go first," Marino said. "Paint chips and tread marks on Porter's silk suit indicate a 2005 to 2008 Chrysler Limited—the 300 series."

"Kind of a man's car," said Tagger.

"You thinking an angry girlfriend is a low probability?" said Julia

Tagger nodded.

"I'm with Johnnie," said Marino. "It's also not the high-dollar car you'd find in that garage."

"So probably an investor, not an investment consultant?" said Julia.

Marino shrugged. "Maybe."

"What about security videos?" asked Julia.

"Cameras went dark just as Porter came out of the elevator," Marino said. "Turns out a guy from Boiler's Electric worked on all the cameras last week. When they checked after the murder they found small pieces of plastic had been spliced into the wiring. He'd installed cutoff switches, which he hid in the electrical conduits."

"Premeditated," said Tagger.

"So," Julia said. "Did they have video of the person as he did his work last week?"

"Probably six foot, thin, wore a baseball cap, dark-rimmed glasses, mustache, brown coveralls," said Marino. "Turns out there's no Boiler's Electric listed anywhere."

"Probably doesn't have a mustache or black-rimmed glasses either," said Tagger.

"What about his car? Julia said. "Surely he didn't drive the Chrysler Limited to fix the cameras."

"No," Marino said. "He drove a small white pickup with Arkansas plates."

"Let me guess," said Tagger. "Stolen."

"Bingo," Marino said.

"Did the feds give you a look at Porter's client list?"

"They're dragging their feet on that score," Marino said.

"How about we get our assistant DA involved," said Julia. "I'll give him a call. Any other leads?"

Marino shook his head.

"Tag, learned anything about Angel?" said Julia.

"Angel made her living as a working girl," Tagger said. "Real name's Sylvia Trisokovich, a runaway from Little Rock three years ago. Just turned eighteen. Been arrested a few times for prostitution. She mostly worked the truck stops, preferred those in west Arkansas and Memphis."

"When's the last time anyone saw her?" asked Julia.

"Course, all the truckers in the area are long gone," said

Tagger. "I found a cleaning woman at the Pilot who recognized her picture. Said she saw Angel in the dining area with a man last Friday. Described him as being a short Mexican, maybe in his thirties, medium build, black hair, clean shaven, wearing a Texas Rangers baseball cap, jeans, and short sleeve pullover shirt."

"That's quite a detailed description," Julia said. "She credible enough to work with a sketch artist?"

"I think so," Tagger said. "She acted as if she didn't like him because he was Mexican. Maybe she looked him over more closely than usual?"

"Or maybe she'll just describe a composite of every Latino she's ever seen," said Marino.

Tagger nodded. "No luck with finding a credit card receipt in the dining room. Must've paid cash. I'm going back tonight to find their waitress."

## Chapter 16

# Elder Abuse

*Monday afternoon…anything for you.* Tagger studied the information on Angel. His phone rang.

"Tagger."

"Johnnie. It's Diane. I could use some help."

"What's going on, Di?"

"Got a complaint of elder abuse from one of the docs at The MED. Frequent trips to the ER. Broken bones, including spiral fractures, as well as older breaks confirmed by x-ray. Doc says this is more than just *a fall down the steps.* I went out to the home to check it out. Couldn't get near the old man because of his son—his angry, very large son."

"So you want me for my body?"

"That, and your gun."

"Where we going?"

"Just ten minutes away. Near the Pink Palace Museum, off Central."

"I don't have anything till tonight. You want to pick me up?"

"Thanks. Be there in fifteen."

***

Sergeants Diane Willingham and Johnnie Tagger drove east on Central Avenue, turning north on Lafayette, then right on Cowden—a quiet street with small, older homes and no overgrown yards. They stopped at the house with a large oak in the front yard. Willingham rang the doorbell. A short Caucasian woman wearing a fashionable warm-up outfit opened the door.

"You again," said Marvell Lester. She looked up at Tagger.

"Mrs. Lester," said Willingham. "I've come back to talk to your father-in-law. This is Sergeant Tagger."

Marvell looked over her shoulder. "Butch is still here," she whispered.

"That's okay," Willingham said, stepping into the living room, Tagger on her heels. "We still need to talk to Mr. Lester."

"Let me get him," Marvell said, walking away.

The room smelled slightly of mold. The furnishings looked worn but comfortable—one decidedly large recliner, one small stuffed chair, and a couch. A large flat screen television dominated the far wall.

Marvell returned. "He said he doesn't want to talk to you," she said softly.

"I'm afraid that's not an option," said Willingham. "We're not leaving until we talk to Mr. Lester."

They heard footsteps, the creak of an old wooden floor. Butch Lester filled the doorway, anger etched on his face.

"I already told you to get out," Butch said loudly. "I know my rights."

"There's been a complaint," said Willingham. "We're not leaving until we check it out."

"What kind of complaint?" Butch demanded.

"Doctor at the MED says your father has way too many broken bones," said Tagger, moving closer to Butch, but not blocking Willingham's line of sight.

"The old man's always falling," said Butch. "Tell 'em, Marv."

"Yeah. He falls a lot," Marvell said, looking down.

"We need to talk to Mr. Lester," Willingham said.

"Like hell," said Butch, moving toward the officers.

Willingham grabbed the handle of her Glock. Tagger moved between her and Butch. Butch kept coming, pulling back a huge fist. Tagger stepped forward, firing a quick left jab squarely into Butch's nose, snapping his head back.

"You bastard! You broke my nose!" said Butch, hands to his face.

"Not so easy when someone fights back," said Tagger. "You need to settle down. Come over here and sit in your chair. Mrs. Lester, he could use some ice, maybe a towel for the blood."

Marvell hesitated, then slipped past Butch cautiously, on her way to the kitchen. Butch moaned, cussing, his face in his hands. Tagger backed up, leaving a clear path to the recliner. Butch looked up, the anger gone from his eyes, then shuffled to his chair. Willingham left to find the elder Lester. Soon Marvell approached looking worried, she extended her hand from a distance, offering Butch a washcloth filled with ice. He took it and pressed it against his nose.

"He didn't used to be like this," Marvell said. "He's a good man when he's not drugging." She touched Butch's arm. When he didn't pull away, she moved closer.

"What kind of drugs?" said Tagger.

"Cocaine," said Marvell.

"You doing blow, Butch?" said Tagger.

"Sometimes," Butch said through the washcloth.

"Where you getting it?" Tagger said.

"Mexicans," Marvell said.

## Chapter 17

# The Almost-Eighty Worries

*4:30 PM Monday…Union Station.* "Lieutenant, your aunt on line two," said Teresa.

"Hey, Aunt Louise," said Julia.

"Hello, dear. You busy?"

"Nah. Now's a good time."

"I've been thinking a lot about yesterday's dinner."

"Yesterday's dinner?"

"I owe you an apology. The three of us got carried away. I'm afraid we ruined your evening."

"Y'all did carry on. But no problem. I guess the seminar got you pretty worked up."

"Partly. We older folk tend to get nervous about every aspect of our future. You know—health, finances, family, friends…death."

"Aunt Louise. You and your friends are in terrific health. Y'all love living at the Haven. No need to get nervous."

"That's mostly true, dear. But we see the signs all the time. Like Dell. Did you notice how confused she got, and how much she depended on Beth?"

"The two of them have been like that ever since I've known them. They're always together, always finishing one another's sentences, always best friends."

"Yes, but Beth has confided in me about how concerned

she is. What used to be cute is feeling more like…dependence. Dell's confusion is genuine. Her long-term memory is still good, but it's hard to tell how much of her current condition is due to a worsening short-term memory or confusion. Neither one is a good sign, and we've seen examples of both."

"You thinking Alzheimer's?"

"We worry about it all the time. But even so, it is only one of many forms of dementia, all of which are scary."

Tears welled in Julia's eyes. She couldn't speak.

"You and Wayne gave my life meaning. I'm so sorry for what you and your little brother had to go through, but I'm so thankful Protective Services sent you both to me."

"We feel the same way, Aunt Louise."

"That's why it's so important that I not be a burden to you."

"Aunt Louise, I promise. No matter what, you will not be a burden."

"I have to hang up now."

"Aunt Louise?"

She was gone.

Julia dabbed her eyes with a tissue, and tried to make sense of the call. I need to see Aunt Louise, she thought. I have to be with her. She left the precinct house drove west on Union Avenue, passed Methodist Hospital, looped around the medical building, and into *Holliday Flowers*. A particularly striking arrangement in the cooler caught her eye. Leaning the large arrangement against the driver's window with the vase resting on her lap, Julia headed east. She kept her speed just above the posted limit, holding the steering wheel with her left hand whenever she had to shift.

A car pulled out of a spot near the entrance to the Haven. Julia pulled in. She eased the big arrangement from the car, and walked quickly to the entrance, grateful for the automatic doors. People smiled as she passed. Julia tried to smile, but a little grin was all she could manage. She hastily scribbled her name in the visitor's log at the front desk and carried her flowers to the open elevator.

Julia stepped inside, repeatedly pushing the button to the second floor, but everything about the elevator was slow—doors closing …the ride…doors opening. I should have taken the stairs, Julia thought. By the time the doors opened, Julia couldn't be contained. She strode to Aunt Louise's apartment door, raised the flowers to cover the peep hole, and rang the doorbell. Several rings and a few minutes later the door opened a crack. Aunt Louise peeked out, her eyes red and teary. Julia lowered the flowers and met her face to face.

"Thought these flowers might brighten your spirits," Julia said.

Louise opened the door wide and reached to hug her, flowers and all. "Not as much as seeing you, dear," she said. Then pulling back and looking down she said, "I'm sorry for hanging up. Isn't it just like an old woman to cry over nothing?"

"Isn't it just like a mature woman to care so deeply for her friends and family?" said Julia. "I'm the one who should apologize. I tried to talk you out of your feelings, when I should have been listening. I'm sorry, Aunt Louise."

"You don't owe me an apology, dear."

"Yes, I do. And now I'm here for you. Come and sit with me. I want to listen."

***

"Would you like to go down to the dining room?" Aunt Louise asked.

"They have wine, don't they?" said Julia, "Something to

counter the artery clogging effects of all those fried foods?"

"They have several nice selections, dear," said Aunt Louise. "And not everything is fried. Remember they always have jello."

Julia smiled. "Let's do it."

Louise and Julia walked into the dining room, arm in arm.

"Over here," said Joyce, waving.

"Yes, do come sit with us," Beatrice said.

"What timing," said Julia, waiving. "Are the *hushpuppy four* always in the dining room?"

"So it would seem," Aunt Louise said. "But they are always nice. Let's join them."

"It's so good to see you, Louise," said Joyce.

"And Julia, too" Shirley said.

"Y'all still in trouble with the director?" Julia asked.

"Trouble?" said Beatrice.

"You remember," Shirley said. "The last time they joined us for dinner, Mrs. Jacobson was on the warpath about—"

"That's right," interrupted Joyce. "The Walgreen's runs. Remember, Lawrence?"

"Yeah," Julia said. "How'd all that turn out, Lawrence? Did you get the—"

"Julia Todd," Louise said, slapping her on the arm.

"I still went," said Lawrence, looking at his water glass. "I just never told her."

"You sly fox, you," said Julia, smiling. "And, ladies, did he get the right stuff?"

"You mean the condoms and lubricants?" whispered Shirley.

"Yeah," said Julia, leaning away from Aunt Louise. "Well, did he?"

The three women looked embarrassed, and began to

giggle. "Yes," said Beatrice, sneaking a look at Lawrence. They broke out in laughter, playfully pushing one another.

"Way to go, Lawrence," Julia said.

"Is this the same sensitive niece who brought me flowers not two hours ago?" said Louise.

"Aww. Flowers," said Joyce.

"How thoughtful," Beatrice said.

"What's the occasion?" asked Shirley.

"Oh, I had a little crying spell," Louise said.

"What about?" said Beatrice.

"Life, I guess," Louise said. "You know. Concerns."

"I think maybe she's got the almost-eighty worries," Joyce said, looking around the group.

"How old are you, Louise?" said Shirley.

"I'll be seventy-eight next month," Louise said.

"Yup," said Beatrice. "The almost-eighty worries."

"What are y'all talking about?" Julia said.

"We see it all the time," said Beatrice. "Folks here have run life's gauntlet."

"And, you know, the life expectancy is eighty-one," said Shirley.

"For women," said Lawrence. "Seventy-five for men."

"So it's normal when you make it past the middle seventies to think your life's almost over," Beatrice said.

"Folks just naturally take to worrying," said Joyce.

"Cancer, heart attack, Alzheimer's, assisted living, being dependent on some horrible machine," Beatrice said.

"Of course," said Shirley. "Someone's dying every month or so around here."

"As the young people say," Joyce said. "It's right in your face."

"Yup," Lawrence said. "Can't miss it."

"If you don't mind me asking," said Julia. "How old

are you?"

"I'm the baby," said Shirley. "I'm eighty-six."

"Beatrice is the oldest," said Joyce. "Eighty-nine."

"I can't believe it," Julia said. "Y'all seem so much younger. How do you do it?"

"Of course, you've got to come from good stock," said Beatrice. "Genes play a big part."

"Yeah," said Lawrence. "Like George Burns—drank, smoked, caroused with women half his age, and lived to be a hundred."

"Lawrence always makes a big deal of the carousing part," said Beatrice, smiling.

"I'm not putting the carousing down," Joyce said, with a wink. "But the Haven has lots of programs to keep us going."

"We have Tai Chi for balance," said Shirley.

"Everyone needs balance," said Beatrice. "Falling is probably more of concern around here than Alzheimer's and the big *C*."

"There's swimming, exercise, painting, memoir writing, foreign languages, current events discussion groups, volunteer activities, and field trips," said Joyce.

"Don't forget bridge," said Shirley.

"There you go, Aunt Louise," Julia said. "You'd probably appreciate the Tai Chi to help you with your balance. Maybe something in there for Dell, too."

"Yeah," said Beatrice. "We all take Tai Chi. Even Lawrence comes once in a while. You should join us."

"It's so relaxing," said Shirley. "It really loosens up my arthritic joints. I do it every morning."

"I've seen people doing it on TV documentaries about China," Louise said. "It looks so beautiful, so peaceful. But there's no way I'd be able to learn it."

"Not true," said Joyce. "Lynn has new people join the class

all the time."

"Lynn?" said Louise.

"That's our teacher," said Shirley. "Just an itty-bit."

"Full of energy and personality," Beatrice said. "You'd love her."

"I don't—" said Louise.

"It's settled," interrupted Beatrice. "We'll come and get you tomorrow morning. Be at your door at nine-fifteen."

"What do I wear?" said Louise.

"Just wear comfortable clothes and flat shoes," said Shirley.

"Now that's taken care of, we should get something to eat," Joyce said.

"What do they have tonight?" said Julia.

"Fried catfish, hushpuppies, French fries, and coleslaw," Beatrice said, her eyes brightening.

"Hope the coleslaw's not deep-fried," Julia said.

Chapter 18

# Slipping Away

*Monday, August 3, 2009…you can only win the game if you're still alive.* Akilah's two months were up. It took only seconds to finish packing, taking care not to search for the tracking devices she knew were hidden there. She would never be far from the probing eyes of the Judge. He'd provided a ticket to Caracas, Venezuela, and the promise of an even larger bonus waiting for her in one of its banks. But that would be out of the question, just one more way to track her. The doorman held the limo door for her and placed her bag in the trunk, probably adding yet another bug, she thought. The driver began his race to the airport. Once there, she checked her bag through to Caracas, and boarded the short connecting flight to the King Khaled International Airport, just north of Riyadh.

***

Akilah moved slowly through the large airport. She found the Venezuelan Avior Airlines counter, confirmed her flight, and proceeded to the nearby restroom. A CLOSED FOR CLEANING sign blocked the entrance to a women's restroom. Akilah went in. A cleaning woman swept the floor on the far side.

"Can't you read?" the woman said.

"I'm sorry," said Akilah. But I don't think I can make it to the next restroom. I'll just be a minute."

The woman produced a bracelet from her pocket. Akilah recognized it as the one Preston had slipped off her arm all those weeks ago. She nodded.

The woman indicated the end stall.

"All right," the woman said loudly. "But I don't want any mess to clean up."

"Thank you," Akilah said, pushing through the stall door.

Inside she found a carry-on and a plastic garbage bag. Akilah latched the door and stripped, comfortable for the first time in two months that no one was watching. Everything went into the plastic bag. She handed it to the cleaning woman. In the carry-on she found western cloth-ing—underwear, pantyhose, a casual dress with a below the knee-length skirt, two-inch heels, a light brown wig with blonde highlights, and make-up. She dressed, then applied clear press-on fingernails as well as a light touch of lipstick and eyeliner. She dug deeper inside the carry-on to find a stack of Euros, along with a French passport and credit cards in the name of her new identity. There were two airline tick-ets and boarding passes—a first class ticket to Munich and a one-way coach ticket from Munich to Paris.

The cleaning woman slowly passed each article of Akilah's clothing across the scanner tucked inside her cart. The san-dals set off the red light. Damn, thought the woman, they found the hidden drawer. Mitchell's a dead woman. She touched the handle of her SIG Sauer as she looked around. Her senses on high alert, she inspected the sandals. The right sandal was clean. The Judge's men had inserted a transmit-ter in the sandal without the drawer. She let out her breath.

Akilah rose to her full height, adjusted her dress, reac-quainted herself with heels, and left the stall. The cleaning woman looked her over, then pointed to the top of her own dress. Akilah fastened the top two buttons. She glanced in the mirror to adjust her wig and saw the door of the first stall open. Fear overtook her. Her knees went weak and she grabbed the sink. Two hands gripped her arm like a vise. Akilah looked to see the cleaning woman release one hand and turn on the water. She shifted her grip and wrapped an arm around Akilah's waist. She leaned in until her lips touched Akilah's ear.

"It's okay," she whispered. "She's with us. The Judge's men will follow her, believing she is you."

A woman stood in the doorway of the stall, dressed in black from head to ankles, exactly as Akilah had been moments before. She bowed her head.

"We'll leave first," whispered the cleaning woman, securing the bracelet on Akilah's right wrist. "She has her own passport for Akilah, and your boarding pass. I have their tracking devices with me. You'll find your American passport in a compartment inside your purse. On behalf of the CIA, the government thanks you for your service. Now we must go. You have just enough time to make it to the Lufthansa flight for Munich, gate seven. Remember, you are now Martine Didier, French citizen. Good luck."

Martine squeezed the cleaning woman's hand, nodded to the woman in black, and watched them leave the restroom. She waited a few minutes, took a deep breath, pulled her shoulders back, raised her chin slightly, and followed. Martine's heels clicked on the hard surface as she strode down the wide hallway—stylishly, confidently. She saw many women clothed in black, but did not see the cleaning woman. The Lufthansa jet took off forty-five minutes ahead of Akilah's scheduled flight to Venezuela.

***

*Now you see her, now you don't*…A man watched from his seat in the far corner, across from the Venezuelan Avior Airlines gate. He checked his monitoring device, confirming strong signals from all three bugs. Several women dressed in full traditional garb stood and sat in the waiting area. No way to pick out Akilah. He watched a cleaning woman collect trash around the seating area until the boarding announcement. Passengers formed a queue, going through the process of showing passports and boarding passes. After the last passenger entered the jetway, the man approached the ticket counter, flashing a wad of bills. He read the manifest, verifying Akilah had boarded the plane.

When the man left, the cleaning woman snapped each of the Judge's tracking devices, and pushed her cart slowly down the hall.

***

*Martine to Akilah, and back again…*Martine Didier's flight disembarked in the Munich Airport where she used her euros to purchase sandals, a black floor-length skirt, a long-sleeve black blouse, and a black hijab. Martine clicked into the women's restroom. Akilah floated out, *her feet not striking the ground.* She purchased a one-way ticket to Zurich with cash.

***

Akilah took a cab to the financial district. In her brief time in the computer room, she had seen the names of several banks used by the Judge—banks from the US and all over Europe, including one based in Switzerland, others with branches in Zurich. She didn't know whether any given bank might be in league with the Judge, but she would avoid the ones she knew. Akilah chose a bank housed in a modest looking building, outclassed by most of its neighbors. She established an account and, after a lengthy process, had the money transferred from the Venezuelan bank where the Judge had deposited $500,000 for her. Leaving the first bank, she walked down the block and crossed the street to a second bank. Akilah padded into the women's restroom in the foyer, Martine strode out.

Martine opened a savings and checking account, depositing one of Akilah's new checks, written to Martine for $400,000. Propped up with a new credit card in Martine's name and a wad of cash, she returned to the airport by cab and used her newly acquired credit card to purchase a one-way ticket to Paris. While in the airport she bought a satellite phone and service contract. Three hours later she landed at Charles de Gaulle, then travelled by train into Paris.

Martine desperately needed to be pampered—5-star accommodations, spa, room service, champagne. She checked into the Renaissance Paris Arc de Triomphe using her CIA-issued credit card, knowing the agency would be happy to learn she's in Paris, where she was supposed to be. After making an appointment for a massage and facial, Martine went shopping for a fully loaded laptop small enough to fit in her purse, and an electronic bug and camera detector. She chose a detector designed to look like a pen. After the Renaissance puts me back together, she thought, I'll need a new name, fresh passports and credit cards, and some intense computer programs. She tapped into her American accounts secured in the computing *cloud,* and began to identify contacts.

She swept her room and clothes that evening, found no bugs or cameras.

Returning to her room on the evening of the second day, she had four hits—a camera in the chandelier and tracking devices in the hem of her favorite dress, the cuff of her jacket, and the lining of her carry-on.

## Chapter 19

# Two Dead. No One Behind Bars

*Tuesday…hunches, disturbing hunches.* For variety, Julia liked to alternate her runs and gym workouts with Yoga. Today would be Yoga, dressed comfortably in her favorite old short sleeve Dallas Cowboys sweatshirt and cotton sweatpants. After an hour of stretches and balances, she wound down by meditating in the lotus position. Julia used this relaxed state to consider issues or challenges of the day. This morning, Sunday's dinner conversation about the elderly being ripped off loomed large. Aunt Louise and her friends had been unnerved. The prospect of being taken advantage of scared them, especially at a time in their lives when they're least able to stick up for themselves. She wondered whether the owner of the Chrysler Limited could be a senior citizen.

Julia opened her eyes slowly, reached for a bottle of water, and focused on re-entering her world of work. She showered, toweled off, dressed. She shook her head doggy style until her hair fell into place. A few finger combs and Julia was ready for the Deliberate Literate.

***

"Morning, Lieutenant," said Millie. "The usual?"

"Absolutely," Julia said. "Your coffee of the day and a *Cup of Gold* nutrition bar."

"Grab your paper. I'll meet you at your table."

***

*Union Station conference room…* The three officers sat at one end of the large table.

"Bring me up to speed," said Julia.

Tag handed out a sketch of the driver last seen with Angel. "Found the woman who waited on Angel and the driver last Friday," he said. "We got descriptions from both the maid and a waitress. The waitress was able to add a scar on his left cheek, and this tattoo of a mini-rosary on his neck. Here's a composite sketch. Both of them thought it was right on."

"Good work, Tag," said Julia. "Send out copies as a person-of-interest."

"You remember we talked about maybe Angel seeing something she wasn't supposed to?" Tagger said.

Julia nodded.

"Well, yesterday Diane asked me to go with her to follow-up on a complaint of elder abuse," Tagger said.

"Can't you two go on real dates like everyone else?" Marino said. "It's not like you don't go out enough. Do you have to make up excuses to see each other during the work day too?"

Julia rolled her eyes, shook her head.

Tagger smiled, embarrassed.

"Can we get to the point?" Julia said.

"Yes, Johnnie," said Marino. "Just what *is* the point?"

"The point is that the alleged perpetrator was the adult son," said Tagger. "He was under the influence when we walked in. Tried to take a swing at me."

"Tried?" said Marino.

"Yeah, well I was faster," said Tagger. "Anyway, his wife starts talking about what a great guy he was before getting into crack. So I asked where he got his crack. Wife says from the Mexicans. Got me thinking. Maybe Angel did see something she wasn't supposed to. Drugs, maybe."

"You may have something, Johnnie," Marino said. "Cartels have been flooding us with dope for decades. First the South Americans and now the Mexicans. A very creative, determined, and dangerous bunch. They use boats and planes, dig lots of tunnels, and have folks simply hump it across the border on foot. They make so much money they can afford to lose a good percentage of the drugs."

"Not to mention the people they also *lose,*" said Tagger.

"People are a throwaway commodity for the cartels," said Marino. "They've got plenty of desperately poor and intimidated people to use any way they wish."

"How about our border agents?" said Julia.

"Since NAFTA was passed in the nineties, opening up trade with Mexico, the cartels have been driving more and more of their drugs through the border crossings, snuggled in between millions of legitimate trucks."

"In 18-wheelers?" said Julia.

"Yeah," said Marino. "But they use anything they can— big trucks, small trucks, and vans painted to look like they belong to legitimate businesses—*Federal Express, UPS, Wal-Mart, DirecTV,* and even US Border Patrol vehicles."

"Brazen bunch," Tagger said. "So, my idea about drugs is not so far out."

"I'd say so," Marino said.

"Stay on that, Tag," Julia said. "How about you, professor?"

"The DA's office lit a fire under the feds," Marino said. "They released Porter's client list."

"Any hits?" said Julia.

"Not yet," Marino said. "I've pulled the list of auto licenses in Shelby and surrounding counties in Tennessee, as well as Arkansas and Mississippi. I'm zeroing in on 2005 to 2008 Chrysler Limiteds. Next, I'll cross match the owners with the client list."

"I was over at the Haven on Sunday, having dinner with my Aunt Louise," Julia said. "The residents were pretty worked up about the banks and investment firms cheating seniors out of their money. Lots of horror stories. Lots of anxiety. Lots of anger. Heck, even AARP sponsored a workshop to warn them about the various cons targeting seniors. Like Tag, it got me wondering. Any chance a senior citizen might have a dog in this race? Maybe a senior owns that Chrysler."

"Damn," said Marino. "I could have gone all day without thinking about grandpa running over Porter."

## Chapter 20

# Knock, Knock

*Friday afternoon…a friendly hello.* Teresa buzzed in.

"Your lucky day, Lieutenant," she said. "Must be that flashy red Mini. This call's from New York, the FBI on line one."

"Todd."

"Lieutenant. This is Lawrence Masterson."

"A voice from the past. Good to hear from you, Special Agent. Is this a social call, or are we in the middle of some murders we don't know anything about. Like last year when you called to alert us to Charleze Mitchell?"

"Afraid it's more like the Mitchell case. I don't know about any bodies this time, but lots of stuff's happening. The Securities and Exchange Commission is zeroing in on some big time investment fraud, and our section of the Bureau's hitting the ground running. The word is you guys in the midsouth are waist deep in it. You probably already heard about Morgan Keegan."

"Yeah. Your FBI buddies were crawling all over Morgan Keegan Friday, made a couple of arrests. Next morning folks found a dead body in their parking garage. Someone ran over one of the investment consultants—several times."

"Probably some poor jilted investor. Now he's going to have to pay twice."

"That's what we're thinking. You coming down to help?"

"Not if I have anything to say about it. Memphis is too damn hot. Almost melted last year."

"We have air-conditioning, now."

"So I've heard. But the FBI's gone high tech. I can sit in my nice cool New York office, click on a few icons, and like magic—conference calls with pictures in real time. Like Dick Tracy, only bigger."

"Tag and the professor will be glad to see you, err, in real time. Speaking of time, you want to schedule a conference?"

"Be better if we wait on that. The Federal Reserve Bank of New York is sponsoring a big powwow of all the alphabets in a week or so—FBI, CIA, OCC, SEC, ICE, ATF, DEA, FinCEN, you know. I'll have more information after that."

"Sounds exciting. Just let me know."

"Done," he said. "Oh, Lieutenant. Don't be surprised if I look a tad heavier. It's this damn computer camera. Adds thirty, forty pounds."

"We'll make allowances," Julia said. "Talk to you soon."

***

Tagger strode into Union Station.

"Got a little pep in your step, Sergeant," said Teresa. "Looks like you got some good news from across the river. Either that, or you really have to go…"

"Good to see you, too," said Tagger, walking past her. He found Marino at his desk.

"Tony," said Tagger. "Just got back from West Memphis. Got a hit on the sketch. A trucker spending the night at the Pilot recognized our guy. He's pretty sure the driver's first name is Diego. The trucker runs a designated route from San Antonio to Newark and back. Says they cross paths frequently on I-35 and I-40. Says he thinks Diego goes into Atlanta, then up to Richmond, maybe Norfolk. Diego's tractor is an old Volvo, painted white, with four super singles on the back."

"Super singles?"

"They're double the width of regular tires. One of the supers replaces two of the single-width tires."

"Does that make an 18-wheeler a 14-wheeler?"

"I guess so."

"Sounds like some kind of neutering," said Marino, making a face. "Getting four of your wheels cut off has to hurt."

"The trucker pulled his log and confirmed he'd stopped in the West Memphis Pilot on July 31st," Tagger said.

"That the same day you've been checking out?" said Marino.

"Yeah, last Friday. Trucker said he parked next to Diego's rig. Said he saw him with a young woman in the restaurant. Motorcycle woke him at two or three in the morning. It pulled up to Diego's truck and the rider banged on the window, whispering real loud in Spanish. Diego let him in. He couldn't see into the truck because he had privacy curtains. The guy on the motorcycle left after only a few minutes, and Diego pulled out right behind him. But he'd pulled down the curtains, and the trucker thought he saw someone in the passenger seat."

"Angel?"

"That's what I'm thinking."

"Get a description of the guy on the motorcycle?"

"Not much. Only that he was a little guy, medium build, dark hair, and speaks Spanish."

"And the motorcycle?"

"Described it as smaller than a Harley. Maybe red. Not sure because those big mercury lamps tend to discolor things."

"Where do you go from here?" Marino said.

"I'll update our sketch with this new information, and get

it posted in truck stops and rest areas all along that route from San Antonio to Dallas, over to Nashville, down through Chattanooga and Atlanta, then up to Richmond," Tagger said. "Maybe we'll get lucky again. How about you?"

"You're not going to believe this," said Marino. "But I got nineteen matches on Chrysler Limited owners and Porter's client list."

"Nineteen?" Tagger said. "I wouldn't have thought there were that many Chrysler Limiteds on the road, let alone all belonging to Porter's clients. What's up with that?"

"Maybe Porter was giving them away to new investors as a signing bonus."

"I can hear the killer now. *Here's your signing bonus, you SOB.*"

"Not so farfetched when you say it like that."

"Or, maybe Porter is part owner of a Chrysler dealership?"

"A dealership," said Marino. "Now there's an idea."

## Chapter 21

# They're Hauling How Much Cash?

*Friday afternoon…Hotlanta.* Teresa buzzed in.

"You've got a long-distance call on line two. A Major Taylor."

"Lieutenant Todd."

"This is Major Taylor. Atlanta PD Organized Crime."

"Yes, Major. What can I do for you?"

"I think the question is what can we do for each other?"

"Okay. Sounds promising."

"Yesterday, we found the body of a man, shot once behind the ear. Looks like a professional hit. No ID. Lying in a field, beside I-75, north side of Atlanta. Been trying to identify him when we found your person-of-interest sketch. It might be the same man, even has a rosary tattoo."

"Last Saturday morning we found the body of a teenage female prostitute beside eastbound I-40, broken neck. She had a reputation for working the truck stops, particularly across the river in the West Memphis area. A cleaning woman and a waitress at a West Memphis Pilot Travel Center saw her with this person-of-interest on the night before her death. No name on him. No other leads. Only that the women described him as Mexican."

"That's our guess. You probably know Atlanta's a hotbed of drug traffic from the Mexican cartels. I've talked a lot to your Memphis guys in organized crime, so I know you have similar problems. It's just that your population is so much smaller. We give them way too much business up and down the east coast."

"So how can we help each other?"

"Knowing he was most likely a truck driver helps. Plus the fact the girl was killed on Saturday morning. Given the usual routes, that would have given your person-of-interest plenty of time to make his drop. That means he was on his way back with something else when he was killed."

"Something else?"

"I see you don't talk to your organized crime folks much, Lieutenant. You don't think they're just going to drive empty trailers back to Mexico, do you?"

"No, of course not. *That* would be dumb."

"The drivers often swap trailers full of drugs with ones filled with guns or cash. Probably half of the cash is sent back inside cars and vans. But the rest goes in trailers. Not unusual for an 18-wheeler to haul seventy-five, eighty million dollars in greenbacks cross country."

"*Eighty million?*"

"Used to be they headed for the border, but nowadays the cartels don't want to take a chance of losing that much money in one bust. So, some 18-wheelers go across the border, but more often they're routed to a secondary counting house near the border, where the money is broken down into smaller bundles, hidden in all manner of places, and moved across the border by a stream of individuals and families. They call it *ruta hormiga,* the ant route. The *ants* simply drop their load at collection sites inside Mexico, pick-up their small cut, and go home."

"What an operation. So simple, so complex. And the image of an unending line of ants speaks volumes."

"Well, there's another image that speaks even louder.

The cartels are a ruthless, murderous group, killing seven to ten thousand people a year. And the pictures include mass murders, with as many as thirty decapitated bodies dropped in the streets in one part of town, their heads scattered in another."

"Damn. I don't think I'll be able to get *that* image out of my head. Let's go back to the cash."

"Most of the cash is used to keep the various businesses going—paying employees, buying more drugs, especially from South America. Another big chunk goes to keep law enforcement and politicians in line. Billions just sit in homes or warehouses waiting to get distributed. Hell, two years ago the Mexican authorities discovered a house holding $207 million dollars, bundled, wrapped, and piled high—one of their own banks. They just take it out as they need it."

"So how much of this is profit?" asked Julia.

"About twenty percent. That's the cash that gets laundered. They unload it at one of their friendly banks, which then wires the amount to other friendly banks. They keep doing that until we can't tie the money to their various enterprises. That way, if we ever do bust 'em, the evidence is untraceable, and the laundered cash is still theirs free and clear to use any way they wish, including hiring lots of high-profile attorneys."

"Looks like I've got some things to learn."

"One more thing. I'm guessing the two murders are connected. We've seen it before. Sounds like the gang bangers who ride shotgun for the cartel's drug smuggling."

"Riding shotgun? Like *Smokey and the Bandit?*"

"You're not far off. Only *these* bandits are very dangerous men. They don't lead the cops on merry chases for the fun of it. They shoot them. You take care now, Lieutenant."

"You too, Major. And, thanks."

***

Julia picked up the phone, punched in the numbers.

"Lieutenant Ayers."

"Ray. This is Julia at the Union Station."

"Hey. Long time no see. What's going on?"

"I think I need a crash course in drug smuggling. Any chance you could drop by and talk to me and my team? Say next week?"

"Not a problem. Anything in particular you want to know about?"

"We found a dead prostitute Saturday. Looks like one of the Mexican cartel's goons broke her neck. Our one person-of-interest just turned up dead in Atlanta. A bullet behind his ear. We need to know what we've stumbled on."

"I've got just what you need."

## Chapter 22

# Trust Me, I'm From the Government

*Day four in Paris…top of the Arc de Triomphe.*

Martine crossed the Champs Elysees, walked down the stairway into the underground entrance under the Place de Charles de Gaulle, the heavily trafficked roundabout surrounding the Arc de Triomphe. She took the elevator to the top of the monument and searched the crowd for a woman dressed in black, wearing a yellow scarf. The French love their black attire and their muted scarves, Martine thought, but I don't remember ever seeing one with a yellow scarf. She began to laugh, but stopped at a smile. Looking out over the Champs Elysees taking pictures was a woman with a long yellow scarf fluttering behind her like a flag. This agent must have graduated from spy school in the bottom of her class on undercover techniques, thought Martine. She walked to the southeast side of the monument and stood nearby. The woman continued clicking photos.

"Welcome to Paris, *Martine*," said the CIA agent. "It took you longer than we expected." Click. Click.

"I did a little shopping," Martine said.

"Shopping. Of course. Well, we're glad you finally made it." Click. Click.

"Me too."

"Hope you enjoyed the spa treatments on Uncle Sam's dime."

"It's not Uncle Sam's dime I'm after. It's my full pardon. The government *is* going to keep its part of the bargain, right?"

"Of course." Click. Click. "Just not yet."

"You're joking."

"It's only one more little thing."

"I've already done a really big thing. That was the deal. Special Agent Davenport promised. There will be no little thing."

"Davenport is no longer in charge—I am. And I have a project for you in Venezuela." Click.

No response.

"It won't be nearly as dangerous, and I understand your Spanish is even better than your Arabic."

No response.

"There'll be a week-long training program as before. We'll pick you up at your hotel today at three. There's enough time for you to get back there and throw your things together. We'll meet you in the lobby." Click. Click.

Martine spun around and joined the queue for the elevator.

***

*Martine meets Marguerite…*Martine hurried through the monument tunnel, deciding it would be faster to walk back to her hotel than waiting around for a taxi. Those SOBs, she thought, I knew they'd pull something like this. The only difference between them and the Judge is *they* never smile. Martine strode through the hotel doors at 1:52. A handful of people sat in the lobby. One eyed her, the others continued looking at tour books, laptops, or cell phones. How many are CIA? she wondered. Maybe one's waiting for me in the room?

Martine took the elevator, pushing 3. She turned on her pen. A tracking bug in her dress signaled, but no camera. She slipped the bug from the hem of her dress as the doors opened, walked to her room door, and tucked the bug under the edge of the hall carpet. Then she moved quickly to the stairs, climbed to the fifth floor, and strode to the first door on the left. Martine inserted a keycard into the reader, removed the NE PAS DERANGER placard, and stepped inside.

The room looked almost identical to Martine's on the third floor. But this was *Marguerite's* room, with a medium-size battered suitcase holding wigs, a variety of clothing and shoes, and a handful of passports. She walked through the room focused on her detector pen for any sign of a camera or tracking device. All clear. Martine fanned five passports on the bed:

Charleze Mitchell — United States of America,

Akilah al Qasim — United Arab Emirates,

Martine Didier — France,

Marguerite Goscinny — Canada, and

Darlene Kaerchner — Germany.

Martine undressed, folding her clothes neatly. She removed her make-up and fingernail polish, lightened her eyebrows. She over-applied make-up—too much pancake powder, too much rouge and lipstick. She pulled on pleated black slacks, a black and gray striped blouse, and heavy black shoes. Finally, she stretched on a gray wig, added wire-rimmed glasses, opened one of the passports to the photo, studied herself in the mirror.

"Bonjour, Marguerite," she said.

***

An elderly woman commanded the lobby, carrying a large purse and a well-worn square-cornered suitcase, her small steps bolstered by a thick black cane, chin held high. She stepped to the registration desk, set down her suitcase, grew to her full height, and surveyed the other side of the counter as if preparing to address a theatre audience.

"I am Marguerite Goscinny," she announced, speaking French with a decided Quebec twang. "I am checking out."

"We hope your stay was a pleasant one, madam," said the desk clerk, pushing the print button. "Your bill, madam."

"Do not rush me," she said, searching her purse for a pair of reading glasses. Marguerite laid the bill on the counter, checked each entry, returned her glasses, meticulously folded the bill and slipped it inside her purse. She looked up. "Is my taxi ready?"

"Oui, madam. Please allow le garcon to assist you with your luggage," he said, tapping the bell and motioning to the bellboy to hurry.

"Be careful with that," Marguerite said. "And don't get too far ahead of me."

Two men sat in opposite corners of the lobby, watching the desk clerk and bell boy deal with Marguerite—one eye on her and one on each other—snickering, shaking their heads. They lost the smiles when their earpieces came to life.

"Martine is not in her room," said the female voice. "She hid the tracking bug under the hall carpet. Find her. Do you copy? Find her!"

***

*Charles de Gaulle Aéroport*…Marguerite Goscinny boarded the plane for Montreal. A fellow passenger loaded her battered suitcase in the overhead compartment and she settled into her business class seat. She ordered a glass of champagne, closed her eyes and relaxed.

Chapter 23

# Filling In A Few Blanks

*Saturday, Arkansas…cheap cameras.* Tagger pulled into the West Memphis Wal-Mart parking lot, and drove to the white security pick-up parked in the northwest corner, far away from the store.

"Sergeant Tagger?" said the uniformed man. "I'm Logan Colgate, head of security."

"Mr. Colgate. Good to meet you. Thanks for the call."

"As I said on the phone, my wife and I go to the Pilot restaurant almost every week. We ate there last night. Had the all-you-can-eat buffet. You're a big guy. I bet you'd like—"

"Colgate," Tagger interrupted. "The motorcyclist?"

"Oh, sorry. Anyway, I saw your person-of-interest flyer taped to the wall. Got me to thinking. So I came into work this morning and pulled our security DVDs from last weekend, looking at Friday and Saturday. That's when I saw the motorcycle. Right here, under this security light," Colgate said, pointing up. "The one with the bullet hole in it."

"I'll need a copy of the DVD?"

"No problem, Sergeant," Colgate said, pulling out a plastic case. "Ran you off one."

"Thanks."

"The picture's not great. Part because of the dead security light, and part because we use one of the cheapest cameras we sell. Welcome to *Wal-Mart*."

***

*Saturday, Memphis…bet you paid too much for your car.* Marino began calling owners on his Chrysler Limited list. It only took two calls. Both cars purchased from Berkman's Chrysler. Both from the same salesman. Marino drove east on Poplar, almost out to Clark Tower, turned south on Mendenhall, then bending left before crossing over I-240 where it opened to a busy six-lane street flanked by car dealerships and fast food. He pulled into Berkman's. An attractive woman approached before he could open his car door.

"Lovely morning, officer," she said, smiling. "I'm Ellie Houston, How can I help you?"

Marino got out, his thick leather belt squeaking. "I'm looking for Andy Fine," he said. "I hear he's the man to see about buying a Limited."

"He is indeed the *man* to see about the Limited. But I'm the *woman* to see. I'll give you a great deal."

"Afraid this is police business. But I'll remember your name."

"I hope you do," she said handing him her business card. "Next time just ask for Ellie."

Marino entered the showroom, scanning the name plates sitting in the cubbyhole office windows until he found Fine's. There were other signs in his window. Walking closer he could see Fine had been named Salesman of the Year numerous times, then for the last two years, Salesperson of the Year. He knocked on the window. Fine looked up from his phone call, smiled, and waved him inside.

Marino took a seat and waited for him to finish his call.

He clicked off, stood and offered his hand, "Andy Fine. I'm sure I can help you, officer."

Marino stood, shook his hand. "I'm Sergeant Marino.

I'm pretty sure you can, too," he said. "I'm investigating a murder."

Fine plopped back in his chair. "A murder? Who was killed?"

"Terence Porter."

"Terry… Yes, I read about it in the paper. Terrible. But how can I help?"

"He was a friend?" asked Marino.

"Yes. A good friend, for many years."

"As many years as you've won Salesman of the Year?"

"Why, yes, I suppose. What are you getting at?"

"I've been looking at Mr. Porter's client list. Seems there're an awful lot of his clients who own Chrysler Limiteds. And as far as I've seen, they were all purchased from Berkman's. In fact, you're listed as the salesman for all of them. Odd, wouldn't you say?"

Fine squirmed, fidgeted with a paperclip. "Not that odd," he said.

"Really? Seems like an awful lot of coincidences to me."

"Do I need an attorney?"

"I don't know. Do you?"

"I mean…are you arresting me?"

"Now, why would I do a thing like that?"

"You just seem to be implying…"

"Implying what?"

"That I've done something illegal."

"Really? And what illegal activity might that be?"

"I want to talk to my attorney."

"You can always talk to your attorney. Heck, you even have the right to remain silent."

## Chapter 24

# Reach Out and Touch Someone

*Saturday…the phone call.* Julia dipped her brush into the soft blue paint for what she hoped would be the final time. The renovation would be complete. It had been almost four months since the car bomb damaged her home. Her phone sounded a generic ringtone. She found herself in a tug of war. Should I apply the final brush load of paint, she thought, or should I answer the phone. It rang again. She placed the brush across the lip of the paint can, climbed down the stepladder, and grabbed her cell from the kitchen counter.

"Todd."

"Well, hello, *Todd*," said Mark.

"Mark. I didn't know it was you."

"Yeahhh," he sing-songed. "Your little ole Svedish boyfriend."

"I miss you, boyfriend."

"We just talked Thursday."

"Really? It seems like forever ago."

"I was thinking about you and how much you love your gourmet coffee. Did you know the Swedes pride themselves in their coffee?"

"I thought it was vodka."

"Yeah, that too. Anyway they have a huge specialty coffee company and they send the stuff all around the world. So I thought if I had top quality coffee at my house, maybe you'd come over more often. So I signed up for six months."

"How much you getting?"

"You can order it on any schedule you like. I went with one bag a month. They have a bazillion blends, including decaf. They even threw in a free coffee maker."

"You don't drink that much coffee."

"That's the point. I'd need help. And you can choose whatever type of coffee you want."

"Well maybe on the weekends. Better yet, you could bring your toothbrush and gourmet coffee over to my place on Friday nights."

"It's a deal. Will I need to bring a paint brush too?"

"Just have one more brush full to finish my second coat."

"One final stroke? That's great. You've been working."

"No one here to distract me."

"Is that what I am, a distraction?"

"Yeah," she said. "Want to distract me now?"

Chapter 25

# You're On Candid Camera

*Monday, 2:30 AM…rest stop southeast of Chattanooga.* Hector parked the Cadillac Escalade in the I-75 rest area truck lanes, accommodating the trailer. His passenger woke up.

"What's going on?" Ernesto asked, bleary-eyed.

"I gotta take a leak," said Hector. "You watch the car."

"Yeah, yeah."

Hector pulled the bill of his ball cap down to just above his eyes and climbed out. He walked inside the restroom, spotting feet under the second stall. He stepped up to the urinal and unzipped. He looked up to see a grainy photograph of the Escalade, Ernesto pushing his motorcycle into the attached trailer. "What the hell?" he said to himself, stepping back and wetting his jeans. He looked over to see a poster taped above each of the remaining urinals. He hastily zipped up and pulled the flyers off the wall, stuffing them into his pocket. No other flyers were visible in the restroom, but he left without washing his hands or his jeans, in case there were flyers in the stalls.

Hector jogged to the Escalade and yanked open the door.

"What's the big hurry?" asked Ernesto.

"Look at these," said Hector, tossing him the fliers.

"That's me!" said Ernesto. "Where the hell'd they get this?"

"I don't know. But we need to ditch the trailer quick, and

probably this car, too."

***

Hector turned off the expressway, driving south on a two-lane highway. He saw an abandoned barn, standing alone. He turned onto the rutted drive, pulled off into tall grass, cut his lights, and backed through the barn's open doors. Ernesto grabbed a flashlight, and they hurried to unhitch the trailer. The two men hoisted Hector's black motorcycle into the Escalade. Then Ernesto wiped his red motorcycle down as thoroughly as he could, while Hector loaded helmets, leather jackets, gloves, and other gear. Hector eased the Escalade from the barn, turned on his lights, and retraced his route to I-75.

***

*4:15 AM...*The phone rang in the in-town Atlanta suburb of Decatur.

"Hello," said Manuel, clearing his throat.

"Manuel? Ernesto. We need help."

***

Hector pulled the Escalade into the three-car garage. Manuel Ramos engaged the automatic door closer.

"Thanks, Manuel," said Hector, handing him a flyer.

"You've been careless," said Manuel. "You've jeopardized the cartel's business."

"I was protecting the cartel," said Ernesto. "That stupid Diego fell behind on his run because he couldn't keep it in his pants. And his whore girlfriend would've been singing to the cops about us."

"And I take it you're the one who killed Diego without checking with me," said Manuel.

"That's right," Ernesto said. "And you'd have pulled the trigger yourself if you'd heard him yapping to anyone in the bar who'd listen. I just helped him outside, then took him

104

for a little ride."

"You know he was hauling guns?" Manuel said.

"Guns," said Ernesto, looking down.

"We almost lost them," said Manuel. "You never think about the big picture, Ernesto. Lucky I found another driver. You could have cost the Conrios cartel big time."

"Hey," said Ernesto. "Nobody told me."

"You didn't need to know," said Manuel. "And what about your cycle?"

"I wiped it clean," said Ernesto. "It's sitting in an abandoned barn out in the sticks. No one's going to find it."

"Weren't you the one assigned to off that banker in Memphis?"

"Yeah," said Ernesto. "I nailed him in the head, twice."

"You sure," said Manuel. "I read about him in the newspaper. Someone shot up his three thousand dollar mirror. Looks like you didn't come close."

"What?" Ernesto said. "I saw the shots hit."

"You saw the shots hit his reflection, you idiot," said Manuel. "El Pequeño Toro is going to be pissed. *The Little Bull*'s got a short fuse. You know how angry he gets. You'd better get your act together, boy, or one of us is going to get a contract email with *your* name and picture. Hell, the Little Bull might cross the border himself—just to deal with you personally. It wouldn't be the first time."

Ernesto's face flushed, first from anger then from fear. "I'll finish Traner off on our way back through Memphis," he said.

"Okay," said Manuel, looking from Ernesto to Hector. "Here's what's going to happen. You're going to stay out of sight. In a few hours my wife'll be taking my kids to school. Then you're going van shopping, at a place that's not going to require any paperwork."

"A good for nothing van?" said Hector. "We need more power than that."

"Your stupidity got your picture plastered in every piss house and cop shop from here to Laredo," said Manuel. "You need to stay off the radar. End of discussion."

***

"Here's the address," Manuel said.

"We don't know Atlanta," said Hector.

"Use your fancy GPS," Manuel said, handing him an envelope. "I've already talked to Jorge. He's got a souped-up black van, lots of power, and plenty of room for two motorcycles *and* your weapons. He'll do a straight-up swap for the Escalade, no questions asked. Give him this ten thousand dollars as a thank-you. And, Hector…"

"Yeah," said Hector, snatching the envelope.

"Make sure he gets all ten thousand," said Manuel.

"I need a new motorcycle," Ernesto said.

Manuel looked at him, hard. "Jorge can arrange that too," he said. "But you use your own damn money."

"You want us to come back here?" said Hector.

"Hell, no," said Manuel. "Get your asses back on the road and check on deliveries. And Ernesto…"

"Yeah?" said Ernesto.

Manuel's eyes narrowed. "I don't want to hear about anymore screw-ups."

## Chapter 26

# The Meeting Before The Meeting

*8:00 AM, Monday…the right way to start the day.* Julia felt good, driving into Union Station with a bag of decadent chocolate éclairs from La Baguette bakery. She gathered her team in the conference room.

"We should do this every Monday, Lieutenant," said Tagger, reaching for another napkin.

"I'll second that motion," Marino said, raising his coffee cup.

"You're welcome, fellas," Julia said. "Now, if you can concentrate enough to bring me up to speed before our conference call with Masterson…"

"I got a call on the updated person-of-interest flyer," said Tagger. "Turns out the head of security for the West Memphis Wal-Mart is a fan of all things deep fried. He and his wife love to eat at the Pilot restaurant. Spotted our flyer and decided to check Wal-Mart's security DVDs for the Friday and Saturday in question. Low and behold he got a hit. The picture quality is poor, but you can clearly make out a large dark SUV pulling a white or light-colored closed trailer. A motorcyclist pulls up and drives up a ramp into the trailer at 2:32 AM Saturday. He climbs into the driver's seat and pulls away.

"That's consistent with the timeframe given by the

trucker who saw the guy on the motorcycle drive off. Right?" said Marino.

Tagger nodded. "And it's consistent with the Medical Examiner's ToD estimate."

"Anything we can use from the DVD?" asked Julia. "Faces, plates, make, model?"

"Nothing I was able to make out," said Tagger. "But I'll take it over to Elwood to see if he can work his computer magic on it."

"Good idea," said Marino. "Elwood's cleaned up some pretty bad videos before."

"I updated the person-of-interest flyer again," said Tagger. "Including the info about Diego having been found dead. Now we have two dead, and a large black SUV towing a trailer with at least one man and one motorcycle."

"That's a high-profile vehicle," said Julia. "Should be easy to spot. How about the Porter case, professor?"

"Something Johnnie mentioned got me to thinking," Marino said. "So I called the first two names on my list of clients with Chrysler Limiteds. Turns out both cars came from Berkman's Chrysler dealership. Both sold by the same salesman, Andy Fine."

"Some coincidence," Julia said.

Marino smiled. "Had a nice chat with Mr. Fine. Seems he and Porter had a standing relationship. Part of Porter's sales pitch was to offer potential investors fifty percent off on the latest Chrysler of their choice for signing up. Most of them chose the Limited."

"That'd be a thirty or forty thousand-dollar signing bonus," said Tagger. "How could Porter afford it?"

"He required a minimum buy-in of a hundred thousand," said Marino. "And since he had no intention of investing any money in the client's name, he had about sixty or seventy thousand free and clear. He simply used the client's own money to pay for the other half of their car."

"So, in effect, the clients paid full price for their new car," said Tagger.

"Right," said Marino. "Then Porter used their remaining money to pay off earlier investors. And if he played his cards right, he'd scam them into investing even more money, chasing the possibility of hitting it big."

"Any chance Fine got greedy?" said Julia.

"Actually, he was an early investor," said Marino. "Porter made sure Fine got hefty returns, even this last year when the market dropped in the toilet."

"You thinking he had anything to do with the hit-and-run on Porter?" asked Julia.

"Motive's not obvious," Marino said. "Doesn't mean there isn't one."

## Chapter 27

# In Real Time

*9:00 AM, Monday…friendships forged under fire.* Teresa set up the large screen monitor in the conference room in preparation for FBI Special Agent Lawrence Masterson's computer-conference call. She angled the computer camera to pick up all three officers. They heard the call-in signal. Teresa clicked on the icon, and Masterson's face filled the screen.

"Hey, guys," said Masterson. "It's great to see you. Ain't technology grand?"

"Hey, big man," said Tagger. "You recover from your Memphis assignment?"

"Johnnie!" said Masterson. "No problem. Soon as I got north of the Mason-Dixon line the uncontrollable sweating stopped. Hey there, Tony."

"Lawrence," said Marino, smiling. "We miss having you around. Well, you and Maria."

"And Lieutenant Todd," Masterson said. "It really is good to see you. To see all you guys."

"The feeling's mutual," said Julia. "Two people are alive because of the team we put together last year."

"I read where Dr. Mitchell skipped on her bail just before the trial," said Masterson.

"After what her attorney told us, I'm not sure she'd have

spent more than a few years in jail for the industrial sabotage and insider trading," said Julia. "He said she had recordings of telephone conversations that would clear her of any involvement in the murders."

"Maybe so," said Marino. "But a guy can hope can't he?"

"How's the little Texas sharpshooter?" said Tagger.

"Yeah," said Marino. "How is Maria?"

"Maria's doing great. We talk on the phone every other week or so," said Masterson. "She's enjoying her assignment on the west coast. And from what I hear, she's holding her own."

"Did you have your big meeting yet?" said Julia.

"This coming weekend," said Masterson. "Meantime, the SEC has been zeroing in on a few of the Memphis banks and investment firms. Like I told the Lieutenant, the FBI sent a considerable contingent of agents your way, first stop—Morgan Keegan. It wouldn't be as big a deal if it were only a matter of sorting out the fraud, but it looks like these guys have been crazy enough to be doing business with some very bad dudes."

"What kind of bad dudes?" said Tagger.

"The worst kind," said Masterson. "The kind who'll hunt you down and kill your family just to send a message."

"We've had one investment consultant killed," said Marino. "But we're not aware of his having family in the area."

"Someone also took a shot at one of your bankers about ten days ago, while he was in his own home," Masterson said.

"I heard about that shooting," said Julia. "Out in Collierville. Didn't realize he was a banker."

"We've been watching this guy," said Masterson. "Herman Traner. A VP at Sizemore Global Financial Solutions Group. He's dirty. Runs a Ponzi scheme and is point man in Sizemore's international money laundering program."

"You're kidding," said Tagger. "Sizemore? He's a major player in charity work in the city, sits on all the big non-profit boards. He even bailed out the annual St. Jude PGA tournament by sponsoring it. *He's* being investigated for fraud? And money laundering?"

"Big time," said Masterson. "A massive Ponzi scheme for the common citizen, and money laundering for terrorists, gun runners, and drug cartels."

"And you think this attempted murder of Traner is tied to...?" Julia said.

"I'm thinking the money laundering," said Masterson. "Because Traner's been seen in the company of one of the biggest international money laundering organizations, run out of the Middle East. But then again, guys like him are so full of themselves they don't have any sense. Hell, he could've convinced the head of one of the cartels to buy into his Ponzi scheme, expecting to rip him off like one of his clueless Tennessee marks."

"You have an idea how we fit into this?" said Marino.

"I think you'll see more murders of financial types and their families in the Memphis area," Masterson said. "You should be suspicious of any shooting or arson in your upper income communities. And one more thing. These guys don't care who's standing next to their target when they start spraying the area with bullets. Be careful."

"Where will these thugs be coming from?" asked Julia.

"Hard to say," Masterson said. "I'm thinking they'll be tied to the drug cartels, mostly Mexican. These guys have a pattern of setting up housekeeping in upscale suburbs, blending into the neighborhood. You know, like Russian sleeper spies from the fifties?"

"You mean a church choir member on Sunday and a hit-man during the week?" said Marino.

"You got it, Tony," Masterson said. "Maybe even a kid's soccer coach. Very hard to spot. So to answer your question, I think they'll come by car—either from just down the street, or driving in from a nearby big city, maybe Dallas or Atlanta."

"Anyone sharing this with the MPD?" asked Julia.

"Being that the Mexican cartels are now considered the biggest organized crime threat to the US, all FBI communications are being run through the organized crime units of the various police departments," said Masterson. "I think they're taking point on this one."

"Thanks," said Julia. "Keep us posted. We'll do the same."

"Agreed," Masterson said. "You guys keep your heads down." He clicked off.

"Nice to see Lawrence," said Tagger. "How come I don't feel so good?"

"Because, my large friend," Marino said, "he was warning us World War III is coming to Memphis."

"And he probably broke ranks to do it," said Julia. "I haven't heard anything about this in department meetings. Those in the know must be playing this close to the vest."

"So where do we go from here?" said Tagger.

"Turns out Lieutenant Ray Ayers is coming over tomorrow," Julia said.

"He's from organized crime, right?" Marino asked.

"Yeah," said Julia. "I asked him to bring us up to speed on how the drug smuggling works in the midsouth. He'll be here at two."

Chapter 28

# Out of the Blue

*Tuesday…I don't have time for this.* Julia winced, pressed her hand on her cheek.

"What's the matter, Lieutenant?" said Teresa.

"This darn tooth," Julia said. "It's been screaming at me."

"Bet it's abscessed. You need to see a dentist. Gotta cut out the infection. Odds are you'll need a root canal. Oh, my God, lots of shots. Make sure you ask for the laughing gas. I know plenty of folk who didn't do that, and they really regretted it afterwards."

"Teresa."

"I'm just saying. My uncle almost died from the infection—"

"Teresa!"

"Okay. But don't say I didn't warn you…Want me to make an emergency appointment with your dentist?"

***

*Looky what I found…*The phone rang. Tagger picked up.

"Sergeant, this is Deputy Sherriff Elliott in Catoosa County, Georgia. I think we found something you've been looking for."

"Our person-of-interest?"

"Not quite. Wouldn't want to make it that easy for you. But we do have the white trailer with a red motorcycle inside."

"Great work."

"Found a copy of your person-of-interest flyer lying in the grass. My guess is your guy discovered it at one of the rest stops. Knew he had to ditch the trailer. Expect he'll do the same with the SUV soon as he can."

"We'll send someone to tow it back. Thanks, Deputy."

Tagger began revising his person-of-interest flyer, again.

Chapter 29

# An Unintended Consequence of NAFTA

*Audacity, creativity, savagery…Union Station conference room.*

"I asked Lieutenant Ray Ayers of the OCU to fill us in on the drug smuggling, especially coming from Mexico," Julia said.

"Happy to be here," said Ayers. "Of course, we're all used to hearing Memphis is a transportation hub for the country. Federal Express is headquartered here, and we've had an increase in train, plane and truck traffic over the years. The fact Memphis is a hub also makes it perfect for smuggling—drugs, guns, U.S. dollars, contraband cigarettes, and illegal aliens, as well as human trafficking."

"Somehow it doesn't seem like such a good thing now," Marino said.

"Fact of life, Sergeant," said Ayers. "There really isn't a place in the country free of smuggling. The Justice Department has identified over a thousand US cities with a cartel link. It's just most places refuse to admit it's happening in their hometown."

"Not something the Chamber of Commerce wants to market," said Julia.

"No," said Ayers. "But realistically, smuggling, like our commerce, is based on supply and demand. If people didn't demand these things, there'd be no profit in smuggling it."

"Nobody but ourselves to blame," Marino said.

"And the Mexican cartels have forced their way into the driver's seat on filling those demands," said Ayers. "They've learned from the Mafia, running their diversified operations like big business—accountants, business plans, lawyers—all backed up by a small, well-armed militia, warehouses of weapons, stockpiles of cash, a large fleet of trucks, and a pay-roll loaded with government and law enforcement officials."

"How the hell'd that happen?" said Tagger.

"Y'all remember NAFTA?" Ayers said. "The North America Free Trade Agreement passed by Congress in 1995 to encourage trade between the US, Canada, and Mexico?"

"I remember," said Marino, "But Tag, here, was playing football for Michigan about then, and I don't think he had time to read the papers."

"Huge layoffs in the Michigan auto plants." said Tagger, shooting Marino a look.

Julia rolled her eyes. "Please continue, Ray."

"Yes, lots of layoffs," said Ayers. "American industry moved many of its factories into Mexico to reduce employee costs. Right away US transportation companies moved to block Mexican trucks from driving on our highways. They put in a crazy-ass three-phase system. Mexican long haul truckers brought goods up to the border at which point they trans-ferred their containers to a separate Mexican trucking firm which drove the goods across the Border and off-loaded them in warehouses just inside the US. American truckers picked up those trailers and made the runs throughout the country."

"So US truckers brought drugs and other contraband goods into this country," said Tagger.

"For the most part unknowingly, but yes," said Ayers. "This

system continued for almost five years before the Mexican government sued, resulting in an arbitration ruling in favor of Mexicans driving Mexican trucks across the border and into the US.

"Did this result in more smuggling?" asked Julia.

"Yes, but probably because at this same time the volume of traffic crossing from Mexico increased to over three million truck containers a year, just into Texas. The vast majority are legitimate. But it only takes a small percentage to keep the drugs flowing, and there's no possible way to thoroughly inspect more than a tiny fraction of that many vehicles. If in fact, the border guards randomly select times of the day when they focus extra officers and dogs on searches."

"The odds have to be better at the Tunica casinos," said Tagger.

"I was talking to one of Homeland Security's ICE agents," said Ayers.

"Immigration and Customs Enforcement?" Marino said.

"Right." said Ayers. "It's a big agency, second only to the FBI. Anyway the agent said the cartels seem to always know when ICE has scheduled intensified searches. Said they believe one or more of the ICE agents are on the take—anyone from a custodian or a secretary all the way up the line in Washington, D C."

"We heard about the cartels sending men to guard the smugglers on their routes," Julia said.

"Yeah," said Ayers. "That's probably why you invited me here. A lot of the guards are recruited from Mexican and Mexican-American street gangs. These thugs ride shotgun, and too many officers have been killed when they stopped one of the cartel's 18-wheelers. But the thugs work both sides. They keep the drivers in line as well."

"Like Diego, our person-of-interest?" said Tagger.

"Exactly," said Ayers. "Apparently, Diego didn't follow the rules."

"What's the deal about these trucks going back across the border full of cash?" said Tagger.

"Some do," said Ayers. "The cartels set up money-counting shops in cities like Los Angeles, Chicago, Atlanta, Boston. They change small US denominations into fifties and hundreds, then vacu-pack them in small packages to hide in cars and vans. Hell, even in teddy bears. Others are vacu-packed in huge bundles. Some 18-wheelers carry ungodly amounts of money, piled high on pallets, packed inside bags of dog food or fertilizer. But not all the returning 18-wheelers carry cash. Some carry guns, explosives. Lots actually have legitimate cargo. For one thing, having a smaller percentage of the cartel's trucks hauling what the feds call *bulk cash* increases the odds of their getting across the border clean, especially since both countries do a half-assed job of checking traffic crossing *into* Mexico. But even so, the cartels are making so much money, getting caught's—"

"Just the cost of doing business," Marino interrupted.

"Exactly," said Ayers.

"We've heard the cartels plant men, even families, in our big cities," said Julia.

"Not only in the big cities," said Ayers. "A while back some hunters stumbled upon a huge marijuana farm up in northern Wisconsin, guarded by guys with AK-47s."

"You have a handle on who's here in the midsouth?" asked Tagger.

Ayers smiled. "Let's say...we have a few people under surveillance."

"Would these be the ones to carry out contract hits?" asked Tagger.

"Good question," said Ayers. "Not usually. They're more

likely to be in a coordinator role, maintaining their undercover position and letting the thugs run the risk of getting caught."

"You waiting for them to do something before you bust them?" said Marino. "Or, is it better to have one in the hand, than diving into the bush trying to catch them?"

"Another good question," Ayers said. "Like in the spy shows, we're able to gather a lot of good intel by just watching and listening. It'd be a shame to lose that source of information and have to start all over with a new cartel sleeper."

## Chapter 30

# The Van

*The counting shop...Boston.* Hector drove. Their new van had all latest gadgets, not too different from their Cadillac. Ernesto sat in the passenger seat, reloading ammo clips.

"How many times you going to do that?" said Hector.

"As many times as I want to," said Ernesto.

"Look, man. You can't undo the past."

"Nobody talks to me like Manuel did."

"Chill out, dude. Manuel's nobody to fool with."

"He ain't no better than me. Puts his pants on just like I do—one leg at a time."

"When you move up the line, you can have a nice house and a fine wife just like him. In the meantime, you need to keep your nose clean. Just do what the man says."

"You didn't like the way he talked to you, like you're going to steal some of the ten thousand dollars. Like you're a common thief. I saw you. He pissed you off."

"Yeah, but you saw me keep my cool. I didn't keep arguing with him."

"We ain't that much different, Hector. We're good at what we do. And we don't like being disrespected."

"True, but I don't want my picture coming up on somebody's Android. And Manuel can make that happen."

Ernesto didn't answer.

"Here's the counting house, up on the right."

He eased the van up to a large iron gate connecting two twelve-foot stone walls. Two guards appeared. One waived them in. After traveling about a quarter mile, two large warehouses came into view, eighteen-wheelers backed up to the docks. Cars and vans parked at the far end of the lot. Hector drove around back. The two men checked their Glock 17s and got out. They nodded to the guards and sauntered inside. They had visited this counting house scores of times—clean bays, and neatly stacked vacuum-sealed packs of fifty-and-hundred-dollar bills. The larger bundles stood six feet high on pallets. Cardboard boxes held smaller bundles of varying sizes. In the far bay, cars and vans stood torn apart as if still on the assembly line. Dashboard and door panels unscrewed, seat cushions piled next to the car, and bumpers lying on the concrete floor—everything ready to hide bundles of cash. Other cars perched on lifts as men with torches welded various size containers to the undercarriages.

Hector jumped when a forklift spun around the corner. The forklift picked up a pallet of bills and headed toward an eighteen-wheeler waiting at the loading dock. At the far end they found the counters and vacu-packers. They approached the foreman.

"We're ready to escort an eighteen-wheeler," said Ernesto. "You about done?"

"You're early," said the foreman. "I've still got two hours. The truck'll be ready."

"No problem, my man," said Hector. "We'll just report back to Manuel about how you run this operation."

"No reason to get him all worked up," said the foreman. "I'll put another forklift on it. You'll be on your way in a half-hour."

Ernesto smiled and fist bumped Hector. "I can't wait to

get back to Memphis. I got some unfinished business to take care of," said Ernesto, scrolling through his Android pictures of Herman Traner and his family—his wife bent forward loading two young children in the car, Traner petting his Weinheimer, his children carrying backpacks to school.

## Chapter 31

# They're A Couple

*Tuesday…Beckman's Chrysler dealership.* Marino sat in the cruiser reviewing his notes, engine running. A tap on his window startled him. He looked over to see a smiling Ellie Houston. She gave the smallest of finger waves. He pressed the power window lever.

"I was hoping you'd come back," she said.

"Afternoon," he said. "Ellie, right?"

"Very good. I don't think I got your name."

"Marino. Sergeant Marino."

"Did your mother give you a different first name than *Sergeant?*"

"Yeah," he said, smiling slightly, a puff of air escaping his nose. "Anthony."

"Do you go by Anthony or Tony?"

"Tony."

"Well, Sergeant Anthony Tony Marino, you decided whether you're interested in buying a car? Or, are you only here to talk to certain salespeople?"

"I'm here on police business."

"What does a girl have to do to be a part of your police business?"

"You already are. It's official," he said, pulling out her business card.

"I want to help. Ask me some questions."

"Okay…It seems to me this dealership sells an awful lot of Limiteds."

"The dealership doesn't, but Andy Fine does. Probably more than anyone else in the country."

"I saw the Salesman of the Year awards plastered all over his office window."

"Sales*person*. And, yes, he's won several of them, thanks to the Limiteds."

"You know his secret?"

"Pretty sure he's got help."

"You mean a junior sales assistant?"

She smiled. "More like a senior sales assistant."

"You talking about the sales manager?"

"Yeah, Marvin Drewer."

"So you think he's showing favoritism?"

"I think he's getting more than one piece of the action."

"And what action might that be?"

"Have you met Marvin?"

"Not yet, but he's on my list."

"Well, it's only a woman's sense, you understand. But I think Marvin prefers to foxtrot backwards."

"You saying Drewer and Fine are a couple?"

"Not Drewer and Fine, silly. Drewer and Terence Porter."

## Chapter 32

# John and Bob

*Tuesday...Union Station.*

Julia's phone rang. "Todd."

"Lieutenant, got something," said Tagger. "I've been watching T-DOT cameras on I-40, looking for the SUV and white trailer from eleven days ago. Thought you'd want to see this."

***

Tagger pressed PLAY. "This is fifteen minutes after they left the Wal-Mart parking lot, coming under the flyover, looks like a Cadillac Escalade. I never found them at the next T-DOT camera, so I thought maybe they got off on Sycamore View," Tagger said.

"You thinking they pulled into a motel for the night?"

"Yup," he said inserting a DVD into his computer. "Went out to check security DVDs. There are at least five motels in that area."

"Don't tell me. You found something in the last place you looked."

Tagger winced. "These little gems just come to you from outa the blue?"

"Yup. That's why they made me a lieutenant. So what'd you find?"

"Compliments of La Quinta Inn, we have this shot of the

Escalade and trailer, and wait for it…Our *two* passengers."

"Great work, Tag. Pretty good shots of them, too."

"They signed in as John Smith and Bob Jones. Lord knows which one's which."

"For one night?"

"Two. The SUV and trailer remained in the lot for five hours. Let me fast forward this thing. Here we are, 8:35 PM Saturday. John and Bob unhook the trailer and drive off in the SUV."

"8:35 Saturday night. You thinking the same thing I am?"

"Trying to earn my lieutenant stripes," he said, returning to the T-DOT cameras. "Here's their Escalade on the Bill Morris Parkway. And here they are getting off on Byhalia Road."

"That'd take them right into Collierville."

"Yup."

"I think you've just found the men who took those shots at Traner. Good work, Tag. Anything more at the La Quinta?"

"They returned at 10:32 PM, hooked up the trailer, and drove east on I-40. I'm guessing they thought they killed Traner."

"Take the DVD over to Elwood. Wait while he cranks out prints on John and Bob, then hand-deliver them to Lieutenant Ayers. I'll give him a heads up. OCU needs to be on the lookout. These guys are coming back."

Chapter 33

# The High-Pitched Drill

*The toothache from hell…*Julia didn't sleep well. It's just a little tooth, she thought. How can it hurt so much? I hate the dentist, even for cleaning, but I can't deal with this pain. At six AM she began calling her dentist's office—only the same recording. Finally, at 8:30 a real person answered. Julia convinced her she had an emergency situation, and received a 9:15 squeeze-you-in appointment.

***

Julia's pain seemed to lessen the closer she got to the dentist's office. Only a light throbbing remained by the time she pushed through the office door, ten minutes early. The waiting room had twelve chairs, only three empty. Julia checked in. The receptionist confirmed her appointment had been made for an emergency. But now Julia seemed unsure.

"It doesn't really hurt so much right now," she heard herself say.

The receptionist smiled knowingly. "Please have a seat, the doctor will be with you shortly."

Julia watched as one hygienist after another showed up in their blue surgical scrubs and called a name. Each one dutifully smiled and asked the *next* patient how they were feeling today. She wondered if she needed to use the bathroom, but she didn't want to leave in case they called her name. She concentrated on holding it, besides it took her mind off her tooth, which had begun to hurt again.

A very young woman in green scrubs came around the corner.

"Ms. Todd," she announced, seeming surprised by Julia's uniform.

Julia stood and walked to her.

"I understand you have a bad toothache," she said loud enough for everyone to hear.

"Yes," said Julia, softly. "It's been acting up the past few days."

"The past few *days?*" she said loudly. "And you're just coming in *now?*"

Julia shrugged her shoulders, feeling powerless to respond to being scolded by this twenty-something authority figure.

***

Julia felt woozy, her bottom lip frozen on the right side. But she felt no pain. She picked up a coffee at the McDonald's drive-thru, and headed to the Union Station.

"There you are, Lieutenant," said Teresa. "Your dental appointment was so long ago, we've been worried."

Julia attempted to speak, but her fat lip and tongue didn't want to cooperate.

"I see you've been trying to drink your coffee," said Teresa, pointing to her own chin and blouse." She pulled a few tissues from their box, handed them to Julia.

Julia touched her chin with her left hand, finding the dribbled coffee. But in a bizarre moment, the right side of her face did not feel her left hand's touch.

"You need to let the novocaine wear off," said Teresa. "I bet you also need some protein. But don't go trying to eat anything. My cousin tried that once after a dental visit. Almost chewed his tongue completely off—"

"Teesa," Julia interrupted. "Peeze."

"Okay. Got it," said Teresa. "I'll walk up the street and get a power smoothie from the Smoothie King. That way you won't have to chew."

"Tanxs," Julia said.

***

"You okay, Lieutenant?" said Tagger.

"Much better now," Julia said. "My lip's tingling back to life, my head's clear, and I can enunciate most of my letters. Tell me where we are on these cases."

"Got an interesting break," said Marino. "Turns out there's a third party involved in this—Beckman's sales manager."

"How'd they run the game?" said Julia.

"You know how car salesmen always tell you they have to check with the manager?" said Marino. "Well, in this case the manager, guy named Marvin Drewer, was in on the scam. Porter sent money for each new car. Drewer sold the Limited at an inflated price, forcing the client buyer to pay well over what half-price should have been. Then he adjusted the official Berkman books to document a significantly reduced selling price. Drewer and Fine took their payment for the deal from the difference between the money actually received and the total figure logged into Berkman's accounting sheet."

"Something's missing," said Julia. "Porter must've gotten something else out of this."

"Actually, Drewer and our Mr. Porter may have been an item," Marino said.

"So, the angry lover theory may not be so far off after all," Julia said.

"Another theory that doesn't seem so outlandish," said Marino.

"Sounds as if we need to get Drewer down to 201 for a

little chat."

"Drewer didn't show up for work yesterday," said Marino. "I dropped by his house. No car. No Drewer. Two newspapers on the front lawn."

"What about our smoking gun?" Julia said.

"You mean the car?"

Julia nodded.

"Haven't found it yet," said Marino. "But Drewer has to have lots of contacts in the body repair business."

"What did Fine have to say about the couple?" Tagger asked.

"He only confirmed Drewer and Porter were good friends," said Marino.

"So, where'd we get the idea about them being an item?" said Julia.

"From Ellie Houston, one of the salespersons," Marino said.

"A female car salesman?" said Tagger.

"Sales*person*," Marino said.

"Tony, this is the first we've heard of this salesperson," Tagger said. "You been holding out on us?"

Julia rolled her eyes.

"I'd have to say Ellie has been very helpful," said Marino.

"Ellie?" said Tagger, his eyes widening.

"Okay, you two," Julia said. "Find Drewer. Find that car. Tag, bring us up to speed on John and Bob."

"Who's John and Bob?" Marino asked.

"The aliases for the two guys in the Cadillac Escalade," said Tagger.

"How'd you get their aliases?" said Marino.

"Turns out the SUV-trailer combo's pretty easy to spot on the T-DOT cameras," said Tagger, passing out 8x10s. "Found the motel they stayed in that Saturday night."

"Let's hear it for the Tennessee Department of Transportation," said Marino. "Which one's John and which one's Bob"

"Your guess is as good as mine," said Tagger.

"Tag found John and Bob headed into Collierville just about the time someone put two holes in Traner's window and very expensive mirror," said Julia.

"Damn," said Marino. "This opens up your Mexican drug theme, Johnnie—from transporting drugs to travelling hit men. This attempted hit might've been ordered from one of the guys Masterson was talking about Traner being hooked up with."

"I ran these photos over to Lieutenant Ayers yesterday afternoon," Tagger said. "Apparently they've had a security watch on Traner's home the last few days. Now it looks as if they'll be setting something up for his family and his work place."

"How many times have you had to update your person-of-interest flyer, Tag?" Marino said.

"A lot," said Tagger. "Fortunately, we got good response from each one."

"This is feeling more real," said Julia. "We need to stay alert."

"Roger that," said Tagger.

## Chapter 34

# Reservations For Two

*Wednesday…Union Station.* Marino picked up the phone and dialed.

"Ellie, this is Tony Marino."

"Hi, Sergeant Anthony Tony Marino," said Houston. "I've been hoping you'd call. This a social call or police business?"

"Police business. I thought you could help me again."

"It seems like I'm doing all the helping. How about we even things out a little?"

"Even things out?"

"Yeah. I'll help you, and you'll take me to dinner."

"That's not standard operating procedure."

"Is that a no?"

"I'm thinking about it."

"Well, while you're thinking about it, tell me how I can do my part of this bargain."

"We're trying to locate a Chrysler Limited, in the range of 2003 to 2008. I'm guessing y'all sell used cars."

"We do."

"If you sell 2003 to 2008 Limiteds, I'm betting one of them is missing. Can you check?"

"Whoa. This sounds like I'd need a really nice dinner to stay even. Say, the *Brooklyn Bridge Italian Restaurant*, Friday, 6:30?

No response.

"You are Italian, aren't you?"

"Yes."

"Oh, good—a *yes*. It's a deal then. I'll check on your used Limiteds. You make reservations."

***

*Wednesday evening*...Julia pulled into the Memphis International Airport. We barely got all Mark's bags to fit inside the Mini on the trip to the airport, she thought. If he brings home more than one embroidered handkerchief souvenir we won't be able to get it all in. She followed the short-term parking signs and found a spot near the Northwest Airlines end of the airport. Mark's plane had been scheduled for touch down at 10:18, a direct flight from Amsterdam. But he would have to clear customs.

Julia watched the stream of passengers coming toward her—hair mussed, clothes wrinkled, eyes red, shoulders stooped. This looks nothing like the group I saw leaving Memphis, she thought. There he is. Julia waved. Mark saw her and smiled. They soon stood face to face. Mark set his carryon on the floor and the two shared a long, close embrace. They pulled away looked in each other's eyes and kissed—a mature-we're-in-public kind of kiss—then hugged again. They held hands on the way to baggage claim.

"It's so good to see you," Mark said, squeezing her hand. "I missed you."

"It's great to have you back," Julia said. "How was your flight?"

"Long. But the plane had lots of vacant seats and I got to stretch out. Much better than the packed flight over. You know these newer planes have smaller seats, less leg room."

"You'll feel right at home in the Mini."

"Oh, yeah, the Mini. I forgot. I'm used to having my knees

in my mouth. I'm sure I can squeeze in."

"I'll put the top down. That should help."

***

They collected Mark's bags and creatively stuffed them into the Mini.

"So, what's your schedule for the rest of the week?" Julia said.

"I'm not going back to work at the Haven till Monday. And I figure I'll be dealing with jet lag for the next eighteen hours. But in between, I'm all yours. I'll be ready for a frozen margarita, Molly's La Casita style."

"That's a date. You can pick me up in your super roomy Prius."

## Chapter 35

# Guarding the Money

*Riding shotgun on the twenty-first century stage coach…*Hector and Ernesto rode close behind the eighteen-wheeler, hauling the cartel's seventy-eight million dollars. The cartel required team drivers, keeping the number of night stops to a minimum. This trip included Gustavo and Mario. Drivers adhered to speed limits and required lane assignments, giving law enforcement no reason to pull them over. But if they were pulled over, the van maintained contact with the eighteen-wheeler through one of Midland's latest two-way hand-held communications devices, effective up to thirty-six miles. The van mostly followed, staying within a half-mile.

"I need to off this dude, Traner," said Ernesto.

"Not on this run," said Hector. "There's way too much money in the truck."

"Everything's been quiet," said Ernesto. "We'd only be off his tail for an hour or so."

"Absolutely not," said Hector.

Ernesto pulled his Glock.

"Don't mean nothing, bro," said Hector. "I'm way more afraid of what Vargas would do to me."

The speaker squelched. "Need to crash for the night," said Gustavo. "There's a Love's truck stop coming up in seventeen."

"That's cool," Ernesto said.

***

They arrived early at truck stops so they could select the most defensible parking spot—one giving the van visual contact, where the truck could not be readily accessed from the rear. At least one man inside the cab, armed. Hector and Ernesto took turns watching from the one-way rear windows of the van. Their stay passed without incident. The truck left at five the next morning, the van on their tail.

***

West of Knoxville on I-40 the highway followed curves, descents, and rises, making visual contact difficult. Hector demanded the truck's 2-ways be put on squelch so he'd be better able to hear any message coming in. The squelch broke.

"Hector," said Gustavo. "Check out the black SUV. Been behind us for the last ten miles."

"Why's that a problem?" said Hector.

"Every other car on the road has passed us," said Gustavo. "Something ain't right."

Ernesto picked up speed, closing on the truck. At the top of a rise they could see the truck and the trailing black SUV. Hector took out his binoculars and began focusing.

"Texas plates," Hector said. "Can't see through the windows."

"Get the MP9s," said Ernesto.

"Think they're cops?" said Hector, laying Ernesto's MP9 on the console between them.

"Don't know," said Ernesto. "But if they're not cops, who the hell are they?"

"There's a parking area coming up," said Hector. "There won't be any cameras or cops there. Should we have Gustavo pull in?"

"At least we won't be going seventy if we have to fight," said Ernesto.

Hector cued his 2-way. "Gustavo, pull off in the parking area," he said.

"Si, senor," said Gustavo.

"Wake up, Mario," said Hector. "Make sure he has his Glock."

"He's sitting right next to me," said Gustavo. "He's ready."

*The wild west on steroids...*Gustavo put on his turn signal and slowed. The SUV stayed behind him, coming within twenty feet of the truck. Gustavo turned at the exit. The SUV followed, the van closing the gap. At this time of day, truckers rarely used parking areas. Gustavo pulled into the small empty lot. He drove to the area furthest from the expressway, beside an open field, the SUV on his tail. Gustavo shut down the truck. Mario handed him a Glock. They unbuckled their seat belts. First Mario, then Gustavo dropped into the area between the seats and moved behind the doors, close to the extended cab's bunk beds, crouching on either side.

Ernesto turned off the highway and eased the van closer to the SUV, staying back, waiting for them to show their hand. A second black SUV approached on the exit ramp, pulled up behind the van. Hector saw it in the side view mirror.

"Shit!" Hector shouted. "There's one behind us."

Hector dropped his seat to full recline, and somersaulted into the back, slipping between the two motorcycles. Ernesto grabbed his MP9, and powered down both front side windows. Hector readied himself at the back doors, raising his machine pistol to shoulder level. He pulled the door handle down, took a deep breath, popped the door open a crack, shoved the MP9 through, and pulled the trigger. A dozen rounds ripped through the windshield of the trailing SUV. Its horn blared. Hector pulled back inside, closing the door.

The lead SUV sprayed gravel as it sprang forward, going around the truck and bouncing through the field. It recovered to the pavement and entered the expressway, tires smoking. Ernesto hit the gas.

"Stop!" yelled Hector. "We can't leave the truck."

Ernesto slammed on the breaks.

"Back up," said Hector. "We have to see who's in that SUV."

Ernesto threw it in reverse and hit the gas, stopping inches from the riddled SUV. Hector jumped out, dropped, and duck-walked to the passenger side door. Ernesto squatted and moved to the driver's door monkey style, his left hand hitting the pavement for balance.

"Now!" yelled Hector.

The two men opened their respective doors, thrusting their MP9s into the SUV. Three men lay dead—two in the front seat, one in the rear seat.

"I know this man," said Ernesto. "He's from the Bacarzo cartel."

"Why would they break the treaty?" said Hector.

"Beats the hell out me," said Ernesto. "But we better get out of here."

"Yeah," said Hector. "And we ain't taking any detours in Memphis."

## Chapter 36

# The Day Began With Promise

*Getting back to the old normal...*With Mark home and no toothache, Julia slept soundly. The daylight woke her before the alarm. She dressed in her exercise clothes and started her run to the InsideOut Gym. Running without the toothache felt freeing. She ran harder just to test it. When no pain came she relaxed for the rest of the run. Julia passed her membership card under the scanner, watched her picture come up on the screen. I've got to get some room for Molly's tonight, she thought, squeezing her stomach. Her workout started with planks and Spiderman stretches, followed by more push-ups, sit-ups, and dumbbells. Then she worked the heavy bag—punching and kicking. She caught her breath and ran home, where she showered and dressed.

***

*A nice surprise...*Julia walked into the Deliberate Literate. Mark sat at her usual table. He waved his fingers in a tired greeting. Julia smiled.

"What're you doing here?" she said.

"You know how jet lag works. I couldn't sleep. So I thought I'd have coffee with you."

"Sorry about your sleep. But having coffee with you will be great."

"I brought my toothbrush."

***

*Union Station…*Marino's phone rang.

"Hey, Sergeant Anthony Tony Marino," Houston said. "You have our reservations? Cause I found your car, and maybe a little something extra. But it'll cost you."

***

"We've got the smoking gun," Marino said.

"You found the car?" said Tagger.

"The 2008 Limited came from Beckman's used car inventory, and it's sitting in an auto repair shop. Seems the bumper got banged up."

"Sounds like you have an inside source. That salesperson?"

"Bingo. She came through big time."

"So, you going to thank her? Properly?"

Marino smiled. "I'm thinking about it."

***

"I swear," Teresa said. "I thought Dr. Blue Eyes would have called by now. You're aunt's on one."

"For your information," said Julia. "Dr. Blue Eyes met me for coffee this morning."

"Already knew that. And I hear you're going to dinner tonight."

"I really need a list of your sources. How do you always know everything?"

"Someone has to stay on top of things around here. Otherwise, it'd just be a place to pay speeding tickets."

"Bye, Teresa." Julia punched the flashing button. "Hey, Aunt Louise."

"Hello, dear," said Aunt Louise. "Is this a bad time?"

"It's a good time."

"I wanted to tell about my Tai Chi classes."

"Yes. I want to hear all about them."

"The women were right, the teacher—"

"Lynn," Julia interrupted.

"Yes, Lynn. Well she's delightful. Never knew a stranger. Very patient. She took time to show me the forms, and then I did my best to follow."

"So, you like it?"

"I think so. There's so much to learn. But I can tell I'm already paying more attention to how I put my feet down, especially around the apartment."

"Sounds exactly what you'd hoped for. I'm happy for you."

"Yeah, I'm waving my hands in the clouds right now."

"Earth calling Aunt Louise? You okay?"

"Oh, perfectly, dear. That's the name of the first form I learned. You pretend to be waving in the clouds. I kind of like that image. Makes me feel taller."

"If you like it, I'm all for it. Now tall person, I'm waving bye-bye to my phone."

"Good-bye, dear."

***

"Lieutenant Ayers on line two," said Teresa.

"What's up, Roy?"

"Hey, Julia. Thought you might like to know the State Police found a fully loaded SUV with three bullet riddled upstanding Mexican citizens."

"Where?"

"Westbound I-40. Parking area, half-way between Knoxville and Nashville."

"A *loaded* SUV?"

"Weapons. Enough to start a war."

"But apparently not enough to win a battle," she said.

"Good one. The feds ran their pictures through their data base. Turns out these guys belong to one of the major Mexican cartels—the Bacarzo cartel."

"And someone knocked them off? Think it's another cartel?"

"We're pretty sure it's another criminal powerhouse," he said. "Can't rule out the usual suspects in this area of the country—one of the many Mafias, or one of the major prison gangs. But, like you say, it could also be a rival Mexican cartel."

"The cartels are fighting their turf wars in the states?"

"Horrible thought, ain't it?"

"It looks as if they were coming this way," she said. "Any chance it involved one of those 18-wheelers loaded with cash?"

"That's what we're thinking. You sure you don't want to come work for the OCU? You've got the nose for it."

"No thanks. These guys have way too many American made military weapons. I'm happy with my little Glock. Not interested in playing with machine guns, C-4, and bazookas."

***

Teresa buzzed in. "Lieutenant. Boss on line one."

"Afternoon, Major Williams," said Julia.

"Afternoon, Lieutenant. I understand you and your team are getting involved with the Organized Crime Unit."

"Well, sir. We've just been following-up on a dead prostitute. One lead turned into another, and we found ourselves in the middle of a Mexican cartel. Thought it'd be good to get briefed by OCU."

"Logical. It's always logical with you, Lieutenant. But it may not be prudent."

"What am I missing, sir?"

"Turf, Lieutenant. Turf. You've stepped on some mighty sensitive toes."

"Sorry, Major. I've been talking directly to Lieutenant Ayers. Not doing anything behind his back."

"Consider this a friendly warning, Lieutenant. The political gods are about to rain on your parade."

"We're cool, Major. In fact, I just told Ayers I didn't want to be involved in a war between Mexican cartels."

"What war?"

"Looks like one cartel ambushed another just east of Nashville. It probably has to do with an attack on an 18-wheeler headed back to Mexico, loaded with cash."

"Where'd you get all this?"

"Actually, from OCU."

"Damn. Okay, I want you maintaining a low profile. At least until I can figure out what games are being played."

"Yes, sir. A low profile. That's what I told OCU."

"So, we're clear, Lieutenant?"

"Yes, sir."

Click.

Teresa appeared at the doorway.

"You still employed, Lieutenant?" Teresa said.

"What?" said Julia.

"Well, the Major seemed to be in a foul mood, even for him. I just wanted to know if I needed to look for a new job, too."

"Teresa. That's almost a compliment. I think."

"Well?"

"He just told me to keep a low profile."

"Damn. He doesn't like the red Mini."

"Not that. He wants me to stay out of OCU's business."

"Wait a minute. Isn't Lieutenant Ayers the one who's always calling and always dropping in here?"

"Apparently one of his bosses is miffed."

"But he's miffed at you instead? Some kind of male turf thing?"

"Let's hope it's something as lame as that."

"When will these boys ever grow up?"

"Say, Teresa. I have to keep a low profile, but that doesn't mean you do."

"What you want me to do? I'm ready for some undercover work."

"We're not going all that far undercover. But it might be interesting to keep an eye on the daily logs having anything to do with OCU, starting six months ago."

"Got it. What am I looking for?"

"That, Ms. Johnson, is the million dollar question. I'm hoping you'll find something interesting, unusual, maybe even a pattern."

"You know me, Lieutenant. I'm all over this like a duck on a June bug. I love these assignments."

"And, Teresa. Mum's the word. I'm trying to keep a low profile here."

"They'll never get anything out of me, Lieutenant, unless they ply me with chocolate."

Chapter 37

# Now This Is More Like It

*Margaritas in Midtown...Thursday evening at Molly's La Casita Mexican Restaurant.*

"Hey, y'all," said the general manager Kelly, giving them a big hug. "Haven't seen you in a while."

"I've got a good excuse," said Mark. "I couldn't afford the cab fare from Sweden."

"That may be the best excuse I've heard in my twenty-plus years at Molly's," said Kelly. "Y'all want your frozen margaritas, right?"

"Right," said Julia.

***

"This is more like it," said Mark. "There's lots of vodka in Sweden. Don't misunderstand. I enjoyed their drinks, but I missed these margaritas." He and Julia clinked glasses.

"Welcome home," Julia said. "Now don't take too big a drink. Remember the brain freeze."

"Ow," he said, holding his head. "Too late. And don't roll your eyes."

"Too late," she said, smiling. "You finally get some sleep?"

"Yeah, four straight hours. I feel much better. You've lost weight since I've been gone?"

"You silver-tongued devil."

"Really. I can tell."

"Must have been the toothache."

"Toothache?"

"Couldn't eat on the right side. Heck. Couldn't eat on either side half the time."

"You go to the dentist?"

"Got a brand new filling yesterday. Knock on wood, it's just great. No pain."

"Good. How's your aunt?"

"She's doing well. Just started Tai Chi classes to improve her balance. Says she can tell a difference after only two classes."

"I've seen Tai Chi do wonders for many of the Haven residents. But in just two classes? That might be a record."

Julia smiled.

"Anything happen at the Haven while I was gone?"

"AARP sponsored some kind of talk about folks getting ripped off by banks and investment companies."

"Good idea. I remember when one of the residents handed me a slick 8x10 color brochure. Said he'd invested with this guy, made over fifteen percent return in the middle of the recession. He planned to host a get-together in his apartment to introduce people to this miracle investor. He wanted me to come. I turned him down. Tried to tell him to be careful, but only ended up offending him. He told me loud and clear he had financial statements for the last year documenting his extraordinary earnings, and he trusted this investor because he worked at Morgan Keegan."

"Morgan Keegan? You remember his name?"

It's been a while. Let's see. I think it started with *P*...Parker, Prichard—"

"Porter?"

"That's it. Porter. Yeah. Tommy Porter. No. *Terry* Porter. So, you know him?"

"Terence Porter's body was found last week, in the Morgan Keegan parking garage. He'd been run over several times."

"Sounds like someone got really angry."

"That's what we thought."

"People get worked up when you mess with their money, especially seniors. It's their life line."

"I think I saw a little of that last weekend. Beth and Dell couldn't talk about anything else. Even Aunt Louise was on the bandwagon about unscrupulous bankers and investors victimizing folks, especially seniors. Said they didn't have a conscience and should be locked up."

"Strong words from your aunt."

"Aunt Louise and I had dinner with the hushpuppy four a few nights ago."

Mark smiled. "You mean Joyce, Lawrence, Shirley, and…?"

"Beatrice. Yeah, those are the ones. They told Aunt Louise she had a case of the almost-eighty worries."

"Haven't heard of that particular condition, but it makes sense. For most of us, if we're lucky enough to make it through the seventies, the end is very near."

The waitress appeared across the table. "You know what you want to order?" she asked.

"Are we far enough away from eighty to safely ignore calories?" Julia asked Mark.

"No question," he said. "In fact, statistics say we're at an age when eating with abandon on occasion is a good thing. Maybe drinking, as well."

Chapter 38

# The Road Atlas

*Saturday morning…Union Station.* Marino walked into Union Station.

"Morning, Sergeant," said Teresa. "Doing a little catch-up?"

"I need a some computer time," Marino said. "Haven't seen my little buddy Jarvis in a while. He doing okay?"

"My nephew's still in Minnesota at that camp for kids with Asperger's. My brother says he's getting good reports from the counselors and teachers."

"Did he ever use the Road Atlas I sent?"

"You didn't hear?"

"No. Raif never called."

"That brother of mine. I really need to teach him some basic manners. If anything, being an MPD major, he should have exceptional manners. Sorry, Sergeant. Anyway, your Atlas was a great idea, a salvation. You remember Jarvis's obsession with earthquakes?"

"Yeah. He knew every detail of the New Madrid Fault, including when to expect the next big one."

"Well, now he has another obsession—interstate highways. Your map helped him get over his fear of going away to camp. He knew every detail of their trip to Minnesota, and couldn't wait to try it out. Raif said he actually took a wrong turn on their way up north, and Jarvis showed him how to get back on the right highway."

"I miss seeing him around here."

"Sounds like we need to arrange another telephone call between the two of you. Y'all talked about earthquakes on the last one. Maybe you can compare notes on highways this time? How about me trying for next Saturday?"

"Works for me. Just let me know."

"Sergeant Tagger came in about twenty-minutes ago. You two trying to impress the Lieutenant?"

"Just trying to keep up with her."

Chapter 39

# Classic Government Silos

*Saturday afternoon, New York City….alphabet soup.* Walter Berness, President and CEO of the Federal Reserve Bank of New York, sat at the head of a large conference table.

"Before we begin, I want to introduce Michel Archambault," said Berness. Monsieur Archambault is the Executive Director of the Financial Action Task Force, with representatives from thirty-four countries. He's come all the way from FATF headquarters in Paris to underscore the international urgency of this case."

Archambault nodded.

"And, of course," said Berness, "mostly from Washington, we also have representatives from the CIA, FBI, SEC, ATF, DEA, IRS, OCC, FinCEN, Justice, and Homeland Security's ICE. Thank you all for coming. Now, to the business at hand. The CIA has made a significant breakthrough in a large international money laundering operation. Special Agent Anita Davenport is to be congratulated on her accomplishments, and her willingness to bring us together. She will brief us on the latest information involving a man called the Judge."

Davenport stood. "Thank you, President Berness. I appreciate your willingness to host this meeting. And I want to thank all of you for coming. I realize the CIA hasn't always been warm and fuzzy. I hope to change our image today. As

I've told you in our phone conversations, the Judge runs a massive international money laundering program for high profile clients." She moved to a large monitor hung on the wall.

"We successfully infiltrated the Judge's operation by way of a specially designed Trojan horse." The screen came to life with a list of the Judge's clients and the amount of money each had invested over the past three weeks, followed by a list of the banks laundering the money. "For all of you doing multiplication in your heads, you already can see the scope of this enterprise is huge—in the neighborhood of a quarter of a trillion US dollars annually."

The group began talking excitedly.

"Ladies and gentlemen, please," said Berness. "Allow Special Agent Davenport to continue."

"Keep in mind these numbers only apply to that percentage of fiscal intake these clients chose to have laundered. In some cases it may represent the bulk of their funds, in other cases, such as the Mexican cartels, it's probably no more than twenty percent of the money they take in."

"This list of banks is unbelievable," said Berness. "Small state banks, as well as large national and international banks with excellent reputations."

"Yes, sir," said Davenport. "It's a complex operation with all the classic laundering tactics—wire transfers, U-turns, layering, spin drying, and even some smurfing—and being pulled off by several heretofore highly regarded banks. But for the first time, we have stacks of evidence—all organized and court-ready thanks to our access to the Judge's computer. And, ever since we planted the Trojan horse in these banks' computers, we've been diverting their dirty money to US government accounts without their knowledge—almost fifteen billion in less than three weeks."

"Please don't spend any of that money, Special Agent" said Archambault, smiling. "That is, until the thirty-four member governments of the FATF determine who the money really belongs to."

"Does this Trojan horse program also keep track of all their transactions," Berness asked, "like a readymade copy of their fraudulent *second* set of books?"

"Absolutely, sir," said Davenport. "If the Judge pulled the plug tomorrow, we'd still have enough evidence that would stand up in court—on him, his clients, and each of these banks. There'd be no need to conduct extensive audits. I hope you can appreciate the beauty of this data collection." She pulled up the next page. "Here you'll find a listing of the clients and their known criminal activities. This is for those of you who don't have any responsibilities involving money laundering, and were wondering why you were invited."

Side conversations began, the noise level rising.

"Please," said Burgess. "We need to push on."

"And the Iranians and North Koreans?" said Aaron Collins, a senior officer in the Immigration and Customs Enforcement section of Homeland Security. "Practically the whole world has levied sanctions on them. Where the hell are they getting all this money?"

"There are several investors hoping to get their weapons grade nuclear material, as well as the rockets needed to deliver the warheads," said Masterson, representing the Economic Crime Unit of the FBI's Financial Crimes Section. "And there are countries willing to pay top dollar to be first in line. In addition, other investors are simply supporting the Iranian government's nuclear weapons plan in hopes of obliterating Israel. That money's being laundered in these banks to maintain the donors' anonymity, and to keep the assets from being frozen."

"A large number of the banks involved are part of the Sizemore Global Financial Solutions Group," said Davenport. "J. Francis Sizemore has banks in Mexico, Houston, Memphis, Miami, and Atlanta, as well as Costa Rico, and a number of the islands—Antigua and Barbuda in particular."

"Some of these European banks on the list are huge, with impeccable reputations," said Archambault. "These banks are making billions of dollars, tax-free, then sending the laundered money back to subsidize more crime and terrorist activities. And of course, the Judge is only one of many operations shoveling this dirty money their way."

"We need to coordinate a massive seizure of assets," said Cole Wallace, Inspector General of the Securities and Exchange Commission. "We should freeze these accounts now and nail the major players—the Judge, the terrorists countries, the cartels, all of them."

"Freezing the accounts would be easy, but getting to the Judge and his clients is another issue. It would take hundreds, maybe thousands of agents, involving complicated planning, and there's no way to keep such a plan quiet, sir," said Davenport. "So much money. Too many on the take. Highly confidential planning will need to begin with a small group. In the meantime, we can continue siphoning off their money. But you're correct. We'll need to arrest the leaders responsible for generating all this dirty money before they go underground. When the upper level planning and coordination is done, we'll be in a better position to implement a coordinated sweep. We have enough hard data to get the banks later, they're not going anywhere."

"How long before one of them learns what's going on?" asked Collins.

"No way of knowing, sir," said Davenport. "Someone could already be suspicious. And you can bet they won't go quietly."

"Quietly?" said Collins.

Davenport became more serious. "Lots of people are going to die, sir."

***

"Thank you for coming," said Berness. "I trust everyone is aware the content of this meeting carries the highest level of confidentiality. Special Agent Davenport will be in touch."

Last to leave were Berness, Collins, Davenport, Masterson, and Archambault.

"Excellent meeting, Special Agent," said Collins. "You conducted your mission with precision. My congratulations to you and your team."

"Thank you, sir," said Davenport.

"We've had many dealings with the Mexican cartels," said Collins. "And monitoring the borders has been no picnic. It will be good to have a real toe hold in this fight."

Archambault motioned to Davenport. "Could we chat?"

"Of course," said Davenport. Masterson nodded and left the room, closing the door behind him.

"I'm having another cup of coffee. Would you like some?" said Archambault.

"Oui, monsieur."

"Crème? Sucre?"

"Non, merci."

"Parlez-vous français?"

"I'm afraid not," she said, grinning. "Just trying to be sociable."

"Your kindness is noted," he said, handing her a cup of coffee. "I have a feeling you know more than you admit. In fact, I'm certain there is much more to you than meets the eye." He smiled.

Davenport sipped her coffee, focused on Archambault's eyes.

"I was wondering, this person who planted the virus…he was a member of your agency? The CIA?"

"Actually, no," she said. "We had a contractual arrangement."

"These things always fascinate me. Was he American?"

"Yes. American."

"Ah. I'm so impressed with how you Americans conduct these secret operations," he said, turning to Collins. "Can I assume you knew all about this, Aaron?"

"Not this time, Michel," said Collins. "The CIA had the lead on this. We're all coming late to the party."

"At least there's a party," said Archambault.

***

Davenport left the building to find Masterson leaning against her car.

"How'd you know which car was mine?"

"I'm a trained federal agent."

"You saw me drive in."

"Hey, good agents have impeccable timing."

"Interesting conversation back there."

"What'd the Frenchman have to say?" said Masterson.

"He wanted to know who my undercover agent was," Davenport said.

"Why would a Frenchman be so interested in the identity of one of your agents?"

"Exactly. I thought he wanted to talk about those major European banks we identified."

"What'd you tell him?"

"Just said it was a contractual arrangement, someone outside of the agency."

"Anyone I might know?"

"Now, Lawrence. We each have these special initials so we can keep secrets. No secrets, no more initials. Consider it a need to know classification."

"Okay. I don't need to know," he said. "Back to the Frenchman, you have anything on this guy?"

"I've thought of him being like the head of the United Nations, dealing with all those countries. An important position, but probably little power and lots of headaches."

"Too many personalities. Too many agendas. A thankless job, with the potential success of a cat herder."

"That's *if* he's a good guy. What if he's not?"

"Food for thought. Collins or Berness have anything to say?"

"Not really. Berness was on his cell and Collins was tanking up on water."

"Tanking up?"

"Yeah, he emptied one whole pitcher and started on a second. I commented about it. He told me his doctor had prescribed a new medication for his chronic back pain and told him to drink lots of water."

"I'm amazed his bladder allowed him to stay for the entire meeting."

Chapter 40

# The Conrios Cartel

*A Fortune 500 business with fire power…the Little Bull.* Alejandro Molinera Vargas, head of the Conrios cartel, sipped Tequila while he listened to his accountants report on his money—how much money, and the profitability of each venture.

Faint knocking at the door.

Vargas tensed, his mouth tightened.

Louder knocking.

"Who the hell is it?" he bellowed.

The door opened wide enough for a man to poke his head inside. "Señor. Señor," said Efren.

"You'd better have a damn good reason for interrupting my meeting," said Vargas.

"Señor, the CIA has our…I mean has *your* money, señor."

"What the hell are you talking about?"

"I just talked to the gringo," said Efren. "The CIA planted viruses everywhere—the banks, Señor Judge's computer. They've been taking money out of the banks and putting it into the CIA's vault for three weeks."

"What?" yelled Vargas, slamming his Tequila glass on the table. "They've got my money? Like hell."

"Three weeks," said Javier. "That would be almost a half-billion dollars of your money."

"Check our accounts! Now!" Vargas roared.

Javier's fingers flew over the keys of his laptop, moving from one account to the next. "The money is right where it's supposed to be," he said.

"Somebody jacking me around?" said Vargas.

"Señor," said Efren. "He said something else…"

"Spit it out," Vargas said. "Before I make a necktie out of your tongue."

"I didn't really understand it, señor," said Efren. "He said all the banks got some kind of horses."

"Horses?" said Javier. His eyes opened wide. "Trojan horses?"

"Somebody tell me what's going on," said Vargas.

"A Trojan horse gets inside a computer like a virus," said Javier. "The Trojan horse gives the computer instructions."

"What instructions?"

"Like, make sure the money transactions are documented in all the banks, confirming the money has been sent and received. But wire the money to the CIA."

"So the CIA does have my money?"

"It's possible."

"You need to talk to my inside man yourself," said Vargas. "Do it now!"

***

"The CIA has your money, señor," said Javier.

"You are certain?" said Vargas. "No mistake?"

"Our man said the CIA bragged in a big meeting in New York about how they'd sent an American spy to take information directly from the Judge's computers," said Javier. "Information about everyone, including Conrios. Then they uploaded Trojan horses in each of the Judge's banks, telling the computers to send everybody's money to the CIA. No mistake."

"I'll kill him!"

"Who, señor?"

"The Judge!" said Vargas. "I was doing just fine laundering my money the old way till he came along."

"Remember, señor," said Javier. "We'd grown so fast with the Colombians out of the way and the United States opening up the border for us. We needed the big banking network the Judge had put together."

"I remember," said Vargas. "I also remember telling the Judge I'd kill him if anything happened to my money."

"What'd he say?"

"Nothing," said Vargas. "He just smiled that damned smile of his. That cocky SOB." Vargas looked off, lost in thought. His focus returned, intense. "Does anyone else know about this?"

"Our man doesn't think so because the money is still flowing to the CIA."

"That means the Judge doesn't know yet. Good. He won't expect us."

"Expect us?"

"Yes. I want to talk to my lieutenants, one at a time. Get Ramon in here first."

***

Vargas handed Ramon a photograph. "This bastard lost me my money. I want his smiling head on my table," he said, tossing a black garbage bag at Ramon. "You take the lead on this."

"Si, señor."

Vargas unfolded a sketch of a seven-story building, slid it across the table. "This is where he lives and works. Guards are posted outside this wall and throughout the building. There's nothing but sand for miles around. They'll see you coming."

"We can travel at night, driving with night vision goggles."

"Select twenty of your best men. Take the jet. I'll arrange to have vehicles fully loaded with weapons and explosives waiting for you in our hanger. You'll find the Judge's computers and extra guards in the building's two underground levels. The Judge lives in the penthouse, on the top two floors. Leave nothing standing."

"Si," Ramon said.

"And, Ramon…"

"Señor?"

"Tell no one," Vargas said. "Any word of this leaks out, you won't come back alive."

Ramon nodded.

"Come back to me tomorrow with your plan."

"Si, señor."

***

"Javier," Vargas said. "There've been plenty of people near the Judge's computer, many from the United States. There's no way to know who planted that Trojan thing in his computer. I want to send a message. No one messes with the Conrios cartel. Get the names of all the US bankers involved with the Judge. I want complete workups—pictures, cars, family members, everything. And I want them on the Android phones by Thursday."

"Si, señor."

***

*Preparations for a battle…* "Luis," said Vargas. "I want the guard tripled around the compound, 24/7. I'm sure spotters have already reported our meetings. They'll be watching closely. I don't want any of the cartels thinking they can take us while our best fighters are gone, especially the Bacarzo cartel. And, Luis…"

"Señor?"

"Shoot any man who falls asleep on his watch. I'll be checking the guards myself. If I find any man sleeping I'll shoot him, and then I'll shoot you."

"No one will sleep, señor."

***

*The Bacarzo cartel compound...The Stallion.* Jose Pena Ramirez Delgado sat on the floor, rolling a large red ball back to his two-year old son. Each time the ball hit his legs, his son broke into a hearty laugh, making Delgado smile. This tender father-son moment belied the violent nature of the man who led the second largest cartel in Mexico, the man known to his friends and enemies as El Semental—*The Stallion.* The door opened and his bodyguard walked quietly to Delgado, leaned over and whispered.

"Send him in," Delgado said.

"Señor Delgado," said the man.

"You have news?"

"Something's going down at the Conrios compound. Vargas's lieutenants have been reporting to El Pequeño Toro today, one at a time. No one is saying anything, but he's increased the guards."

"Shit," said Delgado. "I knew it was coming. This is payback for that screwed-up attempt to jack his money truck in the United States. Double our guards. Be ready for anything."

Chapter 41

# Business As Usual

*Funny how a few pounds weigh...*Julia dressed for her run. Mark said I'd lost weight, she thought. She checked herself out mirror and smiled. She felt strong as she got into her morning run, enjoying the bounce in her stride. She wondered if she should attribute the extra spring in her step to Mark's being home, or to being a few pounds lighter.

***

*Some things are hard to swallow...*Julia sat at her usual table at the Deliberate Literate, sipping a steaming coffee. The Memphis Police Director's face looked out from the front page of the *Commercial Appeal*. He stood behind a bank of microphones talking about yesterday's capture of a ton of marijuana found in an 18-wheeler on I-40. Just over his right shoulder, looking important, stood Major Dorsey Echols, head of the Organized Crime Unit. Julia inhaled instead of swallowing, and began choking. She calmed herself and snuck a look around to see who might be watching. So much for keeping a low profile, she thought.

***

*Union Station...the low profile.*
"Morning, Lieutenant," said Teresa.
"You see the paper this morning?" said Julia.
"If you're trying to keep a low profile," whispered Teresa,

"you should say *Good morning, Teresa. How are you this fine morning?*"

Julia rolled her eyes, then motioned with her head for Teresa to follow.

Once inside her office, Julia closed the door, and motioned for Teresa to take a seat in front of her desk.

"Okay. Good morning, Teresa. Now can we get on with this?"

"Sure. I just wanted you to know I'm taking this assignment very seriously."

"Ms. Johnson?"

"Okay. Yes. I saw today's *Commercial Appeal.* The most interesting thing about it is this is the eighth photo exactly like it over the past five months. Sometimes it's cocaine, sometimes marijuana, and once crystal meth. But the picture never includes any OCU officers except Major Echols. The Major is taking all the bows."

"I guess that's not such a big deal for a group that spends so much time undercover."

"Maybe so. But I don't think Lieutenant Ayers goes undercover. And our own Major Williams is always dragging you up on that platform. Sometimes he even makes you talk."

Julia made a face.

"We can work on your speaking later," said Teresa.

"Teresa…your report?"

"I've been through two months' worth of Divisional logs. It's clear Major Echols has his fingerprints all over each entry. He has to be the micromanager from hell."

"So maybe we were right, it is just a male turf thing."

"I'll keep digging. You keep your low profile. But gagging and choking at the Deliberate Literate can't help."

"Teresa?"

Teresa walked out smiling.

***

*The crime board...*

"The Crime Scene techs have the 2008 Limited with pieces of Porter's suit stuck to the undercarriage," said Marino. "Drewer's prints are all over it. He drove it to the body shop that next day and told them there was no rush, just stick it back in the lot till they have some free time."

"Good work, professor," said Julia. "What about Drewer?"

"Went over to his house with a search warrant. Place looked like the inside of a model home. You know, not lived in, neat as a pin—furniture gleaming, not a hint of dust, magazines fanned out on the coffee table, quality paintings, all the plants just come from a nursery. I felt bad leaving shoeprints on the white carpet, even clean ones. Everything in its place except dinner dishes in the sink, bureau drawers partially cleared out, and the empty desktop where a PC used to sit. Looked like he left in a hurry. We issued an all-points, but haven't heard anything."

"Here's one of Porter's brochures," said Julia, sliding it over to Marino. He handed it out at the Haven several months ago. His claims of rate of return on investment are out of sight. Sounds too good to be true."

"Yeah," said Marino. "Sounds like a Ponzi scheme, or a pyramid scheme. Later investors end up paying dividends for earlier investors, who can be persuaded to sink in even more money."

"That's the stuff Masterson said Sizemore and his VP Traner are mixed up in," said Tagger.

"There's another thing," said Marino. "The salesperson—"

"Ellie," interrupted Tagger.

Marino shot him a look. "Yes—Ellie. She told me Drewer and Porter had talked about smurfing. She said when she googled it all these articles came up about homosexuality. Some crazy stuff about the Smurfs being homosexual, and some slang about certain types of gay men being called Smurfs."

"I had a Smurf lunch box," said Tagger.

"Well, cheer up, Johnnie," said Marino. "When I googled it again I found *smurfing* is actually included in the federal Bank Secrecy Act of 1970 regulations, although regulators tend to call it *structuring*. It's a method of laundering money in small enough chunks of cash to keep under the mandatory ten thousand dollar reporting requirement. If I understood the articles, smurfing originally applied to the use of several people each depositing a portion of the dirty money, named after how the cartoon *Smurfs* all work together to get things accomplished. But sometimes the term smurfing means one person working with small chunks of dirty money, structuring the deposits to keep them under the federal radar."

"Wait a minute," said Julia. "I got all caught up in the cartoon characters. Are you saying Drewer laundered dirty money from Porter's Ponzi scheme?"

"That's what it seems like to me," said Marino.

"So how would that work?" said Tagger.

"From what I read," said Marino, "it's like when the DEA finds marijuana on a yacht. They can use it to prove their case *and* they can confiscate the darn yacht. The same applies to dirty money—it's evidence tying the criminal to the crime, and authorities can confiscate the money. Laundering money breaks the chain of evidence, and at the same time lets the criminal keep the laundered money free and clear. So, Porter would need a way to launder the money he bilked from his clients. He could launder it by depositing it in a bank, which has lots of regulations, like that ten thousand dollar mandatory reporting rule. Or he could figure out a way to wash it through a business which the Bank Secrecy Act doesn't cover and which involves large cost purchases, like property or—"

"Cars," interrupted Julia.

"Bingo," said Marino. "Maybe like the *Smurf* analogy, they had lots of small transactions going."

"How does Porter get his share of the laundered money?" Tagger asked.

"Well, in banking," said Marino, "it's not uncommon for the bank to issue a line of credit, a debit card, or a retail value card to the depositor for the amount of the dirty money, minus any fees for the bank. The depositor then uses the debit card until his laundered money is used up, while the bank quietly covers all the bills."

"But the dealership doesn't issue debit cards," said Julia.

"No," said Marino. "But what if Porter is put on the payroll with a fancy title, maybe as an international sales consultant? Or, maybe he incorporates a consulting firm to receive all the money?"

"I'm getting nervous, professor," said Julia. "You're actually starting to make sense. So, this means we need to look at all the Beckman dealership's books."

"And we need someone who knows what to look for," said Tagger.

"The IRS has a Criminal Investigative Unit," Marino said.

***

*Competing Mexican cartels are using Tennessee as their battle ground...*

"Lieutenant Ayers called to tell me about three Mexican citizens found in a black SUV loaded with an assortment of military-type weapons. Sound familiar? The SUV and the three men had been riddled with nine-mil rounds."

"You talking about MP9 machine pistols?" Tagger said.

"That's their guess," Julia said.

"And these citizens," said Marino. "I don't suppose they

had anything to do with the cartels."

"Actually, the **FBI** identified them as members of the Bacarzo cartel, one of Mexico's two largest cartels. It looked as if they may have been trying to steal an 18-wheeler headed back to Mexico full of cash or weapons."

"Where'd this happen?" Tagger said.

"On I-40, east of Nashville," said Julia.

"I've been reading up on federal reports about Mexican cartels and all the crap they smuggle in and out of the US," said Tagger. "They're estimating over a hundred of these dudes riding shotgun for a dozen or so cartels of varying sizes and power. The ones in our area probably move through the Texas border crossing."

"Over a hundred of them?" said Marino. "All armed with MP9s?"

"And maybe rocket launchers," said Tagger.

"No way to know the numbers without getting a look at the cartel's books," Julia said.

"So when Masterson talked about *spraying* anyone near the target, he meant with machine pistols?" said Marino.

"Or worse," Julia said. "And probably all made here in the good old US of A."

"Great. Just great," Marino said.

*****

*Unexpected news...*The man's other cell phone vibrated. He looked around. Seeing no one, he pulled the cell from his pocket.

"Yeah," the man whispered.

"Thought you'd like to know," said a familiar voice. "We're gonna be free of the bitch real soon. Explain later."

The line went dead.

Chapter 42

# The Benefits of
# Almost Double Dating

*Thursday…the information mill is alive and well at Union Station.*

"Time for you to go home, get dressed for your dinner date," Teresa said.

"How'd you know about my date?" said Tagger, eyeing her.

"I just hear things. Going to Cooper-Young, huh?"

"Yes," he said slowly.

"Looks like a double date."

"What double date? What're you talking about?"

"You and the Lieutenant will both be eating dinner in Cooper-Young. She'll be with Dr. Blue Eyes and you'll be with—"

"Never mind who I'll be with," he interrupted. "It's none of your business."

"Anyway, you four have a wonderful time," she said smiling. "Say hey to the Lieutenant for me."

Tagger swore under his breath, and left.

***

*John and Bob register again…*The van shadowed a new set of trucks coming across the Texas border, headed for Richmond. Their Androids lit up.

"You check it," said Hector. "I gotta drive."

"We got a contract," said Ernesto. "Over in Memphis."

"Hell, we can get started on this tonight, maybe wrap it up by tomorrow. Least by Sunday."

"I'm in for that. Might even be able to take out Traner while we're there."

"Who's the mark?"

"It's a cop."

"A cop?"

"Yeah, and her old aunt, and a boyfriend."

"A lady cop?"

"Yeah. Not bad looking, either. And, hey, she's got a flashy red Mini Cooper."

"We should be able to find that easy enough."

"How long before Memphis?"

"Looks like we should be crossing the river about five or five-thirty."

"How about *John* and *Bob* check into that motel on the east side of town. We can take care of business from there."

"Let's do it, *Bob*."

***

*East Memphis…the La Quinta Inn parking lot.* They unloaded motorcycles from their van as quickly as possible, hoping not to draw attention.

"You sure you took care of the camera?" said Hector. "I don't want to see my picture staring back at me the next time I take a leak."

"And I don't want to have to deal with Manuel's smart mouth again. Yes. I took care of it."

"Let's find the cop's house first. I've got it in my Android GPS. Make sure your two-way works, and keep your speed down, we don't need to get stopped by the cops."

"Yeah, yeah."

Hector and Ernesto rode side by side west on I-40, back

toward midtown Memphis, jumping four lanes of traffic to follow Sam Cooper Boulevard till it ended at East Parkway. They turned south, following the Google map route. Coming to Julia's street, they split up, one riding in front of her house, one on the street behind.

"Two cars in the driveway," said Hector. "One's a red Mini, the other's a gray Prius."

"The Prius belongs to the boyfriend," Ernesto said.

"A two-fer," Hector said, passing Julia's house. "Wait, they're coming out of the house. Can't stop here."

"Meet you at the corner," said Ernesto.

Mark waited for two cars to pass, then backed out of the driveway. Hector and Ernesto rode away from the on-coming cars, turning back on the next parallel street.

"You follow them, pull up alongside, and take 'em out," said Ernesto. "I'm going to blast that Mini. There's just something about hot red that gets the toro in me all worked up." Ernesto turned his cycle around.

"Got it," said Hector, hoping to catch the Prius. But he'd turned onto a dead-end street. He revved up his motorcycle and reversed course, catching a glimpse of the tail lights as Mark made the traffic light and turned south onto Cooper. By the time Hector rode down Cooper he saw the couple walk into the Tsunami Restaurant.

***

Ernesto slowed as he came to Julia's house. He heard barking and looked down to see a dog nipping at his boot, not much bigger than a Chihuahua.

"He won't hurt you," yelled Mrs. Woozley from her porch. "He thinks you're a lawn mower."

Hector didn't respond. He saw other neighbors watching. "Can't do it, man. Too many neighbors, and this damn dog."

"No problem," said Hector. "I lost them in traffic. They

went into a restaurant. Have to wait till they come out."

"You wait for them. I'm going to find Traner," said Ernesto. "Stay in touch, bro."

***

Mark pulled the Prius into Tsunami Restaurant's small parking area. He squeezed Julia's hand. They kissed lightly, got out of the car, and walked into the restaurant. Glasses of Steele Cuvee Chardonnay awaited them.

"Are you ready to order?" asked the waitress.

"I'll have the sake-steamed mussels for an appetizer, and the scallops for the main course," said Julia.

"And I'm going to make a meal out of two appetizers," said Mark. "The mussels and the calamari."

***

Cars filled the curb parking spots bumper to bumper near the Blue Fish Restaurant, on the corner of Cooper Street and Young Avenue. Tagger drove north on Cooper looking for a spot. He found one about a block away, across the street from Tsunami. Johnnie Tagger and Diane Willingham walked back to the Blue Fish for a large platter of their favorite Blue Point oysters, and whatever entrée struck their fancy.

***

Tagger and Willingham left Blue Fish, strolling up the sidewalk, her arm in his. The Cooper-Young district was busy, even on this Thursday evening. Lots of pedestrians, slow moving cars. The traffic opened at Tsunami, and they crossed the street. Tagger unlocked the car with his key fob. As he reached to open his door he heard a motorcycle. He turned. A black motorcycle came toward them on the other side of the street, moving slowly, the black helmeted rider clearly looking away to his right. Tagger turned to see what the rider might be looking at. Julia and Mark pushed through the doors of the restaurant. Tagger's eyes shot back to the motorcycle, his mind flashing on the cartel's hit man. He forced his long legs into a hard sprint. In four steps he crossed the center line. The rider raised a large handgun.

Closing on the rider, Tagger yelled, "Lieutenant! Down!" He brought his left arm across the rider's throat, lifting him off the cycle and dropping him flat on his back, but not before the rider got off two rounds. The force of the impact on the street split the rider's helmet. But the blow from Tagger's arm had already crushed his windpipe. He lay in the street, dead, his MP9 beside him.

***

At the sound of Tagger's warning, Julia looked to see the motorcycle rider bringing up his MP9. She wheeled and tackled Mark, who hit the sidewalk with a loud oomph. She heard the shots and felt a hot sting. Julia lay pinned to a stunned Mark. Neither could move.

***

Willingham took off immediately after Tagger left, making a beeline for Tsunami. She slid to one knee beside the couple, her off-duty piece in one hand, keeping pressure on Julia's back with the other, protecting them from the line of fire.

"Johnnie!" Willingham yelled. "Talk to me."

"Clear!" yelled Tagger. "He's down. Anyone hit?"

Willingham's hand felt wet. Her stomach clenched. Blood soaked Julia's shirt. "The Lieutenant's been hit! Call it in! Officer down!"

***

A paramedic treated Julia for what he called "a rather ugly looking wound" where the nine-mil round had torn through her side, ripping through her belt in two places. Both Julia and Mark had scrapes from hitting the sidewalk. Tagger held an ice pack on his left forearm. Diane adjusted the second ice pack held around his shoulder with self-adhering elastic wrap.

"The lieutenant needs to go to the emergency room," said the paramedic.

"Can I ride with her?" asked Mark.

"Not a problem. Climb in."

"Tag, find out what the hell's going on," said Julia.

"On it, Lieutenant."

"And, Tag," Julia said, softly. "Thanks for saving our lives. And Sergeant Willingham, thanks for keeping us safe."

"Yes," said Mark. "Thank you both so much."

The ambulance doors closed. Mark held Julia's hand and said, "And thank *you* so much for saving my life. Just remind me never to play football with you."

Tagger watched the ambulance pull away. "We'll have to double date more often," he said.

***

Ernesto followed his Google map into Collierville, slowing as he approached Traner's street, clutching the grip of his MP9. Everything looked familiar from his last visit, everything except the white unmarked van, one that didn't fit in this upscale neighborhood. Ernesto stopped, and watched. Something felt wrong. A shadow moved between two houses. He turned his motorcycle around and left. At the next corner he slowed and called Hector—no response.

"Hector," he said to himself. "Where are you, bro?"

***

*Outside Julia's room at the Methodist ER.*

"Thank God you were there last night, Johnnie," Marino said.

"Just dumb luck," said Tagger. "What are the odds?"

"I know if you hadn't been there, the lieutenant would

174

be dead."

"I don't want to think about that."

"I don't get it. Why would a Mexican cartel want to knock off the lieutenant?"

"And how would someone in Mexico know to find her at a midtown restaurant?"

"You think maybe the doc was the target?"

"That's just as crazy."

"Meantime, we need to watch both of them."

"Think we can convince him to spend the night at the lieutenant's house so we can watch them at the same time?"

"I got a feeling he's already planning to do that."

A woman walked toward them—brown slacks, colorful t-shirt, unbuttoned beige long-sleeve shirt, sandals, and toe-nails painted in an array of neon colors.

"Hey, Doc," said Marino. "Love the toes."

"Sergeants," said Dr. Tonya Proctor, nodding. "I had play therapy sessions all day. I work in small groups trying to teach kids empathy in little ways, like nurturing others. Kids get a kick out of painting my toenails. Just don't look too closely. It's hard for three-and four-year olds to stay inside the lines. So, how's our girl?"

"Darn lucky," Marino said. "I'm sure she could use one of your debriefings."

"She's always in the middle of it," said Tagger, pointing. "This time it's a nine-mil, here on her side, through and through, no vital organs or bones."

"Thanks to Johnnie," said Marino. "She and Dr. Sanders are both alive."

"Mark, too?" Proctor said. "Is he injured?"

"Just some scrapes from where the Lieutenant tackled him on the sidewalk, taking him out of the line of fire," said Tagger.

"My God," Proctor said.

"If they survive as a couple, it has to be true love," said Marino, smiling.

"The nurse just left," said Tagger. "You can go in."

***

"Tonya," Julia said. "What a nice surprise."

Proctor hugged her gently. "You made the breaking news on TV," Proctor said. "I thought you might be here."

"How's the family?" said Julia.

"They're all fine. More to the point, how are you?"

"I believe this is where I say it only hurts when I laugh."

"Yeah, well, I'm going to ignore your laughing off the fact you almost died tonight. I know this is serious, cause your two sergeants are outside looking extremely concerned."

"Mark and I ate dinner at Tsunami. We'd just walked outside when I heard Tag yell. I looked toward the sound of his voice and saw a rider on a motorcycle moving slowly. He looked like he had a gun aimed at us. I jumped on Mark to get him down. That's when I felt it. Fortunately for us, Tag took the guy out before he could unload his clip."

"Your first instinct was to save Mark?"

"No time to think."

"I'm sure he's grateful."

Julia smiled.

"What've you been thinking about since?"

"Trying to figure out why. Why me? Why is a goon from a Mexican cartel trying to kill me?"

"And?"

"And…will there be others taking his place."

"And?"

"And…how can I protect myself if I don't know why or who."

"And?"

"And...Mark could have been killed just because he was with me."

"And?"

"And I could've been killed...and I may still be a target... and Mark may yet be killed because of me."

"Yes, dear friend, you could have died. And, yes, it may not be over. And, indeed, the only way you can protect Mark might be by making sure you're never around him. Now that's going to be a real dilemma."

Chapter 43

# The Executioners

*From the jungle to the desert…* The jet landed just after midnight and taxied to a medium-size hanger. Ramon and twenty-one men wearing desert camouflage fatigues and boots disembarked. A black pickup and three black SUVs awaited them, along with crates of equipment: Saab Next-Generation Light Anti-tank Weapons, Israel's new Micro Tavor Assault Rifle-21s, helmets, ammo belts, first aid kits, gas masks, and night vision goggles.

"This is brand new, called the N-LAW," said Husam al Din in broken Spanish. "One man fires from shoulder. The N-LAW shoots missile, accurate to six hundred meters, and target not have to be tank. Not like old LAWs, these can load again. But today you might not have time to reload. So, we load all ten. Use one, throw away. Use another, throw away. Push this switch and the N-LAW can use for close, like between buildings or inside building. Watch for back blast. It will fry anyone behind."

Ramon motioned two men up front. "Teach these men the N-LAWs," he ordered.

The remaining men followed Husam to a stack of three wooden crates. He pried off the lid and pulled out an automatic rifle that looked as if the barrel had been sawed off.

"These are small but powerful," said Husam, demonstrating.

"Built for fight inside city— swing easy side to side when go around building, or search inside room to room. They can be assault rifles or machine guns. I change these to machine guns with thirty-two round magazines. Hold tight when fire automatic. Barrel go up when you shoot automatic. Use short bursts."

"Helmets in crates there," said Husam, pointing. "Everybody get one. Make sure fit good."

"I didn't see the Huey," said Ramon.

"Helo behind building," said Husam. "You bring pilot, yes?"

"He's standing right beside you," Ramon said. "Someone needs to orient him and the machine gunners."

"No problem, señor," said Husam.

***

*4:00 AM…time to rock and roll.* The helmets, gear, N-LAWs, and MTAR-21s transformed Ramon's band of men into a crack strike force. They turned out the lights in the hanger, allowing their eyes to adjust to the dark. The men knelt on one knee or squatted, maintaining silence—some praying, some staring blankly. Ramon stood facing away from his men, then raised a clenched fist about head high. The men stood. He brought his hand down sharply, pointing with four fingers to the vehicles. Five men quickly filled each SUV, three in the pickup. The drivers adjusted their night vision goggles. Ramon climbed into the passenger seat of the pickup and put on his goggles—everything now appeared through a veil of green. The pickup eased ahead, the three SUVs followed. It gained speed as the driver's vision adapted, slowing when the green wall and buildings came into focus, reducing the engine noise.

***

*4:25 AM…the Judge's compound.* A faint mechanical hum

broke the still desert night. Guards stationed on the roof spotted an approaching convoy through their night vision scopes—a pickup and three SUVs. They alerted guards at the gate and front door. Sharp loud knocking and glaring lights awakened the Judge from a deep sleep. He struggled to orient himself. His bodyguard spoke loudly as he jogged toward him.

"Someone comes, sidi," Fahad said. "No time to change from your bed clothes. You must leave now!"

His AK-47 in one hand, the other gripping the Judge's forearm, Fahad led the way cautiously but with haste. He quickly located the disguised lever, opening a concealed steel-reinforced door inside the kitchen pantry.

***

At about three hundred meters out the pickup stopped. Two men rose from the truck bed, N-LAWs on their shoulders. The men stretched over the cab, steadying their aim.

"I'll take the roof," whispered the first man. "After my shot, you take the left side of the gate. Now get out of the way. I don't want to set your ass on fire with my back blast."

The two men fired their missiles in sequence. The gable of the roof exploded, as did the wall on the left side of the gate. They grabbed two freshly loaded N-LAWs. The first man fired again, taking out the wall on the right side. The driver stomped the gas pedal to the floor. The SUVs kept up. The pickup burst through the gaping hole where the gate used to be, driving directly to the front door of the Judge's seven-story building before slamming on the brakes. The two men rose once more and fired through the glass doors into the lobby. The SUVs slid in, either side of the pickup, doors flying open. Men armed with MTAR-21s poured out, dashed toward the building, followed by the men carrying a new set of loaded N-LAWs. Guards fired down from their position on the roof. One man dropped, another screamed, grabbed his shoulder.

***

*An escape route he hoped he'd never have to use...*Two yards inside the hidden escape door sat the opening to a spiraling slide, sufficient width for one man, too narrow for two. The Judge flinched at the deafening explosion, reaching for the wall to steady himself as the building shook. Fahad slammed the heavy metal door shut and pushed the Judge forward. He dropped to a seated position, Fahad closely behind as they began the steep eight-story descent to sublevel one. Movement sensors turned on lights ahead of them. Explosions and unending machine gun fire echoed off the walls of the slide. The building shuddered with each explosion. After seven floors the slide flattened out, depositing both men behind a steel-plated wall separating them from the computer room on sublevel one. Fahad punched in a four digit code on a keypad. A heavy door opened to a hallway just wide enough for the two to walk side by side. The Judge ran through the door first. Fahad cleared the opening and punched in the code on the other side. The heavy door banged shut, sealing them off from the seven-story building.

***

The sounds of automatic weapon fire and explosions masked the noise of the approaching UH-1H helicopter. The distant hum grew into a roar as it closed on the compound, M-60 machine guns on each open side door. The pilot fired two rockets at the rooftop, making quick work of the guards. The helicopter began to circle the building while the machine gun on the port side sent all its rounds into the penthouse floors.

## Chapter 44

# Beware

*Thursday evening…La Quinta Inn.* The ten o'clock Breaking News showed pictures of Hector's motorcycle. The newscaster said he'd been killed by a cop—a Sergeant Johnnie Tagger. And that Hector had wounded the lady cop. They labeled her condition as guarded. That means she'll pull through, Ernesto thought. An internet search yielded no additional information. He downed the alcohol from the mini bar. What the hell happened. I can't believe Hector's dead. I need to ice that cop for him, finish the contract, get Traner, and blow this place. Oh, shit. What about Manuel? I'll call him after everything's taken care of. Ernesto stayed awake the entire night.

***

Ernesto called the front desk the following morning at five. The *Commercial Appeal* wouldn't be delivered until six. And the free breakfast room wouldn't be open until six-thirty. Ernesto paced the room like a caged tiger, inventoried his ammo for the fourth time, and cleaned his MP9. He ran a search on Johnnie Tagger and Google mapped his address. At 5:50 AM he went down to the dining room until the *Commercial Appeal* dropped off a bundle of the day's newspaper. The front page carried pictures of Hector's motorcycle, his cell phone shattered, and a big story on the shooting.

Ernesto's phone rang. He recognized the number.

"Yeah," he snapped.

"What the hell happened?" said Manuel. "And why am I learning about it from my computer. Your mess made national news. The whole world has been alerted to the work of the cartel. I'm expecting to see my name flash on the screen next."

"I don't know what went wrong," he whispered.

"I thought you two worked as a team. Where were you when they killed Hector?" Manuel asked.

"Hector said he had the cop, and told me to ride out to look at one of the other sites," Ernesto lied. "The old folks' home, where the aunt lives and the boyfriend works."

"What should I do with you, Ernesto? I told you, no more screw-ups."

"I didn't screw up," Ernesto shouted. He quickly surveyed the dining room. No one but him.

After a long pause Manuel said, "What do you want to do?"

"I want to kill the cop who took out Hector."

"Too risky," said Manuel. "The cops'll be on high alert, guarding him and that lieutenant. Hell, the cops may be tightening up on all the people El Pequeño Toro ordered killed. We've got nine other teams with contracts too. They didn't get a quick start like you two. They haven't taken out anyone yet. Now they may not be able to get near their marks."

"I can't just do nothing," said Ernesto, raising his voice, adding in a whisper, "They killed Hector."

"Okay. You get one swing at this one. Go to the old folks' home. Take out who's ever there—the aunt, maybe the boyfriend. But that's all. Then get back in your van and hook up with your trucks. Call me after they make their drop. I'll have a new partner for you."

No response.

"Ernesto. I didn't hear you."

"Si, señor." Ernesto clicked off.

Manuel pulled up Ernesto's picture and sent it to the phone of another hitman, with information about the route he'd be taking, and the final drop site in Richmond.

***

*Friday morning…recuperating at home.* Mark rose early, made a pot of coffee, flipped on the local news. He heard the short, uneven sliding of slippers, and turned to see Julia bent forward, one hand on each hallway wall.

"What're you doing up?" he said, moving to help.

"Can't stay in bed forever," she said, leaning into him as he guided her to a comfortable living room chair. "Besides, I smelled the coffee. Can't sleep now." She winced as she lowered herself into a chair.

"I checked your fridge. Not much to eat. How about a cheese-egg sandwich?"

"I'm afraid to ask…but what's a cheese-egg sandwich?"

"Growing up, our Mom always scrambled eggs, melted cheese on top, and put it between two slices of toast. Voila. Cheese-egg sandwich. Now all the fast food joints sell some variation of it, usually including meat."

"Well, if you're cooking, I'm eating."

Mark brought her a large coffee and turned up the news broadcast. By the time he returned with two cheese-egg sandwiches, the weather forecast had finished and another of the noisy *breaking news* introductions blared in.

"Look," he said. "There's the motorcycle from last night."

The camera panned from the cycle lying on the street to the front window of the Tsunami Restaurant, showing a single bullet hole. The newscaster conveyed the importance of the story by giving unusual emphasis to every third or fourth word.

"Thankfully, we had already left the scene," Julia said.

The newscaster told how Lieutenant Julia Todd had been wounded and taken to the MED's trauma center, but the alleged assailant had been pronounced dead on the scene, killed by an off-duty MPD officer who came to Todd's aid. The camera scene changed to the MED's parking lot, empty squad cars parked randomly, blue lights flashing.

"Oh, no," Julia said. "That's me. You're pushing me in a wheelchair? My God. Did I give an interview? I had so many drugs in me I really don't remember."

"Actually," Mark said. "You did a very good job. And, well…you'll see."

***

*Friday morning, MPD Headquarters, 201 Poplar…*

"Major Williams," he answered.

"When you gonna reign that prima donna in?" yelled MPD Major Dorsey Echols.

"Good morning to you, too, Dorsey."

"I'm dead serious, Williams. You know the procedure. No one talks to the press except the Director, and on rare occasions one of the division commanders. Hell, Todd's got her mug on TV and in the paper all the time. And I want it stopped."

"You talking about the wheelchair interview at the MED last night?"

"That's just the most recent. No other cop would dare talk to the media after getting shot. I want to know what she was doing at that restaurant anyway."

"I think they call it dinner."

"You know what I mean. Looks like she's been in bed with a Mexican cartel, and for all I know, she has—literally."

"You're way out of line, Dorsey."

"I seriously doubt it. And last week her grandstanding interfered with one of our investigations."

"The Organized Crime Unit had a claim on the dead prostitute found by the side of I-40?"

"Damn straight. Hell, before we could say a word she's plastered person-of-interest flyers from San Antonio to Richmond. That's not the way you conduct an OCU investigation."

"But it *is* the way you conduct a murder investigation."

"I'm warning you. Keep her face off the TV and out of the papers."

"Like last year when the national association presented her with the Officer of the Year Award?"

"What a pile of bogus crap. An officer, three civilians, and a security guard are murdered by that Wall Street broad, and Todd gets an award? Who the hell pushed that?"

"Our Director."

***

*Friday late morning…Union Station.* Julia shuffled gingerly into Union Station, carrying a small pillow.

"Lieutenant," said Teresa. "Don't you ever scare me like that again."

"Promise," Julia said.

"Do I need to give you lessons on how to keep a low profile?"

"I don't seem to be able to do that, do I?'

"That's an understatement. You need to chill for a while, Lieutenant. I need more time to cover your backside."

"Okay, no more drives in a noisy Prius, and no more high visibility dinners."

Teresa softened. "You ain't moving too good," she said. "You got a doctor's note saying it's okay for you to be here?"

"Doctor says it's no big deal. Says I can get back to exercising in a few days. I'm a tad sore, but it won't be long."

"What's the pillow for?"

"I just stick it against the back of the chair. Helps me sit up better, less pressure on the exit wound."

Teresa winced. "The guys are here," she said. "They took turns watching your house last night, and assigned other officers to follow you and Dr. Blue Eyes to work. I'm supposed to tell them when you come in."

"Sure. Please have them bring a cup of coffee to my office."

"Oh, I get it," said Teresa, smiling. "Kinda like having the men boil water when the baby's about to be born. Just giving them something easy to do, something they can't screw up, something to make them feel involved, but still keeping them out of the way of the main event."

Julia managed half an eye roll.

***

*Be careful what you delete...*Julia placed her pillow in the chair and slowly settled in. She turned on her computer and clicked on EMAIL. The small hour glass popped on the screen as the computer churned away for what the receiving box said was going to be a single email. Holy cow, Julia thought. This email is taking up a gazillion dino-bites. Someone must be sending a complete cold case file, or maybe a resurrected JC Penney's catalog. Finally, a single email slid in on the left side of the inbox screen.

FROM: IOU

SUBJECT: Beware.

"No. Not a virus," she said, moving to delete the email. On the right side of the split screen Julia saw the top of a photograph in the body of the email. She scrolled down on the right side of the screen without opening the email. A man looked out at her from his front porch. The street number clearly visible above the door. A name underneath, Herman Traner. Still hesitant, Julia scrolled down to find a picture of his family—wife, two young girls, and a Weinheimer. More pictures of the girls and wife. Other pictures followed of Traner in his car and entering the Crescent Center parking garage in east Memphis.

Marino and Tagger arrived at Julia's door, one carrying a cup of coffee, the other a donut.

"How you doing, Lieutenant?" Tagger asked.

"I'm fine, thanks to you. What in the world were you doing there anyway?"

"Diane and I had just finished dinner down the street. The only parking place we could find happened to be across the street from Tsunami."

"This has to be the first positive testimonial for the lousy parking in Cooper-Young."

"Really, Lieutenant," said Marino. "You're at work after taking a slug from an MP9? You have any idea what one of those does when it hits flesh? Jesus, Mary, and Joseph. We just talked about that yesterday. You should be home."

Julia shrugged her shoulders. "I'm okay. I promise. Thanks for standing watch last night, fellas. I really appreciate it."

"We couldn't rule out Dr. Sanders being the target," said Marino. "So it was a lot easier when the two of you stayed together."

Julia blushed. "I hate to bring this up," she said. "But if they could find little ole me, they'll sure be able to pick you out of crowd, Tag. And since you just killed one of their own…"

"I figure I'm in good company," Tagger said.

Julia looked at him, shaking her head. "Anything on the shooter?"

"No identification," Tagger said. "He had a cell phone on his hip. The street busted it to smithereens, no registration on the motorcycle, only extra ammo clips in the saddle bags. A photo to the FBI came back with a match on a Hector

Alonso, a Mexican citizen affiliated with the Conrios cartel."

"What have we stumbled into?" Marino said. "This can't have anything to do with Porter, can it?"

"Maybe this crazy email I just opened will shed some light on this," she said. "Pull up chairs, guys. And bring the coffee and doughnut."

They sat on either side of her.

"Someone calling themselves *IOU* sent this email with *Beware* in the subject line,"

Julia said, clicking open the email to the full screen. "I thought it was some kind of virus email. Now I don't think so."

"What's your guess as to who's the author?" said Tagger.

"No clue," Julia said.

"This the guy Masterson was talking about?" said Marino. "The one somebody took a couple of shots at in his home?"

"Same name," said Julia, continuing to scroll. The next set of pictures were of J. Francis Sizemore, followed by a man, then a woman. Each in a similar format: house, family, car, Crescent Center.

"Don't recognize these names," said Marino. "Maybe they work with Sizemore."

The next pictures sent chills through Julia's body. She rocked back in her chair.

"What the hell's going on, Lieutenant?" said Tagger. "This is you at your house, with your new Mini, and at Union Station. These pictures had to be taken recently."

"And a picture of you and Sizemore," said Marino. "What is this? The St. Jude Golf Classic?"

"Yes," said Julia. "Sizemore Global Solutions Group took over sponsorship for the PGA tournament. Aunt Louise bought me a ticket for opening day this past June. I remember seeing him there, but I never so much as waved at the man."

"Someone trying to set you up, Lieutenant?" asked Tagger.

"Keep scrolling down," said Marino.

"Mark," Julia whispered, eyes wide.

"The same deal," said Tagger. "You're with Mark at his home, his car, and the Haven for Seniors, where he works."

The next picture showed Aunt Louise at the Haven, followed by people unknown to the men.

"You know these folks?" Tagger said.

"My brother Wayne," Julia said softly, her mouth dropping open. "His home, wife, kids, car, place of work."

"I don't recognize the area," said Marino.

"It's Olympia, Washington," said Julia. "This is my family." The pictures ended. A sentence followed.

*Photos emailed to hitmen from the Conrios cartel.*

"That's the cartel your shooter belonged to," Tagger said.

"And those reports I've been reading? They say the Conrios cartel is the largest cartel in Mexico," said Marino.

Julia sat quietly, staring.

"This is personal, Julia," said Tagger. "We're family, too."

"That's right," said Marino. "And we're not going to let anything happen to any of you."

## Chapter 45

# It Takes A Family

*Shuffling priorities…* Julia gripped the arms of her chair, her eyes wide, lips pursed. She jumped up, wincing.

"Where're you going, Lieutenant?" asked Tagger, standing up in front of her.

"I've got to warn Aunt Louise," she said, turning away from Tagger.

Marino stood up, blocking her in. Julia turned back to Tagger, eyes wide.

"Last spring, when that car bomb went off in my face, Tagger said. "You jumped up beside me in the ambulance. You remember? I couldn't think straight. And you ordered me to the hospital where I needed to be. Well, I'm not ordering you anywhere, but I do believe our heads are clearer than yours right now. The three of us need to think this through before anyone leaves this room."

Julia nodded, sat slowly, and took controlled, deep breaths. When she looked up again her eyes had narrowed, determination had replaced fear. She grabbed each man's arm, looked from one to the other.

"Let's do it," she said. "Priorities. What are our priorities?"

"Keeping you, your aunt, the doc, and your brother and his family safe," said Marino.

"Letting the head shed know about this email," said

Tagger. "Let them decide who to send it too, approve security for you, your family and Dr. Sanders."

"And the others?" asked Julia.

"We'll leave them to the powers that be," Tagger said. "Our family's our priority."

"The email gives no timeframe," said Marino. "But according to last night, these creeps are already here."

"I'll call Aunt Louise, my brother, and Mark," said Julia. "Get them to lie low till we get a handle on this."

"I'll take a few officers over to the Haven," said Marino. "I'll let the director know she'll be seeing more cops thanks to a freak rise in crime in the neighborhood. We don't want a panic. Then I'll help your aunt move in with one of her friends for a while. We'll get the doc to take some time off as well. I'll station officers on the grounds."

"I'll forward a copy of this email to Major Williams," said Julia. "He'll know who should have a copy, and how quiet to keep this. We could be dealing with countywide hysteria if we're not careful. Then I'll fire off a copy to Masterson, and ask him for some help in Olympia."

"And I'm going wherever you go," said Tagger. "I'll grab a couple uniforms, too."

***

No sooner had the emails been sent, then Teresa buzzed in. "The boss, Lieutenant," she said. "Line two."

"Major Williams," said Julia. "Thanks for calling so quickly."

"What the hell's this?" said Williams. "Last night you get shot by a goon from a Mexican cartel. And today you and your family members are on an international hit list?"

"Like I said in the email, sir," said Julia. "The sender of this email believed it was a hit list from the Conrios cartel. That cartel turns out to be the same one responsible for the attempt on my life last night. I don't have a clue who sent this, or why I or my family are included."

"You know this looks as if you're involved with the cartel. Looks as if Echols has something on you."

"I understand that interpretation. But, sir, I—"

"I don't believe it for a second, Lieutenant," Williams interrupted.

"Thank you, sir."

"But if, or should I say *when* this gets out, the media will go wild."

"The department doesn't need any more bad press. I'm sor—"

"Don't even go there," he interrupted. "I want to know what you're doing to keep yourself and your family safe."

"Sergeant Marino has already taken a detail to the Haven, and my aunt will move in with one of her friends for a while. I talked to my brother in Olympia. He's taking a few weeks, heading out of town with his family today. I was about to call Dr. Sanders when you phoned."

"And you?"

"Sergeant Tagger is, well, *tagging* along after me. As for the other people with photos in the email, I'm hoping Organized Crime will be putting together a plan."

"You thinking these are all the pictures?"

"I'm guessing these are only related to Memphis. There have to be bankers and investment consultants involved from all the big cities. There's just too much money floating around."

"Any idea of the timeframe?"

"No, sir. But we now know the cartel's hitmen are already in the area, and maybe in other cities."

"I've shared this email with the Director. He'll decide how widely we disseminate it."

"Thank you, sir."

"Lieutenant."

"Sir?"

"I want you and your family in one piece. That's an order."

"Yes, sir."

*****

Julia called Mark. "Hey sunshine," Mark answered. "Howyadoin? How's the side?"

"My side's doing okay," she said. "But I have something very important to tell you."

"Your aunt Louise? Is she okay?"

"Just listen, please. I received an email warning me I'm a target for hitmen—"

"Hitmen?" Mark interrupted. "You mean that guy last night?"

"Mark. Listen. The target includes my family—Aunt Louise, my brother Wayne and his family. And Mark. It includes you."

"Me? My God. Are you serious?"

"Dead serious. Now listen carefully. We're setting up protection. Sergeant Marino should be at the Haven by now. Go to Aunt Louise's apartment to meet him. I just talked to Aunt Louise. She's a wreck. She'll need someone to calm her down."

"I don't understand. Who's doing this? When's it going to happen? How will you be safe?"

"Sergeant Tagger will be watching me. It appears to be a Mexican cartel. But I have no idea why we've been targeted. And no, we don't know when."

"I love you," said Mark.

"And I love you. Now don't wait. No time to finish any paperwork or make any phone calls. Just go."

Julia hung up, overcome with guilt and fear. *My family could all be dead because of me,* she thought. Mark almost died last night *because of me.* Julia felt as if a boulder pinned her to the chair. She took a deep cleansing breath and rolled her chair back enough to open the top drawer. She fanned through the overlapping stacks with her hand, uncovering a dog-eared business card accented with coffee stains. She pulled it out, closed the drawer, and punched in the numbers.

"Private investigators," said Jackson Frederick.

"What happened to Detective of the Heart?" said Julia.

"I'll be damned. Lieutenant Todd. Long time no hear, sweetness."

"What's this about private investigators with an *s?*"

"Oh, I just thought it sounded better. People are more likely to do business with you if they think you're good enough to have employees. Just like all those TV ads for attorneys. There's never just one."

"What about truth in advertising?"

"You just gonna keep bustin my chops? Or are you gonna put me to work? Be happy to clear my calendar, just for you."

"Actually, Jackson, I am looking to hire you. I've got a time-sensitive job I'm hoping will be right up your alley. "

"Now you're talking, sweet cheeks. Let's do some business."

***

*Seeking an IT consult...*Memphis Police Information Technology Specialist Elwood Banks bent over his laptop, his fingers flying across the key board. Data flashed on his monitor. Julia stood, looking over his shoulder.

"Can you do it, El?" Julia said.

"Working on it, Lieutenant." said Banks. "I've been itching to try these programs I pulled from the laptop you confiscated last January." He stole a quick glance at Julia.

"I thought you told me those hacking programs were illegal?"

"Not really illegal. More like…ill-advised."

"Come on, El. I really need to know who sent this email."

"Whoa!"

"What?"

"Just hit a firewall—one of the government's firewalls. I'm guessing CIA or FBI."

"Can you break through it?"

"A watched pot, Lieutenant. Go get some coffee, maybe even a doughnut. I'll be right here."

***

"This IP address belongs to Special Agent Harrison Cornell of Homeland Security," said Banks. "I can't get any further without a password."

"Cornell?" said Julia. "That name's familiar. Homeland Security…Special Agent Cornell…That's it. Cornell is one of the clowns from Homeland who busted Charleze Mitchell free last year. Waltzed right in and snatched her away before we could ask her a single question. Said the government needed her services, enough to keep her out of jail."

"Maybe he thinks he owes you."

"Yeah. Maybe."

## Chapter 46

# This Is For Hector

Ernesto fitted a silencer on the MP9, slipped it into its holster and took Sycamore View to I-40 west, heading for the Haven. He stayed in the right hand lane, taking the flyover and merging south onto the I-240 loop. Up ahead he saw a red Mini Cooper convertible take the cloverleaf at exit 13, reappearing on the Walnut Grove Road bridge, crossing over I-240 heading east.

"Todd," Ernesto said out loud. He zipped in and out of traffic, leaving the expressway at Walnut Grove, but losing sight as he followed the long cloverleaf exit and looped back over the bridge, crossing above I-240. As he reached the crown of the bridge, he thought he caught a flash of bright red heading south on Brierview Street, just before Baptist Memorial Hospital East. He waited with others for the traffic light, then raced from the bridge, zipping across two lanes of traffic exiting from the expressway. He turned right on Brierview, a busy two-lane street in a heavily treed neighborhood, with large expensive houses and well-manicured yards. Stop signs punctuated the route. Ernesto took a right on River Oaks, following a winding street with several dead end coves. No sign of the Mini. He swore, pulled to the curb and reset his GPS back to the Haven.

As he began following the GPS directions, he spotted the

red Mini Cooper, her short brown hair whipping in the wind. Weaving in and out of traffic he passed several cars. Now only three cars separated them. The traffic thinned. Cars turned off. Ernesto moved his motorcycle closer, his hand on the MP9 pistol grip. He saw her right hand turn signal and decided to come along side the Mini. As she slowed for her turn Ernesto sped up, pulling the MP9 but keeping it low, the butt sitting on his right thigh. Ernesto squeezed the trigger on full auto as he passed. The Mini drifted into a telephone pole, the horn blaring, radiator steaming. The motorcycle continued on.

***

*The Haven for Seniors…more excitement than a heart can take.* Mark grabbed his laptop and cell phone, and rode the painfully slow elevator to Louise's floor. He walked down the hall and rang the bell. The door opened.

"Sergeant Marino," said Mark. "Julia said I should come up here."

"Come on in," said Marino.

Mark took a step when he heard the stairwell door click shut. He turned to see a small man in motorcycle leathers and helmet walking quickly toward him. He almost leaped inside and slammed the door closed.

"He's right behind me," Mark said loudly.

Marino grabbed Mark's free arm and pulled him to the side. "Hug that wall like it's your best friend," he said. Marino moved to the opposite side wall, crouching, his Glock drawn.

Mark watched in horror as a moving line of tiny eruptions punctured the wall to his left, the only sound coming from his right as glasses and china exploded. The wall at his back seemed to push him forward, closer to the eruptions. Quiet. Then he heard the metallic sound of ammo clips being exchanged, the new clip being locked, a round chambered. The next burst of five silent rounds destroyed the door lock.

Mark's face turned white. His eyes widened. His breaths came in short gulps. His laptop and cell phone dropped, clattering on the floor. Ernesto kicked the door open and stepped into the apartment in one motion. Mark willed his body into the wall, trying to disappear. Ernesto swung his MP9 right, toward the sound he'd heard. He saw Mark. Two ear splitting shots rang out. A shout escaped from Mark's body. Ernesto flew sideways against the door jamb, melting to the floor, his machine pistol clanking on the hardwood. Marino moved in, smoke rising from his Glock. He kicked the MP9 away, keeping his eyes on Ernesto. He bent down and checked for a pulse. He found none. Marino looked up at Mark.

"You okay?" Marino said.

No response. Mark stood against the wall—body tense, fists tight, face pale.

Marino holstered his weapon, picked up the MP9, and walked to Mark. "Come on, Doc," he said, taking him by one arm. "Take a seat over here. Two attempts on your life within twenty-four hours are enough to shake up anyone."

Mark stared.

Marino called for assistance.

***

*Union Station…*Teresa pushed her chair back and limped-ran as fast as her bum leg would allow. She burst into Julia's office, eyes wide, winded.

"Lieutenant," she gasped.

"Teresa? What's wrong?" said Julia as she hurried to her, pulling up a chair.

"I was going over the daily logs," Teresa said, "like you told me. An accident investigation team just reported a car and driver riddled with bullets in east Memphis. The car was a red Mini Cooper. I thought they'd killed you."

The two embraced.

"Who died?" asked Julia, softly.

"A female student at the University of Memphis."

***

*The latest crime scene*…Mark sat glued to Julia on Aunt Louise's bullet punctured couch, color returning to his face. Crime techs worked the scene. Ernesto's body lay in its original position, covered with a sheet. Officers kept residents away, even those with apartments nearby.

"Lieutenant," said Marino. "Is this a good time?"

"I can multi-task, professor," Julia said. "Let me begin by thanking you."

"Yes," said Mark. "I'll never be able to repay you. Thank you so much."

"Believe me," said Marino. "I'm glad I was able to nail this SOB."

Tears dripped down Julia's cheeks. Mark wiped them with his thumbs.

"This character over here is Ernesto Torres, another goon from the Conrios cartel," said Marino. "He had a motel key on him. We tracked it back to Sycamore View, the same La Quinta Inn. A cell phone in his saddle bag had your pictures, Lieutenant, as well as those of your Memphis family. Just like we saw in that email."

"And, Wayne?" asked Julia.

"Your brother's picture was not there. Scrolling back, we found Traner's pictures. This confirms Johnnie's discovery of Bob and John in the neighborhood. I think we've nailed both the guys who tried to kill Traner a few weeks back. Found his van in the motel parking lot, filled with an assortment of weapons. Ernesto probably believed he'd killed you in the Mini Cooper. Then he came here to finish his contract on your family."

Chapter 47

# Getting the Word Out

*Communication is a good thing...*Haven Director Geraldine Jacobson hurriedly called a residents' meeting for all those living in the main building. Her custodial staff tracked down every chair and filled the multi-purpose room except for two sections at the back for residents using the type of walkers which could be turned around and used for a seat. People filled the room slowly. The noise level increased as folks settled in. On the stage with Mrs. Jacobson sat Julia, Mark, Marino, Tagger, and Louise.

Jacobson stood at the podium, tapping on the microphone. "Is this on?" she said.

Heads nodded around the room.

"Thank you for coming on such short notice," said Jacobson. "As some of you know, we had a serious incident on the second floor in Louise Todd's apartment this afternoon, involving Dr. Mark Sanders. As you can see, Dr. Mark is fine," she said pointing back to him.

Mark waved modestly, forcing a half-smile.

"I thought it would be important for us all to hear about it at the same time," she said. "Some of you have friends who don't hear so well. Please get with them afterwards and make sure they have the correct information. Flyers are being handed out." Jacobson took a drink of water.

201

"I'm sure many of you know Louise Todd, or at least have seen her around the Haven. Louise has been with us since last January. Her daughter Julia is a lieutenant in the Memphis Police Department. She is well-respected and has won awards for her bravery. Lieutenant Todd is here with Sergeants Tagger and Marino." Each raised a hand in turn. Jacobson took another drink. "Lieutenant Todd and Dr. Mark were shot at last night when they came out of a restaurant in Cooper-Young. How many of you saw it on television or read about it in the *Commercial Appeal*? Raise your hands." Jacobson scanned the audience. "That's most everyone."

"You may have read about Sergeant Tagger bravely tackling the murderer."

Heads nodded.

"It turned out the man on the motorcycle in Cooper-Young had a partner. That second man went looking for Lieutenant Todd and Dr. Mark." Jacobson paused. "The police thought he might come to the Haven."

There were gasps, and side discussions. A few heads nodded.

"That's when Sergeant Marino came to the Haven to protect all of us. The second murderer came upstairs and began shooting through the walls of Louise's apartment. Sergeant Marino shot the man dead."

Jacobson waited for the talking to subside.

"It is important y'all know you are safe, thanks to the quick thinking of the police, and the actions of Sergeant Marino."

Someone began clapping, and gradually everyone was applauding. Jacobson joined them, turning to look at Marino. Louise and Mark joined in.

"Of course, Louise's room is a mess," said Jacobson. "But the carpenters are already working to replace the damaged walls as I speak. Now, it's going to be dusty and noisy with lots of hammering, and there'll be workers coming and going. So for your own safety, unless you live near Louise, please stay away so the carpenters can make the repairs."

"Are there any questions?"

A man in the front row stood.

"Yes, Morton?" said Jacobson.

"How do we know there are no more partners?" Morton asked.

Julia stood. "We've been trailing these two men for weeks. We have photos and videos of them driving through town. They've always been together, no other accomplices. Once we knew they'd returned to Memphis, we were ready for them. But just to be on the safe side, we'll have a round the clock police presence for the next week."

"Yes, Cerilla," said Jacobson.

"I want to know how the Lieutenant is doing," said Cerilla.

"I'm doing fine," said Julia. "I was in the office today, and the doctor told me I'd be back to running and exercising in a few days. Thanks for asking."

***

If there are no more questions—" said Jacobson.

A woman in the back raised her hand.

"Yes, Gladys."

"Are we still going to have happy hour?"

"For those who couldn't hear, Gladys wants to know if happy hour will take place at the usual time. The answer is yes. I think we could all use a drink."

## Chapter 48

# Watch Your Back

Julia's cell rang. The ID read, Williams.

"Morning Major Williams," said Julia.

"I have two things to say to you, Lieutenant," said Major Williams.

Julia waited.

"First of all, I'm truly grateful you, your family, and your team are safe."

"Thank you, sir. I owe so much to Tagger and Marino."

"I know, and I intend to contact them shortly. Unfortunately, you didn't keep a low profile."

"Sir. We were being shot at."

"I realize that, but giving an interview from a wheelchair?"

"Actually, sir. I was too doped up to even remember doing that. Couldn't believe it when I saw it on the news this morning."

"Doing interviews in your sleep? That's even worse."

"No argument here, sir."

"And now the media are asking the questions I'd feared."

"Sir?"

"Why is a Mexican cartel shooting up our city, trying to eliminate one of our police officers and her family? You can hear them thinking—*She must be dirty*."

"Oh, those questions."

"The Director is on the hot seat. He needs answers. And Major Echols is feeding him unflattering information."

"Like what, sir?"

"Like you think no jurisdictions apply to you, you're always tramping in other people's business. And case in point, you've been going over his head to deal with Homeland Security."

"But I—"

"Let me finish, Lieutenant."

"Yes, sir."

"Like the fact that you and your family were included on a major hit list targeting people believed to be involved in money laundering. And that you and your team interfered with a case OCU had been closely involved with."

No response.

"You can talk now, Lieutenant."

"Oh. Well, as to the first allegation from Major Echols, I didn't go over his head. The email I received came as a one-way communication. Even Elwood Banks couldn't figure how to respond to the email. Only that it came from Homeland Security's Special Agent Cornell, who died yesterday in a shootout with cartel thugs. As to the second allegation, I have no idea how I was included. And neither I nor my family has been involved in laundering anything but clothes. I'm still unsure how one does launder money. And finally, the only two cases in which we might have overlapped with OCU involved murders—murders committed in our own backyard, murders that had to be investigated. And if OCU was indeed involved, my counter question would be why OCU didn't prevent the murders?"

"Not bad. That's pretty much what I told the Director."

"You did? Oh. Thank you, sir."

"There's one other thing. I think Echols is threatened

by you."

"Me? Major, I've only met the man once."

"Not a physical threat, Lieutenant. You've been a rising star in the MPD. Some say it's because you're a minority—a woman."

"Can't change that, sir."

"Wouldn't want you to. But for more than a few, you represent a threat to their ability to rise in the ranks—real or imagined."

"And Major Echols is one of those few?"

"I believe so."

"But his trashing me and my family feels more like resentment than fear."

"Good point. Maybe there's something else. Anyway, this is not for dissemination."

"Understood, sir."

Chapter 49

# Feeling A Little Rusty

*Friday…even the Tin Man needed oil.* Jackson Frederick felt something he hadn't felt in a long time—desire. He flashed back. Some forty years ago I made a gargantuan mistake, he thought. Got too close to a case…invested everything—hell even my own money—to find a teenage runaway, a girl I'd never met. Lost everything—my career, my reputation. I lived in a bottle all those years. Then eight months ago, Lieutenant Julia Todd bulled her way into my life, refusing to go away, despite all the shit I gave her. She cleared up the forty-year mystery of my runaway teen and gave me the spark I needed to get back in the business. This one's for the lieutenant.

He began to hit the neighborhood bars. Nothing new. Except this time he was working a case. He dropped in several of the old bars in midtown, then headed downtown, staying away from the flash of Beale Street. He found a friendly face in the *Bardog Tavern* on Monroe, a block from Front Street.

"The usual, Jackson?" said the elderly man behind the bar."

"Not tonight, Carl," said Frederick. "I'm on a case."

"Really?"

"Yeah. Feels a little strange. But good."

"Been there. Done that," said Carl. "Wish I had some

special 3-in-One oil for people trying to get back in the race like you. It'd help you work through the rust."

"Good one, Carl," said Frederick, flexing his arthritic fingers. "I know what you mean. Say, I'm looking for someone."

"This someone got a name?"

"Nope. Just a talent. This guy's good at taking pictures. Pictures of people who don't know they're being photographed. High quality shots. Probably has a fancy zoom lens. I figure he's a PI."

"Well, you're in the right bar. Check with Burns over there. I bet he'll know, or at least know someone who will."

***

"So you think one of these five guys is my best bet?" said Frederick, looking over his notes.

"Yeah," said Burns. "If I wanted someone tailed and pictures taken, these are the guys I'd go to first."

"Thanks, man," said Frederick. "Love to be able to send a twenty your way, but I don't have one."

"No problem, man. I always heard about you, how you were back in the day…Anyway, glad you're getting your hand back in the game."

"Appreciate it."

"You know you're not the first person this week who asked me this same question?"

"No shit."

"Yeah. Monday, I think. A Mexican. Gave me a Benjamin."

"Who'd you send him to?"

"Gave him the first two names on your list."

Chapter 50

# What Happened to My Dongle?

*Friday…Langley.* D. J. Wallace monitored the money flowing into the CIA from a dozen or so banks, and dreaming about what kind of computers he would buy with his department's share of the confiscated money. He lazily glanced at his other screen, the one monitoring the Judge's computers.

"What the…" he said. He rolled his chair to a different keyboard and began querying his program. His fingers moved more quickly with each outcome. He grabbed the phone.

"Special Agent, this is Wallace," he said.

"What's up?" said Davenport. "Money still rolling in?"

"The money's coming in fine. It's the Judge's computer. It stopped functioning."

"Stopped functioning. What does that mean?"

"Either his central computer got fried, or they discovered our Trojan horse, or they switched computers for some reason. Either way, the signal has stopped."

"But the money's still coming in?"

"Yeah, they're completely separate things. The money's coming because of the program we uploaded in each of the banks. The information from the Judge's computer kept us up to date as to who he's been dealing with."

"We need his information for court, right?"

"Right. We still have everything through today. But we're

not getting anything more."

***

Davenport called her Middle East contact.

"It's no wonder your computer feed isn't working," said the agent. "Someone attacked the Judge's stronghold. The entire building's been destroyed, computers wrecked, lots of bodies."

"One of those the Judge?"

"We didn't find his body, nor his bodyguard's. Maybe he escaped."

"Who did it?"

"Don't know yet. One of our usual informants is missing, a heavy duty player named Husam."

"Stay on this. I need to know."

Chapter 51

# A Headless Return



*Friday, the Conrios cartel compound...*

"You come limping back to me with only four men, three of them wounded," said Vargas. "Where the hell's the Judge's head?"

"We never found the Judge, señor," said Ramon.

"You failed!" said Vargas.

"Not one of the Judge's men lives," said Ramon. "The building is a shambles. His computers are destroyed. Not even an ashtray survived the helicopter's assault on the penthouse."

"Yet the Judge lives," shouted Vargas. He jerked out his SIG Sauer and pointed it at Ramon. "Tell me why I shouldn't kill you."

"If the Judge had been there, he would be dead," said Ramon, eyes intense. "The attack was perfectly planned, perfectly executed. My men fought bravely. We could not have done better. Their widows deserve to have their pay."

"I should give *your widow* your pay," said Vargas.

Ramon took a deep breath. He relaxed his body, lowered his head, and waited.

"You are my best man," said Vargas, holstering his weapon. "Find replacements for your unit quickly. Once Delgado hears about the losses of your best men he will not hesitate. He *will* attack."

"I'll have replacements in seventy-two hours."
"That may be too late."

Chapter 52

# Live To Launder Another Day

*Good to have a backup plan…* The two men walked briskly through the long paved tunnel, the Judge cursing and yelling with every explosion behind them. Fahad spoke into his two-way.

"We are near," Fahad said. "Have the guards ready. No one goes outside the building. Do not let anyone see you. They are well-armed."

"Understood."

A wall came into view. A door opened.

"Sidi, come," the first guard said, reaching for him.

"Don't touch me, you fool," the Judge said. "I am perfectly capable of walking."

"Respect al Hakam," yelled Fahad.

The men fell back.

The Judge had never used this tunnel, but he knew it well. He had designed it. Two mirror image buildings, four hundred meters apart. One seven stories, one four. To his right on Subfloor One sat the base of the smaller building's spiral escape slide. The hidden door across from the tunnel entrance stood open. He hurried through the steel-plated wall. In front of him: an identical computer room, complete with a body scanner outside the door. Computer operators scrambled into the room. Guards hurried to their positions.

"I must assume our comrades in the main building have all been killed," bellowed the Judge. "And the computers have all been destroyed. They might know about this second building. You guards have got be vigilant. Our business must continue at all costs. I want this room up and running at full capacity in five minutes."

The Judge, Fahad, and four guards took the elevator to the top penthouse level on the fourth floor. Fahad positioned the guards—one outside the door, the others throughout the penthouse. The Judge pushed through a door, an exact replica of the bedroom he'd just been wrenched from. Grabbing a fresh set of clothes he walked into the bathroom where he threw water on his face, and changed from his night clothes.

"Fahad," the Judge said. "I want to know who the hell did this. He will pay. He will pay with his life."

"Yes, sidi," said Fahad. "With his life."

"Send a woman and a young child to search the first building. They'll be less likely to shoot them, if they're still here. We need to know the extent of our losses, and the number of their men.

"It will be done, sidi."

"Fahad."

"Yes, sidi."

"You saved my life. I will not forget."

Fahad bowed.

"I can trust no one else, Fahad. Find who's behind this. You must lead this search personally."

"I will not fail you, sidi."

The Judge reached behind his bed, pulled out an MTAR-21, and slung it over his shoulder.

***

*Virginia…*The cell phone sat between the makeup bag

214

and hairbrush in Davenport's bathroom, as she brushed her teeth. It rang. She hurriedly spit everything in the sink, gave her mouth a quick wipe, cleared her throat, and answered.

"Davenport," she said, checking her mouth in the mirror.

"We're back online," said Wallace.

"I don't understand," said Davenport, wiping toothpaste off her chin. "I just got word the Judge's entire building's in shambles, bodies everywhere, and the computers blown to kingdom come."

"Well, he must have a backup system, because after a break of less than a half-hour the information is flowing again."

"Even after losing the central computer, the one with the dongle?"

"Yeah. Remember, they're separate things. The dongle carried the Trojan horse program. It's the dongle that's been part of the central computer—like, physical to physical. I designed the Trojan horse to work its way into the Judge's computer programs and files. Their backup system must've been networked in. So our Trojan horse is alive and still kicking ass."

***

The Judge sat on a cushion eating dinner, the table raised just above the floor. He swung his MTAR-21 off his shoulder at the sound of approaching footsteps. Fahad appeared in the doorway.

"What have you learned?" the Judge said, re-slinging his weapon.

"The woman reported she saw no one left alive," said Fahad. "I took men and we searched carefully. She spoke the truth. All our people are dead. The computers have been destroyed. Nothing remains whole in your penthouse, on either floor. The invaders suffered many losses. They appear to be South American or Mexican. None of their weapons were found."

"One of the cartels? I want a name. Go!"

***

The Judge rapidly clicked through security cameras displayed on his large monitor, searching for any sign of another attack. He relaxed slightly and clicked on the camera positions that used to show Akilah. His sense of sadness puzzled him. I miss her, he thought. I miss her beauty, her body, her intelligence, her confidence. I miss her courage.

A guard cried out, "Sidi. Fahad comes."

"Sidi," said Fahad. "We found the traitor—the gun runner, Husam."

"The same Husam who sold me this MTAR-21?"

"The very same, sidi."

"Who's he working for?"

"Husam always works for the highest bidder. In this case, the Conrios cartel."

"What? The Conrios cartel? Why would Vargas attack us?"

"Husam did not know. I am sure of it. He told us everything, just before I sent him to meet Allah."

"Set up a meeting with the leader of the Bacarzo cartel, Señor Delgado. Caracas, Venezuela is about midway."

"It will be done, sidi."

## Chapter 53

# Their First Date

*Friday evening....Bridgette is larger than life.* Marino and Houston arrived on time for their dinner reservation at the Brooklyn Bridge. Both had changed into casual clothes—Marino in slacks and a blazer. Houston in a sun dress, wedge sandals, and her long brown hair held back on the sides with blue barrettes. Marino held the door for her, and followed into the dining room. No sooner had he entered when the female half of the married proprietors shouted out, strode forward, and gave Marino a kiss and a monster hug.

"Woo hoo! Tony," said Bridgette. Taking him by the arm she pulled him into the dining room and announced loudly, "Hey, everyone. This is Sergeant Tony Marino, the man who saved all those people at the retirement home today." Bridgette began applauding, and the customers joined in enthusiastically. Bridgette hugged Tony again. "I'm so proud of you," she said. Then she hugged Houston. "Ellie. I didn't know you two knew each other."

"We just met," said Ellie.

Bridgette turned to Marino. "Your dinner is on the house, and I have just the table for you guys. I'll have a nice Chianti sent over."

"Ohh, Bridge," Marino said. "You don't have—"

"Hush," Bridgette interrupted. "It's from Vince and me.

We're honored to have you here." She gave Marino a gentle pat on the back and left.

"What did you do?" asked Houston.

"Sometimes you're just in the right place at the right time," Marino said, looking down.

"You going to tell me or do I need to bring Bridgette back here?"

"My lieutenant got shot last night."

"The woman in Cooper-Young?"

Marino nodded.

"But you weren't the cop that saved her, were you?"

"No. It was my partner, Johnnie Tagger."

Houston waited.

"The same people who tried to kill her also threatened to kill her family. Her aunt lives in The Haven for Seniors. I went over with a detail to watch her. I happened to be in her apartment when a gunman started shooting up the place."

"You shot him?"

Marino nodded.

"Did you kill him?"

"Yes," he said, barely a whisper.

"Were you hit?"

"No. He didn't hit anyone."

"The thing that's made me a successful salesperson is being a good judge of character. I knew that first day you were a good man. But I never dreamed you'd be doing things like this."

Marino looked down.

"Are you all right?"

"I will be."

"Don't they usually take your gun and put you on paid leave or something?"

"Yeah, and you usually go through a debriefing."

"With a psychologist?"

He nodded. "But this time it's our whole team. The lieutenant's been wounded, Johnnie killed that first guy, and then there's me. They'll probably have a joint debriefing in the next day or so. No one's said anything about putting us on leave."

"You have your gun with you now?"

He nodded. "You want to go home?"

"Why would you think that? I'm with one of the bravest police officers in Memphis. Besides, dinner's free."

***

"I had a good time, too," Houston said. "I'm so glad you said *yes*."

"That mean you'd be open to doing it again, even if it didn't involve police business?" said Marino.

"No question, Sergeant Anthony Tony Marino." She moved closer and kissed him.

He kissed back.

"Let's make it sooner rather than later," she said.

## Chapter 54

# There's A Leak

*The FBI and CIA in real time...*Lawrence Masterson and Anita Davenport had a face to face meeting of the minds, in cyberspace.

"So we agree, Anita," said Masterson. "The hit on the Judge is connected to the Conrios cartel's contracts on these people who've visited the Judge's compound, mostly from the Memphis area."

"Everyone but the Lieutenant," said Davenport. "I still don't get that connection."

"I can vouch for the Lieutenant. She's straight arrow. No chance she's involved with the Conrios cartel or the Judge. Remember, she's the one who alerted everyone to all the Memphis area contract hits, giving us enough time to intervene. They rounded up a number of Vargas's goons."

"Okay, Lawrence. I give. The Lieutenant's a good guy. But who sent that anonymous email?"

"The Lieutenant told me her IT guy traced it back to a Homeland Security agent by the name of Cornell. But it turns out Cornell died in a shootout with one of the cartel thugs the next day."

"It doesn't make any sense for a Homeland Security agent to send emails to one of several intended victims, and not send a copy to the rest of us."

"You think Homeland was trying to take credit for breaking up the cartel's drug shipments?" Masterson said.

"You know as well as I do that none of the federal agencies are beyond playing dirty pool," Davenport said. "It's a daily battle for funding and a higher ranking in the pecking order."

"Can't rule it out. But, still, I don't see any benefit going to Homeland."

"Let's get back to the Saturday meeting with the alphabets. This all happened within five days of that meeting. The attack on the Judge had to have taken several days to plan and set in motion—gathering vehicles and weapons, flying a strike team in from Mexico."

"According to the cell phones we recovered," Masterson said. "Vargas's contract hits went out on Thursday. Only the one on Lieutenant Todd was initiated that same day. Perhaps it's simply a matter of chance. That particular shotgun team happened to be in the Memphis area when they got the contract."

"And the attack on the Judge took place in the wee hours of Friday morning," Davenport said. "So the strike team had to have left no later than Thursday."

"Let's say someone reported the content of our meeting to Vargas. And let's say the little bull went off the deep end about losing all his money. Why take it out on the Judge? And why only the bankers and investment consultants in the states, he's connected all around the globe?"

"Vargas's reaction seems almost reflexive," she said. "He must've blamed the Judge. Maybe he demanded the Judge cover his losses?"

"And the Judge gave him a quick *up yours?*"

"Yeah, but if the Judge knew about the Trojan horse he would have terminated it himself days earlier."

"Maybe Vargas never trusted the Judge, and he jumped at the chance to take him out."

"And targeting the Americans?"

"Didn't you tell me Archambault wanted to know if your spy was an American?"

"That's right. No way for Vargas to know *which* American, so he calls for the elimination of *all* the Americans who came near the Judge's computer."

"So how did Vargas find out? A bug?"

"Not a chance," said Davenport. "We swept the room and the surrounding area, then set up sensors to detect any listening devices. No, sir. No bugs."

"If no bugs, who's the plant?" Masterson said. "Lots of heavily vetted folks. Maybe a subordinate? Maybe Archambault?"

"Do we dare investigate these people? What happens when they find out what we're doing?"

"What happens if we don't at least check them out?"

"The plant keeps reporting back to the bad guys."

"The Bureau vetted most of them," said Masterson. "I'll look at their files personally. Then we'll make a very discrete check of telephone calls and emails."

"Okay. And I'll see what I can find out about Archambault. But promise me, Lawrence, you'll be extremely careful, or they'll have our hides *and* our pensions."

"As for the Judge," Masterson said. "You're pretty sure he's still alive?"

"Lots of bodies at the Judge's building, but his wasn't one of them. We had a break in the data stream from the Judge's computer. We're guessing the duration of the break follows the timeline of the attack. Apparently our program survived the attack because the data's flowing again. Our IT guy says it means the Judge had a networked backup system, and the operation's still pouring dirty money into the banks at about the same rate, minus the Conrios cartel's contribution. I'm betting the Judge had a contingency plan. He simply changed locations, flipped a switch, and kept the money flowing."

"And you're still siphoning the laundered money to the CIA?"

"Still coming in," she said. "Buckets of it."

## Chapter 55

# If You Want Something Done Right...

*Saturday morning…Memphis.* Julia had not been cleared for exercise—no running, no weights, no hitting the heavy bag, no yoga, and of course, no showers or baths. The best she could do was to sit in her beanbag chair and meditate. She slipped into an optimistic mindset, visualizing her body repairing itself, growing stronger. She considered all the members of her extended family, feeling grateful. What can I do or say to help them adjust to the trauma of these last few dangerous days? she thought. Like the old folks say, the only person you can change is yourself, and put your own gasmask on before helping others. So, I need to take care of myself first, I can stay calm, say nothing to increase their anxiety, not talk about my wound, and reassure them the danger is over. My God, she thought, opening her eyes. Is it over? How will we know when the danger's over? I still don't know who put us on that hit list. These two assassins might be dead, but the person with the agenda is still out there. I have to talk to Ayers, maybe Masterson.

***

*Saturday morning…Decatur, Georgia.* Thoughts and fears ricocheted off the walls of Manuel's brain. Too many contract hits, he thought. Too many things could go wrong. He flipped through the all-night news channels. One story from Memphis. What the hell happened? Ernesto's dead. That bitch cop's still alive. No news from any of the other contracts. Vargas is really going to be pissed. He'll carve me up like a hog.

Manuel paged through his lists of hit men and assignments. Todd needs to be dead by the end of today, he thought, but nobody's available. I'll have to do it myself. His mind raced as he hurried into the garage. He reached up and pulled a small lever. A hidden door clicked open, revealing a room filled with weapons and ammunition, as well as a Ninja Kawasaki 650r, a loading ramp, and riding gear. I'll take the *Ninja*, he thought. It'll give me more flexibility to move around the neighborhood streets. Manuel loaded the motorcycle into his GMC Yukon, selected an MP9 and four loaded magazines, punched in Julia's address and Google mapped it—estimated drive time: six hours, forty-six minutes using the route Hector and Ernesto used, through Chattanooga and Nashville.

***

*Saturday afternoon...Memphis.* Julia's cell played music— the Cantina scene from *Star Wars*.

"Good afternoon, sleepyhead," answered Julia.

"Sleepyhead?" Mark said. "I've been at the Haven since 9:00."

"I thought you planned to skip work today,"

"Yeah, well I decided keeping busy at the Haven would be preferable to me sitting home chewing my fingernails."

"That makes sense."

"You see the doctor this morning?"

"Just walking to my car now. The doctor had a medical student following him around today. The kid got real excited inspecting my two wounds. I thought he was going to take pictures on his smart phone and sell them to his classmates. The doctor had to calm him down."

"Julia, sometimes you're just so full of it. Give me a straight answer."

"The doctor said the wounds looked good, and he had nothing but nice things to say about the job the ER doc did. In fact, he'd thought about plastic surgery for my bikini, but said it wouldn't be necessary. I told him it'd be okay because I didn't own a bikini."

"Julia. You know this isn't funny."

"I know, but I promised myself I'd be positive."

"Heaven help us."

"What? You're into positive psychology. You're always talking about it."

"Your definition of positive comes diagnostically close to the one for denial, but I'll give you the benefit of the doubt."

"That's my positive shrink."

"I saw your aunt Louise. They're moving quickly on her apartment. All the walls have been replaced and have a first coat of paint. The furniture and china are another thing. I bet she'd like some company while she shops for replacements."

"Not shopping. I'm trying so hard to be positive."

"Be creative. Involve Beth and Dell somehow. You can sit at home and pick out types of furniture and place settings she'd like. Then let the three of them make a day of it checking out the sales."

"Not bad. I'm impressed. I just may do that."

***

*Memphis*…Manuel made good time even though he kept under the speed limit all the way. He crossed the Shelby County line at 1:47. Now, nearing Memphis, the posted limit dropped to sixty-five, then fifty-five. He slowed, but cars blew by him in a steady stream. Just like Atlanta, he thought. He took I-40 straight toward midtown, becoming Sam Cooper Boulevard, then dead ending at Overton Park. He followed the traffic south alongside the urban park and turned right on Poplar Avenue, passed the golf course, entering the park by the south entrance. He cruised around until he found a secluded spot in which to extract his Ninja.

***

Julia drove her chili red Mini Cooper up the rise of her driveway, turned off the engine, and heard a puppy bark. She swung out of the mini with only a twinge of pain. Parsley bounded up to meet her. She bent down and scooped him up.

"Hey, boy," Julia said. "Where's your mommy?"

Parsley kept licking Julia, and moving every excitable fiber of his being.

"Let's go around the fence and find Mrs. Woozley."

Parsley wriggled, twisted hard. He broke free of Julia's arms and jumped to the ground, barking and running as fast as his short legs would carry him, down the slope of the driveway, beside the wooden fence to the sidewalk where he stopped to defend his territory. Julia started after him, laughing. Then she heard it, too—the faint purr of a cruising motorcycle. Julia froze, her body remembering Thursday night. She grabbed her Glock and dove painfully to the ground right behind Parsley, hidden by the fence.

The sound grew louder. Julia focused on the street. Both hands steadied the Glock. Her resolve clear. Her pain gone. Parsley's barking blocked from consciousness. Julia concentrated so intently all movements appeared in slow motion. The front tire came into view just over Parsley's head, the spokes barely rotating as the tire passed the fence line. Then the small slanted racing windshield, followed by the muzzle of the MP9 almost touching its top. Both black leather gloves appeared, the black leather sleeves, the dark visor, the black helmet. It seemed to Julia that seconds passed before she saw the rider.

Manuel looked beyond the barking dog up the driveway to the red Mini and the house. He lifted his MP9 above the windshield, pointing over his left arm, turning his upper body toward the driveway. She saw his helmet jerk the instant he spotted her. The MP9 muzzle dropped in her direction. Julia squeezed the trigger—CRACK! CRACK! Manuel rocked back—feet in the air, helmet bounced on the street, his MP9 clattered away on the blacktop. Parsley barked, venturing no farther than the sidewalk. Julia pushed herself up, her side bleeding. She pulled her cell and called for assistance as she slowly stepped off the curb, her pistol pointed at the man lying in the street.

## Chapter 56

# Making The Case

*Some things get old in a hurry…*Julia sat on the curb staring, absentmindedly stroking Parsley. Tagger and Marino worked the crime scene. The coroner's team loaded Manuel into their wagon.

"Damn, Johnnie," Marino said. "When does this shit stop?"

"These guys keep coming like army ants," said Tagger. "And the odds are stacking up against us. I don't think we can get through another attack without someone taking a lethal hit."

"Look at her sitting there. This is sucking the spirit right out of her—attacked twice, shot once. Someone's painted a bull's-eye on her chest. Two attacks on her and one on the doc. How's she holding it together?"

"We need to find the head of this snake and cut it off."

They walked to the other side of the street. Marino sat on Julia's left, Tagger on her right.

"Lieutenant," said Tagger, "you're bleeding."

"He never got off a shot," said Julia, still staring. "I must've pulled a stitch when I hit the deck after Parsley started barking."

"Isn't that the same dog that saved you from the car bomb?" said Marino.

"Sure is," Julia said, looking up. "Parsley, meet Sergeants

Tagger and Marino."

"You two leap over the fence this time, too?" Marino said.

"Nah," said Julia. "We're getting too old for that. I just laid down beside the fence this time and hid behind him."

"You need to tie this dog to your ankle," said Tagger. "Don't leave home without him."

"You got that right," Julia said. "He's saved my bacon twice, now."

"This clown's from Atlanta," said Marino. "And we've got a big ole Yukon in Overton Park with Georgia plates, an Atlanta Braves sticker, and no driver. What are the odds?"

"This one of those cartel sleepers we've been waiting for?" said Julia.

"Maybe so," said Marino. "His Android's full of contracts and hitmen. Almost looks as if he could be one of the higher-ups."

"Come on," said Tagger to Julia. "I'm taking you to get your side looked at."

"I just saw my doctor this morning," said Julia. "I should go back there. Not sure about the bikini anymore."

"I don't think I need to know what that means," Tagger said.

***

"Todd," she answered the phone.

"This is Major Taylor, returning your call, Lieutenant."

"Thanks for calling back," said Julia.

"I'm at my daughter's soccer game. What's the emergency?"

"There's someone here in Memphis I believe you know—Manuel Ramos."

"Ramos? Yeah. I know Ramos," he said, standing and making his way down from the bleachers. "What's he doing in Memphis?"

"Right now he's lying on a gurney."

"He's hurt?"

"No, sir. He's quite dead."

"Talk to me, Lieutenant."

"He rolled into my neighborhood on a Kawasaki and aimed his MP9 at me."

"Holy shit. In your own neighborhood? Why you? You hurt? Who killed him?"

"Taking your last question first, I shot him. And I hurt myself when one of my stitches popped loose doing it. One of the stitches I got last Thursday because Hector Allonso shot me. Allonso happened to be the partner of Ernesto Torres, who tried to kill a friend of mine and one of my sergeants yesterday."

"Allonso and Torres are two of the Conrios cartel's hit men. They in custody?"

"No, sir. They're dead."

"You know I have to ask. Why you?"

"We haven't a clue why my name and members of my family have been part of these cartel contract hits. My involvement started with our finding that dead teenage prostitute, the one linked to our person-of-interest, the one you and I talked about on the phone."

"Tell me more about Ramos."

"We recovered his cell. It contains a wealth of information, enough to look like he's in charge of a cadre of hit men. We're thinking he's one of those high-ranking cartel sleepers."

"That I can confirm, Lieutenant. We've been watching Ramos for over a year. He's always been so careful. It's totally out of character for him to break cover and come after you himself. Someone really wants you dead."

## Chapter 57

# OMG, A Smart Phone

*A 1960s detective faces the twenty-first century without a cell phone…*Frederick tried to call some old friends he thought might still be in the business, but their numbers no longer worked, and their names weren't in the phone book. What the hell's happened since I've been gone? he asked himself. Folks getting old. Folks dying. He began to pace, feeling the need for a drink. As he passed the window he saw two young teenage boys on the sidewalk, one African-American, one Caucasian, looking at their cell phones. Maybe they've got those smart phones I've been hearing about, he thought. He grabbed three cans of *Coke* from the fridge and walked outside.

"Say, y'all," Frederick called, holding up the *Coke*. "I could use some help."

The two boys eyed him, and continued walking.

"No, really. I'm thinking about buying a smart phone, but I don't know anything about them." Frederick sat down on the step. "Come on. I'm too old and fat to hurt you. Tell me about your phones."

The boys exchanged looks, and walked toward Frederick.

"It's not for me. It's for my grandniece," said Frederick. "She'll be twelve next week. I thought maybe I'd get her a phone."

"She's already got a phone, old man," said the first boy.

"How do you know?"

"Duhuh. She's twelve."

"Yeah," said the second boy. "Every twelve year-old I know has a phone."

"It's just a phone, right? I mean, you just call people, don't you?" said Frederick.

The boys laughed. "You for real, mister?" said the first boy. "I almost never call anyone, and no one calls me."

"That doesn't make any sense," said Frederick. "Why have a phone and never call anyone?"

"We text," said the first boy.

"What?" said Frederick. "Test?"

"No," said the second boy, spelling loudly, "T-E-X-T. Here look." Using his thumbs he typed *hello*, and pushed SEND. The second boy's phone came to life beeping. He pushed a button and showed it to Frederick.

"You just sent him a telegraph?"

"OMG," said the second boy, shaking his head in disbelief. "I sent him a text."

"So you can send answers to your friends in class when the teacher's not looking."

The boys laughed. "Sometimes," said the first boy.

"So this is why they call it a smart phone."

"No, said the first boy. "You can get on the internet, look things up, use apps, tweet, get email. You really don't have a cell phone, do you?"

"Afraid not," Frederick said. "How about you show me some of that internet stuff? What if I gave you a name? Could you look it up? Tell me all about him?"

"Easy peasy," said the second boy. "What name?"

"How about if I give a different name to each of you? We can see who has the fastest phone."

"Sure," said the second boy. "What names?"

"You take Murphy Sanderson," said Frederick, spelling the name. "And you take Lou Wright. They are both private investigators here in the Memphis area. Ready? Go."

The boys watched the information appear on their screens. They narrowed their searches.

"Got him!" yelled the second boy.

"Me too," said the first.

"Wow," said Frederick. "You guys are incredible. Let me see." After a quick lesson on scrolling, Frederick looked for anything he could use, taking notes."

"So?" said the second boy. "Are you going to get her an upgrade?"

"Yeah," said the first boy. "Kids can always use an upgrade."

"I think that will be the perfect gift," said Frederick, wondering what an upgrade could be. "Thanks so much, boys."

The boys left, punching one other in the arm and laughing. They waved when they got to the sidewalk. Frederick responded in kind, with a large smile. He sat back down on the step and leafed through his notes. He had addresses, phone numbers, and office hours. There had been a headline he didn't have time to read. Maybe I can get it from the library's newspaper files, he thought. They still have libraries, don't they?

## Chapter 58

# Out P.I. the P.I.

*Saturday evening...the north side of Memphis,* Two elderly men walked slowly down the rutted alley that split the block lengthwise. The fenced backyards of modest 1950s-style homes lined either side. Shrubs and weeds dominated the fences. The alley provided access to garages set behind each house, and allowed garbage trucks to make their weekly rounds out of sight.

"Now why am I here," said Bubba Allison.

"We're here because you still owe me a favor," said Frederick.

"My memory ain't so good no more, Jack. You sure you saved my ass in a bar fight back in the day?"

"If I hadn't stepped in, that pissed off husband would have crushed your skull with a baseball bat."

"Right...You sure this dude's not home?"

"I set the meet myself, Bubba. He'll be in southeast Memphis trying to find his new client. You bring your tools?"

"Always got my picks."

"This house'll have a security alarm. You know how to deal with those, right?"

"Yeah, yeah. I just shine my super bright mini-flashlight on the keypad and find the four dirty keys. Then I start pushing them."

"What? That really sounds stupid. How many times you figure out the code?"

"Most of the time."

"Shit."

"Look, the letters and numbers on a keyboard or a phone are typically side by side, raised or level with the face plate. But on most security keypads each button sits inside its own little cup, and is raised above the edges. The keys themselves might be dirty, but more typically dirt collects just inside the lip of four of the cups. The first number and the last number will be the dirtiest and maybe the most worn down, cause people hit them the hardest—especially men. So I start with one of the dirtiest ones, hit the two cleaner ones, then hit the other dirtiest one. If the buzzer is still going, I do it again, reversing the two cleaner ones. Then if the buzzer is still going I start with the other dirtiest one and do everything backwards. I figure I got eight chances to get it right—if I'm fast enough."

"You serious?"

"Is the Pope Catholic?"

"What if it's a new system? Or, the guy's a neat freak? Or, it doesn't have those little cup things?"

"We're SOL."

Frederick let out a long breath. "How long we got once we get the door open?"

"Most alarms give people forty seconds to put down packages and stuff. Some are shorter, some longer."

Allison opened the lock on the gate. The two men walked to the back door and he picked the deadbolt.

"You ready?" Allison asked, pulling out a small UV flashlight.

"What the hell's that thing?"

"I've found the UV light helps me find the dirt and

fingerprints. Now are you ready?"

"Ready as I'll ever be," said Frederick.

A piercing, loud noise greeted Allison as he pushed the door open. "Close the door before we tell the whole neighborhood we're here," he whispered loudly.

"Thirty-two seconds left," said Frederick, holding his flashlight on his watch.

"Here we go. The two dirtiest keys, most worn are 6 and 1, the next dirty ones are 7 and 9," punching 6-7-9-1. The noise continued. He hit 6-9-7-1. Still blaring. He reversed the dirty numbers: 1-7-9-6. No change.

"Ten seconds," said Frederick.

Allison punched 1-9-7-6.

Quiet.

"Damn, Bubba," said Frederick, shaking his head. "Damn."

"Remember that last series of numbers, the date of the bi-centennial, or we'll never get out clean without setting off the alarm."

## Chapter 59

# A Helping Hand

*The previous Thursday…. I-55, south of St. Louis.* A Lincoln Navigator followed about a half-mile behind an 18-wheeler. Two men from the Conrios cartel rode shotgun for three tractor-trailers loaded with marijuana and cocaine—one truck destined for Saint Louis, the other two for Minneapolis. They pulled the Navigator off the expressway for gas.

"I swear on my mother's grave," said Sergio. "If I ever meet the SOB who designed this car that only gets fourteen miles a gallon, I'll shoot him."

"No problem, bro," said Alberto. "I get to fill up on snack cakes every time we stop for gas."

"Hell. You ain't no better than this damn bus."

Both their phones began ringing.

"Looks like a contract hit," said Alberto, reviewing the series of pictures.

"You shitting me?" said Sergio. "This mark lives in Washington."

"That's cool. We'll get to see the White House."

"The state of Washington on the Pacific coast, you idiot, not Washington DC."

"Oh. My bad. How far is it?"

"It's a hell of a long way, and we still gotta put these shipments to bed. Maybe a day and a half non-stop from

Minneapolis. But more important than that, it's in the Bacarzo cartel's territory. El Semental ain't going to like us doing business on his turf."

"Why do they call him *the Stallion*? He ain't so tall."

"It's not for his height, stupid."

"Not for his height? Oh, I get it."

"Ain't you gonna take this serious?"

"I've got something for El Semental right here, and it has a thirty-round clip. Besides, aren't we going to drive by some cool places we've never seen before?"

"I'll google this address, and plot a map. You get your snack cakes."

***

*2:15 AM Sunday…outside of Olympia, Washington.* The Navigator crept along the street, headlights off, then parked next to the curb.

"Should be the third house down, the dark colored one," said Sergio, checking his MP9 machine pistol. "Take a quick look in the garage. Make sure his car's there."

"No matter who pulls the trigger," said Alberto. "We split the money like we agreed. Right?"

"Yeah, yeah. Now go."

Vertical shoulder holsters held their handguns and over-sized magazines. Loose fitting jackets hid the MP9s from any casual onlooker. Nineteenth century-style streetlamps provided little usable light, giving them the confidence to walk down the sidewalk, hands on their weapons. Sergio confirmed the house number and waved Alberto to check out the garage. Alberto pulled a small high intensity LED flashlight from his jacket pocket, peering through the window. The light revealed a black Acura. He gave a wave and jogged to catch up, as Sergio picked the lock, turned the knob, and eased the front door open, leading with his MP9.

He squatted, stepped inside and swung his gun left. The streetlight offered little help with the dark room in front of him. Alberto followed, a hand on Sergio's back, his gun covering the right side of the room.

"FBI!" a female voice yelled. "Freeze!"

Sergio wheeled immediately, pointed the MP9 in the direction of the voice, squeezed the trigger. The machine pistol sent several rounds within the first second, the barrel jerked upward with each discharge, causing his shot pattern to rise. Alberto turned, but less aggressively, straining to find his target.

CRACK! CRACK!

The two men dropped to the floor like sacks of gravel, their guns landing heavily. FBI Special Agent Maria Louisa Lopez remained still, waiting to make certain her rounds had hit their targets, and no more gunmen lurked outside. Neither man moved. The unique outline of the MP9s was clear in the faint light washing through the open door from the closest streetlamp. No noise from outside. No movement.

Lopez moved cautiously from her hiding place behind the dining table, knees bent, holding her gun tightly in both hands, and pointing it in the direction of the motionless men and the open door. She eased to the far side of the front window to her right and looked out, keeping the downed men and door in sight. Nothing. She reversed her steps, circling well away from the two men and coming up on the far side of the other front window. No sound. No movement. Releasing one hand from her weapon she reached over and closed the front door. Lopez snapped on a lamp.

The image reassured her—both men lying on their stomachs, blood pooling beside their heads, machine pistols near their hands. Lopez kicked the pistols away. She circled Sergio, approaching from the side, Alberto still in full view.

Holding her Glock near his head she checked for a second piece, finding it in an ankle holster. She moved around to Alberto's far side. He, too, had a handgun in an ankle holster. She switched on other lights. Neither man would be moving—ever. Lopez plopped on the couch, blowing a clump of curly hair from her eyes. She pulled her cell and pressed three on speed dial.

"It's over, sir," she said.

"Maria? This you?" said Masterson. "You okay?"

"Yeah, it's me, sir. My heart's still racing."

"As long as it's still beating. What the hell happened?"

"Two guys came through the front door carrying MP9s."

"Jesus. They weren't messing around. You get hit?"

"First guy squeezed off a few rounds before I shot, but they missed. Heard 'em cracking over my head."

"How'd they see you first?"

"Well, I was stupid enough to yell *FBI, freeze.*"

"You never yelled *freeze* when you hunted rattlesnakes back in Texas."

"Good point, sir."

"Damn it, Maria. You're not in the classroom anymore. You could've been killed."

"You're right, sir. I don't remember anything like this at Quantico."

"Okay. Walk me through it."

"They had the automatics, but I had better night vision, having sat in the dark for all that time."

"So, he's on automatic and squeezes off a few. What'd you do?"

"Had the first one in my sights all the way. Shot once. Saw him rock back. Swung to the second man and shot before he got off a round. Saw him jerk, then fall."

"You haven't lost your eye, or your guts."

"Haven't shot anyone since Memphis. Heck, I haven't even pulled my Glock."

"Like I said in Memphis, this was a good shoot, Maria. I couldn't be more proud of you."

"Thank you, sir. I think I can handle this shooting better than I did the first one."

"Still a good idea to check in with a shrink to clear you for active duty."

"Yes, sir."

"Back up a bit. Fill me in on your meeting with the lieutenant's brother."

"Well, after you called, I drove over to meet Wayne Todd. He seemed pretty worked up, but he clearly planned to do whatever his big sister told him. His wife hardly said a word, kinda in shock. The little boy and girl ran around, laughing and playing with their big ole sheep dog. After a reminder from Wayne, they added their backpacks to the camping gear in the driveway. Wayne packed everything in his wife's SUV, keeping his Acura in the garage."

"Good idea to keep it off the road where it could be spotted."

"I watched everyone pile in the car, including their dog. I parked my car on the next street over, walked back, and went inside to wait."

"How'd you position yourself?"

"Fortunately, their house isn't that big. With just a little adjustment I could see both the front and rear doors. Their dining room table has large drop leaves along the sides. I figured it would give me better cover than a chair or couch. Of course, if these hombres had armor piercing rounds it wouldn't matter. But I convinced myself it would be safer."

"You're a piece of work, Maria."

***

*Sunday 5:20 AM…waking to the dreaded phone call.* A phone rang.

"Julia, it's your phone," said Mark.

Julia felt disoriented. She reached toward the light of her phone. "Hello," she said.

"Lieutenant, this is Masterson."

Julia sat up, awake, holding Mark's hand. "Is it Wayne? Tell me."

"Everything's fine. Wayne and his family are still out of town and safe. Just got off the phone with Maria. She'd made sure the family left town and then took up a position inside the house. About an hour ago two cartel assassins broke in. Maria shot and killed both of them. One got off a few rounds, but Maria's fine. She told me she plans to get a carpenter after the crime scene techs are done. She wants the house to look exactly as it did when the family left. Your family is safe."

"Oh, God. Thank you so much. Please give me Maria's phone number, I want to thank her, too. I owe her so much."

## Chapter 60

# The Promotion

*Sunday afternoon, Beckman's Chrysler Dealership…balloons everywhere.* Signs announcing a new manager and mega deals. Marino carried a small picnic cooler.

"Hey, Sergeant Anthony Tony Marino," said Houston. "I'm so glad you could come,"

"This is for you, Madam Manager," said Marino, handing her the cooler. "Congratulations."

"You didn't have to do this," she said, opening the cooler. "Oh, Dinstuhl's. Best chocolates in the midsouth. Good idea protecting them from this Memphis heat."

"I'm proud of you, Ellie," said Marino. "It's so cool to be the first female manager of a Chrysler dealership in Tennessee."

"Your kind words saying I played a major role in the cleanup of the dealership made a huge impression on the powers that be. Of course, the real issue is Chrysler HQ had to scramble to counter all the bad publicity pulling the rug out from under one of the most successful dealerships in the country. They were desperate, and gambled on the positive image of a female manager. And I fully intend to show them this woman can overcome the negative PR and get the dealership back in good standing."

"I don't have any doubt."

"Thank you, Tony," she said, squeezing his hand.

"This all happened so fast."

"The marketing folks decided to rush this announcement so we wouldn't have to compete with the upcoming Labor Day auto sales blitz.

Marino smiled. "Quite a turnout. Are people buying cars?"

"Yes, and the majority are women. I made a few last-minute hiring decisions. We now have half saleswomen and half salesmen."

"But all salespersons."

"You got that right."

"Any dignitaries show up?"

"Actually, a marketing team from Detroit has been here taking pictures, interviewing customers, and getting a feel for the Memphis shopper. I expect they'll have a nice package of commercials and ads we'll be running for Labor Day weekend."

"Those folks over there don't seem to be shopping for a car."

"Oh, those gentlemen. They're managers from other dealerships, welcoming me to the men's club."

"How nice of them. Especially since you're going to blow them all away with your success."

"Interesting."

"What?"

"That's Lindsey Olds, the manager at Caraway Buick. Not far from here."

"What's interesting?"

"I remember seeing him with Drewer and Porter."

"When was this?"

"Not long before Porter's death."

***

*Shake the tree…see what falls out.* Marino crossed the lot, Lindsey Olds in his sights.

"Mr. Olds? I'm Sergeant Marino. Okay if I ask you a few questions?"

"Anything for our MPD," said Olds.

"I understand you knew Terence Porter?" Marino asked.

"Who?"

"The investment consultant from Morgan Keegan. The man someone ran over a few weeks ago."

"Oh, yeah. Terence Porter. I may have met him somewhere. I just don't remember."

"And Marvin Drewer?"

"Oh, sure. I know Marvin. We belong to the dealership managers' organization. We raise a lot money for St. Jude."

"Drewer is a person-of-interest in the Porter murder."

"What? I don't believe it. Marvin's a kind soul. He'd never do anything like that."

"Actually, I've never met Drewer. Haven't even seen him. What's he look like?"

"A man you could trust. A good friend, kind face."

"Okay, but what's he look like?"

"He's shorter than we are, Sergeant, with less hair, maybe a little overweight."

"You're the manager at Caraway Buick, right?"

"Yes."

"Your dealership ever do business with Boiler's Electric?"

"What? Boiler's you say?" Olds said, eyes widening.

"Just trying to get another reference."

"Can't say as I've ever heard of them. They do good work?"

"I think they pulled off their last job quite well."

"I'll look them up."

"You do that, Mr. Olds."

***

"Johnnie. Tony," said Marino.

"What's up?" said Tagger.

"Hey, I know it's Sunday, but I've got a new lead and I'm looking for a wingman."

"Okay, Tom Cruise. Where and when?"

***

Olds lived in an area called Cordova, on the city's far east side—a mixture of rural and urban. Marino and Tagger drove out I-40 east, turning south at the Highway 64 exit, then right on Houston Levee Road. They turned onto Pisgah, a narrow, winding two-lane road, no sidewalks, and lots of wooded acreage peppered with homes of varying ages and sizes. After a short distance Marino turned left. Olds's house sat on the left—a one and a half story structure built circa 1940 with a long, gravel-covered ribbon driveway, several large trees guarding the house, and the yard sparsely grassed. A rooster crowed.

"Bet they've got dogs," Tagger said.

"If they don't their neighbors will," said Marino.

"What're you thinking, Tony?"

"I'm thinking this guy's the man in the Boiler's Electric coveralls, and I'm thinking he's working with Drewer."

"And you think he'll run?"

"I do."

"So I need to hurry 'round back without getting attacked by the dogs."

"I haven't seen many brothers out this way. You could get shot by the white neighbors."

"Thanks. Now I feel much better about the dogs."

"Ready?"

"Let's do it."

Marino put his blue flashers on, hit the gas, pulled into the driveway, and slid to a stop. Both doors popped open—Tagger jogged to the back of the house, Marino strode to the front door, their hands on the grip of their Glocks. Dogs barked. Marino pounded on the front door.

"Memphis police!" he yelled. "Open up!"

Marino saw movement through the window shears and heard quick footsteps moving away. "Heads up, Johnnie," he yelled.

The backdoor banged open. "Freeze!" ordered Tagger, pointing with his left hand, his weapon remaining holstered. "On your knees! Hands behind your head."

The man offered no resistance. Tagger handcuffed him and the two walked around to the front.

"Ah," said Marino. "Johnnie. Meet Marvin Drewer."

Chapter 61

# Follow That Car

*Sunday afternoon…frustration, rage, revenge.* A black Nissan Pathfinder cut in and out of traffic, heading south on Covington Pike as it became Stratford Street and dead ended into Summer Avenue. A banged-up brown Oldsmobile followed, eight cars back.

"Don't lose him, Bubba," said Frederick. "Faster."

"Keep your shirt on, said Allison. "I've logged a lot more years doing this than you. Tell me again why I'm still doing things for you on this case?"

"Well, you were pretty tanked when you challenged the bouncer back in the sixties. I'm gonna say he was probably six-three or four, two hundred fifty pounds, and biceps the size of your thighs. I thought he'd kill you. I just stepped in and talked our way out of the bar, drove you home, and deposited you safely on your bed to sleep it off."

"You sure about that? Doesn't sound familiar."

"I'm telling you, you were so soused I didn't think you could even stay on your feet. Hey. He's turning right."

"I see him, I see him."

"Did he look like he was packing when he came out of the house?"

"He moved pretty fast, but no mistaking the bulge. Not a big piece, but I'm sure it's big enough."

"There he is. Just ran the light at Highland."

"Yeah. Yeah."

"I bet he's headed for midtown. Summer Avenue becomes—"

"North Parkway Boulevard," Allison interrupted. "I've lived here my whole life, Jack. I know the streets that change names. They're everywhere."

"There he is. Just popped out around that *Hostess* truck, down there in front of Rhodes College."

"I got eyes, damn it. If you don't shut up, I'm stopping to pick up a six-pack."

"I'm thinking he'll turn south on McLean or maybe Evergreen."

"What makes you so sure?"

"You saw his pictures. I think he's after Lieutenant Todd. She just shot another assassin yesterday. He's got to be pissed she's still alive. And her home is near here."

"Why didn't you say something?"

"I did. Didn't I?"

"No. You did not. I'm certain of it. I haven't had as much as a beer since I've been joined at the hip with you. No blackouts. No seizures. You haven't told me shit, except how much I owe you for things I don't believe ever happened."

"Well, if I didn't say it, I was thinking it. There. He turned south on Evergreen."

"Please do not tell me Evergreen becomes Belvedere."

"Well it does."

"What're we going to do when he stops in front of the lady cop's house? No way to sneak up on him."

"We drive by to see if she's home. If she's not, we've got time to figure something out."

"And if she is?"

"We go in. You've got a gun, don't ya?"

"I don't carry no gun. Bad things happen when you carry a gun. You gotta gun?"

"Not exactly."

"What the hell's that mean? Not exactly."

"It's just a squirt gun. But it looks real."

"It don't shoot very far, now, does it? Christ. Who carries a squirt gun around? You could get killed by someone who thinks it's real. Damn, Jack."

"He's crossing Union Avenue. He'll be turning right up ahead. Easy now."

"I've got it. I've got it. Don't get your drawers all in a knot."

"There. He's stopped. Drive by and let's see if the lieutenant's car's there."

"Does he know you?"

"No. You?"

"I don't think so."

"Let's go. It's the house with the new wooden fence beside the driveway."

"Pretend to be talking on your cell phone."

"I don't have a cell phone."

"What do you mean, you don't have a cell phone? You leave it at home with your real gun?"

"I'll just put my hand up to my face. Look. No car. She's not here."

"Okay. Plan B. What *is* plan B?"

"We'll need your super-bright flashlight and my squirt gun. Got any handcuffs?"

## Chapter 62

# New Digs

*Sunday open house at the Haven…you can hardly see the bullet holes.* Louise ladled punch into new crystal cups. Residents circulated, carrying beverages or balancing small plates of appetizers, searching eagerly for signs of the shooting. Julia and Mark made a tour of the dining room, not speaking. Mark moved to a corner, staring at the wall, his hand inches away, as if not wanting to disturb it. Julia nuzzled into his side.

"Penny for your thoughts," she said.

"My best friend," he said.

Julia waited.

"Sergeant Marino told me to hug this wall like it was my best friend."

My God, Julia thought. This is the first time Mark's talked about the shooting. I need to be here for him. I need to listen, be strong.

"All I could think of was you," he said. "I pressed into this wall like it was you."

Julia lost a half-breath. Me? she thought. Like it was me?

"You're always so fearless. I tried to pull those qualities from the wall. It seemed to work for a little while, but panic took over. I forgot how to breathe. I dropped my laptop making a huge noise, and the killer knew just where to find me when he blasted through the door."

One tear, then another splashed on her arm. What the…? she thought. So much for being strong.

"I believed I was going to die. Terror overwhelmed me." He looked at Julia. "My last thoughts should have been of you. But I didn't even have the courage to do that."

The next thing Julia knew she found herself with both arms wrapped around Mark, pinning his arms at his sides, her head buried in his chest, silent tears flowing.

Aunt Louise watched, a hand covering her mouth. Her tears joined Julia's.

Julia recovered enough to speak. "Let's get out of here."

Chapter 63

# The Leak

*Sunday evening…a quiet restaurant near the Liberty Bell in Philadelphia.*

"Thanks for making the trip down, Lawrence," said Davenport.

"Meeting in neutral territory is probably safer, Anita," Masterson said.

"Yeah. Something doesn't feel right in DC. People are more uptight than usual. Even the pigeons are crapping on different statues."

"You think they know I've been checking on them?"

"Either that or the word's out there's a spy in our midst and they're distancing themselves from everyone else."

"Trying not to be collateral damage, huh?"

"Yeah, I guess. Anyway, what'd you find?"

"I personally went through all the Bureau's background reviews on everyone who sat around that table, except the Frenchman."

"Including me?"

"No stone unturned, Anita. Everyone looks good," he said, patting her hand.

"I guess I feel better."

"Anything on the Frenchman?"

"Everything looks clean," she said. "He's been the

Executive Director of the FATF for three years. Their record looks good, busted several worldwide rings. He spends a lot of time in different countries, and works closely with Berness."

"One interesting tidbit," he said. "Telephone activity shows over two years of on-going calls to DC from northeast Mexico."

"Who're the calls going to?"

"Don't know. Each call's received by a different phone about every three weeks, give or take."

"That's a lot of burn phones. Even *we* wouldn't be able to justify that kind of waste in our budget."

"Our guys tracked the phones to a manufacturer in Mexico."

"You mean someone is sending burn phones *from* Mexico?"

"Looks like it," he said. "That would mean our spy either has a large stash of throwaways, or he's getting regular deliveries.

"Neither of those strategies is very smart. Too easy to discover."

"You'd think so. But to date no one has."

"So where do we go from here?" she said.

"I decided to focus on the three-week delivery scenario. I'm thinking the spy would shy away from any obvious pattern. It could mean a roving drop point. But still he'd have to pick it up."

"And get rid of the old one. Hell, maybe he's polluting the Potomac with plastic."

"Good point, but that would mean involving yet another alphabet agency."

Anita made a face. "So, you're actually following each person around every day?"

"Not every day. Just a few days on either side of that three-week window. Which, by the way, started yesterday."

"That mean one of your guys followed me here?"

"I cut you some slack," he said, smiling. "I'm watching you today."

Davenport punched him in the arm.

"And just for the I-told-you-so record, Lieutenant Todd made a great find with Ramos's cell phone. Looks like all the alphabets have joined in, ready or not. I told you we could trust her."

"You did, indeed. I stand corrected."

"I assume you guys are a part of this massive bust on the Conrios cartel's smuggling network?"

"No choice," said Davenport. "You?"

"We've been told to stay on our protection details for the bankers and investment types, in case those contracts are still active."

Chapter 64

# Tying Up Loose Ends

*Union Station, Monday morning…rode hard and put up wet.* Tagger and Marino sat across from Julia in her office, everyone exhausted. Red eyes, minimal talking, lots of staring. The coffee didn't seem to be working.

"It's been a rough week," said Julia. "I couldn't be more grateful or more proud of you two. I am in your debt."

Tagger spoke up, "Like we said, Lieutenant, we're family. Family does for one another."

"Well said, my friend," Marino added.

"I feel the same way, fellas," she said. "I did get some good news yesterday. My brother and his family are safe. And wouldn't you know, our favorite Texas sharpshooter nailed two cartel thugs to make that happen."

"Maria? Really? She shot two of them?" said Marino.

"Did she do it in the dark again?" said Tagger.

"Around 2:00AM. Pitch dark," Julia said. "They had MP9s. But they didn't know who they were going up against."

"She's okay, right?" Marino said.

Julia nodded. "One got off a few rounds, but shot over her head. Maria's fine."

"We were busy yesterday, ourselves," said Marino.

"Cued in by Tony's salesperson, again," Tagger said. "We're going to have to put her on retainer."

"Ow," said Julia, grabbing her side. "Don't make me laugh."

"Okay, I'll give you the short, unfunny version," said Marino.

"But you'll have to have a pencil and paper to keep up with this," said Tagger.

"I'm ready," Julia said. "Let me have it."

Marino took a deep breath. "Ellie—"

"That's the salesperson at Beckman's," Tagger interrupted.

Marino gave him a look. "Ellie got promoted to sales manager at Beckman's."

"Way to go, Ellie," Julia said.

"I drove out there to congratulate her," said Marino, glancing at Tagger. "She spots a guy she remembers being with Porter and Drewer—a guy named Lindsey Olds, sales manager at Caraway Buick. Turns out he's a perfect body type match for the guy in the Boiler's Electric coveralls. So I have a chat with him. He's clearly involved. Something he said got me to thinking that Drewer might not have left town after all. So I gave Johnnie a call. Woke him up, as I remember."

"It was Sunday afternoon," said Tagger. "I was stretched out on the couch watching cartoons."

"Anyway, Johnnie and I drove out to Olds's house in deep Cordova, out in the country part of the city. We found Drewer."

"And even though we read him his Miranda rights, it didn't stop Mr. Drewer from telling all," said Tagger. "He couldn't help himself."

"We were right about the multiple drive-overs being the result of a lover's spat," Marino said. "We just had the wrong lovers. Olds caught Porter fooling around with his long time companion, Drewer. According to Drewer, the murder was Olds's idea. Drewer agreed to procure the used Limited, and after the deed was done, he drove it to one of his body repair sites for *safekeeping*."

"See how easy it is when you know who to ask," Julia said. "Speaking of asking the right person, did Drewer talk about the money laundering?"

"Yeah," said Marino. "He told us about his arrangement with Proctor and his dedicated computer with all the transaction data. Pretty elaborate deal. I had a hard time following it."

"And if the professor couldn't follow it, you know *I* got lost," said Tagger.

"The heart of the operation involved a shell corporation set up by Porter supposedly to buy and sell used cars," said Marino. "Keep in mind that used cars are regularly rotated around the country from dealership to dealership in hopes of improving the odds of a sale. They don't stay in any one place for long. He and Drewer then ran their own used car exchange, piggy-backing on the Beckman dealership used cars' VIN numbers."

"Huh?" said Julia. "Walk me through that."

"Drewer would identify two used cars the Beckman dealership had scheduled to be rotated off their lot, and off their books," Marino said. "Porter would send dirty money to Drewer to buy the first used car. Drewer would buy the second car from Porter at the same price minus a ten percent commission. But get this. No cars were ever physically involved, and nothing showed up on the Beckman dealership records beyond the usual documentation that the cars had been legitimately transferred off the lot. Porter's and Drewer's phantom transactions were recorded only on their hidden off-the-books accounting spreadsheet."

"How'd Drewer hide this from his boss, from the accountants?" asked Julia.

"That part's fuzzy," said Marino. "But I understood him

to say they began initially with keeping separate books on the sale of Chrysler Limiteds for Porter's new clients. On the tally sheet for the client Drewer would show the highest possible price for a fully loaded Chrysler Limited, getting Porter's new client to pay top dollar for his half. But on the official books for the Beckman dealership he'd enter a greatly reduced sale price by applying the maximum discounts available. Their working cash came from the difference between the two totals, which greatly reduced the amount of Porter's money that was actually applied—sometimes freeing up as much eleven thousand dollars of his contribution. Drewer and Fine took their cut, and then Drewer entered the amount of the remaining money on the hidden accounting sheet as being his purchase of a phantom used car from Porter. And the last step involved depositing the remaining money in one of Porter's corporation bank accounts."

"This was how they began," said Tagger. "Later they got braver and more sophisticated in their fraud, just buying and selling phantom used cars whether or not a new client purchased a Limited. Drewer got to making multiple deposits in separate banks every week. He said Porter had over four million laundered dollars in his accounts, which he transferred to a bank in Saudi Arabia."

"So where's the smurfing?" asked Julia.

"Drewer's deposits to Porter's various corporation bank accounts never exceeded the ten thousand dollar reporting limit," said Marino. "That's the smurfing, or structuring of the deposits. It's mind boggling how quickly these relatively small structured deposits added up."

"Someone put in a call to the IRS to go through Drewer's computer?" Julia asked.

"The ADA handled that," said Tagger.

"Great work, y'all," said Julia. "And great work, Ellie."

***

Teresa buzzed in.

"Major Taylor from Atlanta PD, on one."

"Just wanted to bring you up to speed, Lieutenant," said Taylor, "we rolled up to Ramos's house with a search warrant within an hour of your telephone call Saturday. Found a laptop full of information—names, warehouses, money counting sites, trucks, routes, meth labs, and even marijuana fields. Turns out Manuel Ramos held a high rank in the Conrios cartel. He coordinated their business for the entire eastern half of the United States, from tornado alley to the Atlantic. Once we broke through his password, we alerted the National Organized Crime Initiative. Within twenty-four hours locals teamed with the various federal agencies, descending on cartel warehouses, trucks, farmlands, and gunmen throughout the eastern half of the country. The haul is already so massive I'm sure you'll see the President himself on the news, bragging about it. Great job, Lieutenant."

"Thanks," said Julia. "I'm hoping this will end their attacks on me and my family."

"I'd like to tell you everything's over for you, but I just don't know. We pieced together a rationale of sorts for all the others, but we never found your name in Ramos's computer except as part of the contract hits. Putting your name on the hit list doesn't make sense."

## Chapter 68

# Special Delivery I

*Monday mid-morning…a game changer.* "Major Williams on line two," said Teresa.

"Lieutenant," Williams said. "Yesterday afternoon I received a special delivery package. Does the name Wilbur Sanderson ring a bell?"

"Wilbur Sanderson? Yes. A mean character, loved to beat up senior citizens. He tried to kill me in my aunt's home a few months ago. We nailed him for one murder, several aggravated burglaries and batteries, and one attempted murder of a police officer. He copped to our sizeable list of crimes, with the exception of murder. The ADA pled him to twenty years without parole."

"Well, it turns out Sanderson has a brother named Murphy who's credentialed as a private investigator. You know him?"

"No, sir. Never heard the name. Didn't know Wilbur had a brother."

"His specialty is divorce cases. They say he's an expert at gathering incriminating pictures. P.I. Sanderson was my special delivery."

"I don't understand, sir. Your special delivery?"

"Yesterday afternoon I get a call saying there was a man with a gun parked outside your house."

"*My* house? You're sure? My house?"

"The caller said I needed to make the scene, personally. I called around and met a team of officers at your house."

"You're sure it was my house? I can't believe it. What time?"

"Four forty-five. You weren't there. But it *was* your house and there *was* a man sitting in a car parked out in front, gift-wrapped."

"I was at my aunt's apartment. Who was the man, and what's this have to do with Sanderson?"

"P.I. Sanderson was the man sitting in the car, handcuffed to the steering wheel, and extremely agitated. A cardboard box sat in the back seat. Among other things, it included Sanderson's Charter Arms Pit Bull .40 caliber."

"What other things?"

"A detailed letter stating that a member of the Conrios cartel hired P.I. Sanderson to create a complete photo history on a handful of bankers and investment consultants, including their families. The whole nine yards."

"You mean the pictures in that Homeland Security email?"

"According to this letter."

"So Wilbur's brother puts pictures of me and my family with the group of bankers and investors targeted by the cartel?"

"The letter alleges P.I. Sanderson saw a chance to pay you back for putting his little brother in jail."

"And then what? He decides to finish the job himself, so he shows up at my house?"

"So it would seem. But there's more. The package also included a thumb drive, reportedly taken from Sanderson's computer. There are copies of emails between this P.I. Sanderson and our Major Echols. If this letter is factual, Major Echols and the Sanderson brothers are in fact cousins, raised by Echols's parents."

"My God. They're practically brothers."

"Indeed. One more thing—a number used frequently on P.I. Sanderson's phone has been traced to a burn phone. The latest call made the Monday before you were shot."

"If it's a burn phone, how's that helpful?"

"Turns out this burn phone's registered to our Organized Crime Unit. One of many available for use by undercover officers. It'd be easy for Echols to get his hands on one from the equipment room."

"And you think Major Echols knew Sanderson had included my pictures on this hit list?"

"So far, he's denying he knew anything about the cartel pictures."

"You've already started an investigation, sir?"

"Internal affairs is investigating Major Echols's role in this. But we're on hold with P.I. Sanderson."

"Why's that, sir?"

"Because he's sitting in an interrogation room at 201 waiting on you to get down here."

"Me? That's great, sir...But do you think it's wise for me to be involved? After all, he tried to kill me, my aunt, my brother and his family, not to mention my..."

"Dr. Sanders?"

"Yes, sir."

"Of course it'd be inappropriate. That's why Lieutenant Ayers is cooling his heels until you can stand outside the two-way mirror and watch everything."

"I'll be there in twenty, sir."

"Don't get any tickets. Oh, Tagger and Marino are also invited to the party."

"Thank you, sir."

***

*Monday evening...plausible deniability.* The phone rang.

"Private investigators," answered Frederick.

"Jackson. This is Todd," said Julia.

"Hey, Lieutenant. Good to hear from you."

"I just got back from observing an interrogation of a colleague of yours—a licensed P. I. named Sanderson."

"No kiddin'. P.I., huh? Can't say as I know the guy."

"How'd you know Sanderson's a man?"

"I didn't. It's just the only P.I.s I know are men."

"He claimed he was assaulted while sitting in his car. Says one elderly gentleman blinded him with an extremely bright flashlight and another squirted him in the eyes with water from a squirt gun. Then they handcuffed him to his own steering wheel. He's still complaining about seeing major spots in front of his eyes."

"The crime in this city is outrageous. Squirt gun, you say?"

"Yeah. According to Sanderson, they tried to frame him with a cardboard box full of crap he'd never seen before."

"Really? A flashlight, a squirt gun, and a cardboard box? Not exactly high-tech."

"Among other things, the box contained a loaded Pit Bull revolver, registered to P. I. Sanderson."

"That's odd. Most P.I.s I know who own a gun carry it on their person, not in a box."

"Also in that box were files, letters, and pictures that seem to have come from Sanderson's private residence…almost as if someone broke into his home."

"Like I said, can't get away from the crime. We really need more cops."

"And something else."

"That would be…?"

"He was parked in front of my house."

"Your house? I thought you lived in a nice neighborhood, Lieutenant."

"Parked in front of my house with a loaded gun. Like he'd

been waiting for me."

"That's horrible."

"But since you've never known P.I. Sanderson, I guess you wouldn't have any knowledge of his house being broken into, or his being assaulted with a flashlight and a squirt gun."

"Sorry, Lieutenant. I'm at a loss."

"By the way, did you ever get a chance to follow-up on that job we discussed last Friday?"

"Been busy with another case. But there's a post-it note on my fridge. I'll get on it tomorrow, first thing. I promise."

"So, I don't owe you any money yet?"

"Not a nickel, Lieutenant."

"Well, I'm still interested in keeping our arrangement, and I'd be eternally grateful for anything you could help me with. I'll expect a full report by the end of the week."

"No problem, Lieutenant. Maybe over dinner?"

"I'd like that, Jackson. I'd like that a lot."

## Chapter 66

# Payback

*Just because you're paranoid doesn't mean someone's not out to get you...the Conrios cartel compound.* Vargas opened the bedroom door and flipped on the lights. The woman in the bed awakened, shielding her eyes.

"Alejandro," she said. "I just got to sleep."

"You need to get up, get dressed, then get the children ready."

"What's wrong?"

"I'm expecting an attack."

"Who's coming?"

"I think the Bacarzo cartel, maybe others. You need to be in the bomb shelter."

"The bomb shelter? For how long?"

"One or two days, maybe a week."

"A week. You know how much the children hate that place. They will not want to go."

"This is not open for discussion. You make them go. I want all of you inside in a half-hour. Fernando will be here to help. Now hurry."

***

*Chomping at the bit...*Delgado's men, doubled in number with the addition of fully armed fighters courtesy of the Judge, surrounded the Conrios cartel compound. Returning the favor to Vargas, the Judge sent along two US Maine Corps AH-I Cobra Attack Helicopters. They approached from the north, armed with rockets, three-barrel 20mm Gatling guns, and TOW 2A bunker busting missiles. Delgado paired the Judge's men with his own, giving the Arab fighters a guide through the foreign jungle terrain. Delgado spread a hand drawn map on the ground.

"The main compound is here," he said, pointing with his knife. "Underground bunkers we know about are here, here, and here."

"There may be others?" Fahad asked.

"Si. El Pequeño Toro is always improving his defenses. That's how he stays alive."

"How many men?"

"These two are the largest," Delgado said, pointing. "Maybe twenty in each. This one's about half their size."

"The entrances are well hidden?"

"They're camouflaged, and each bunker has tunnels extending to four or five entrances, like a tarantula. There are sensors and cameras throughout the area linked to monitors in the bunkers and the main compound. The men can easily move in and out of the bunkers and be deployed as needed in an attack."

"And perimeter defenses?"

"There are snipers and the surrounding area is filled with landmines, booby-traps, and claymore anti-personnel mines."

"How do we get through?"

"The same way they do. My men have tracked their movements for months. The safe paths are marked in red."

"But funneling men through those narrow paths makes them vulnerable to ambush."

"Worse than that, claymores are positioned alongside

these paths, and can be triggered from inside the bunkers."

"So the bunkers have to be knocked out first."

"We've never been able to do that, and that's why no one has ever penetrated Vargas's defenses. But thanks to Señor Judge, the Cobras will do that for us. Then we send men inside each bunker to finish the job."

"Then we take the compound."

"The compound has a bunker of its own, for Vargas, his family, and his key men."

"Does he have the same capabilities to set off claymores and other devices from inside the bunker?"

"Of course. I'm sure from inside the bunker he can also destroy any computers or accounting books he wasn't able to take into the bunker. I know I can do that from inside my bunker."

"Any ideas how we can get a hold of his records?"

"I've been thinking about how to do that for years, my friend. The only way we get his records is if he lets us."

"My two best men should be in position by now to take out their radar, making the way clear for the Cobras."

"Everyone hold your position until the Cobras destroy the bunkers," said Delgado over the radio. "Then follow your assignments. I want Vargas taken alive. You can do anything you want to his men."

Fahad repeated the message to the Judge's men, in Arabic.

## Chapter 67

# Easing the Emotional Trauma

*Tuesday evening…a group debriefing.* Julia, Tagger, Marino, and Willingham sat in psychologist Dr. Notting's spacious office.

"The purpose of the debriefings," said Notting, "is to encourage folks to talk about the event and their feelings. It's not always easy, but we've found officers recover faster after they've talked about their experiences. We have three separate crime scenes to address. Can we begin with you, Sergeant Tagger? What do you recall about that event in Cooper-Young?"

"I'd just unlocked my car when I heard the faint sound of a motorcycle," Tagger said. "Even though it wasn't loud it grabbed my full attention, maybe because I'd been working a murder case involving a motorcyclist. I saw this guy cruising slowly on the opposite side of the street, his head turned away from me. I looked in that direction and saw the lieutenant and Dr. Sanders. The next thing I remember I was right beside him and his arm was fully extended, pointing a damn big gun. I swung. I swung as hard as I could."

"You reacted so quickly," said Notting. "That seems unusual to me. Can you think of any reasons for it?"

"I've asked myself the same question ever since Thursday," said Tagger. "I don't have a good answer."

"Talk about what you've considered," said Notting.

"Like I said, I'd been really focused on this murder case. But there's something I can't explain. About five months ago, the lieutenant and I were almost killed in separate incidents. I happened to be there for her when she came stumbling out of a burning house, and she was there for me after a car bomb blew up, right in front of me. It's like we got some kind of bond."

Julia perked up, leaning forward in her chair.

"So how did this bond play out on Thursday?" Notting asked.

"Our secretary at the precinct is very good at her job, but she can be a real busybody. Last Thursday she started in with her usual jabber, saying the Lieutenant and I should be double dating because we both had dinner plans in Cooper-Young. I blew it off, but then I found myself looking for her red Mini Cooper."

"You've picked up on the lieutenant's *spidey sense*, Johnnie," said Marino.

"You talking about Spider-Man?" asked Notting.

"Yeah. His ability to anticipate things, before they happen," Marino said. "The lieutenant does that all the time."

Notting looked at Julia. "Is this true?"

Julia shrugged. "Sometimes it seems to happen like that. I can't explain it. And it's not like it happens with any regularity."

"Johnnie and I went to junior and senior high school together," said Willingham. "The football coach was also our world history teacher. He nicknamed Johnnie *Damus* because he seemed to sense which way the other team's play was coming. He said he had the same kind of ability to predict the future as Nostradamus."

Notting's eyes widened. He paused. "So you had two

things on your mind," he said, "the motorcycle murderer and the possibility that the lieutenant might be in the
neighborhood."

"I guess so," said Tagger.

"And you instantly put those two things together and
sensed danger?"

"Danger?" said Tagger. "Yeah, I felt *something* bad was about
to happen."

"And you acted. Immediately."

Tagger cocked his head, shrugged his shoulders.

"And what about you, Lieutenant?" asked Notting. "Did
you have any sense of foreboding?"

"Like I said, it doesn't happen all the time. And I'm
here today because last Thursday night Tag had the sense,"
said Julia.

"What made you aware of the danger?" said Notting.

"Tag yelled," Julia said. "I looked toward his voice and saw
the rider pointing a gun at me."

"And your first instinct was…?"

"To protect Mark. I tackled him."

"One bullet struck you. Correct?"

Julia nodded. "I felt a hot sting in my side, but I also
banged up my elbows and knees on the sidewalk. I didn't
think about having been shot."

Notting gestured for her to continue.

"I checked Mark to see if he was okay. I'm afraid I hit him
pretty hard."

"I can attest to that, Lieutenant," said Willingham. "He let
out a huge oomph."

Julia blushed.

"We could have used you on our team when we played
Ohio State," said Tagger.

"What do you recall next, Lieutenant?" Notting asked.

"I tried to get up but it felt like someone was standing on my back," Julia said. "I couldn't move, and my side hurt."

"Someone on your back?"

"That would be me," said Willingham, grinning slightly.

"Oh," said Notting. "Well, now you're in the picture, Sergeant, go back to the beginning. How'd you come to be standing on the lieutenant's back?"

Willingham smiled. "I'd just left Johnnie's side as he clicked open the door locks. I saw him take off running. I figured something bad had happened. Johnnie and the motorcyclist were to my right, the lieutenant directly across the street. I just started running to her."

"Y'all are so instinctive," said Notting. "So responsive."

"I sure didn't have any of that spidey stuff," Willingham said. "I just saw Johnnie sprinting like a man processed and I knew I needed to be running too. I got to the lieutenant right after shots fired. I slid into her and the doc, planted my hand on her back to keep them down, then stood guard."

"And I'm so glad you did," said Julia.

"So you ran into the line of fire?" said Notting.

Willingham managed a half grin, as she shook her head.

"What were you feeling?"

"Things happened so fast," said Willingham. "I just thought that's where I needed to be, no time to be fearful. But I was relieved to hear no more shots. The lieutenant and the doc were moving so I thought they were okay. I was worried about Johnnie until I heard his *clear*. Then my hand felt wet and I knew the lieutenant had been hit. That's when the fear hit me. I swallowed hard and applied pressure to her back wound."

"And everyone's feelings?" said Notting.

"Grateful."

"Relieved."

"Angry."

***

"This is a different scenario for you, Sergeant Marino," said Notting. "On Thursday everything happened within seconds. But you learned about the threats to the lieutenant's family before things started popping at the Haven on Friday."

"True," said Marino. "I'd have to say in my case anger came first. As Johnnie said Friday morning, we consider ourselves part of the lieutenant's family, and we took the threats personally."

"Walk us through the Haven shooting," said Notting.

"I took three officers to the Haven," said Marino, "stationing them in various positions outside the complex of buildings. Turns out, I didn't bring enough people to cover the grounds. The lieutenant had already talked to her aunt, and then to Dr. Sanders. All I had to do was accompany her aunt to a friend's place, clear out all the nearby apartments, and wait in hers. The doc came up about fifteen minutes later. That's when the shit hit the fan."

"So you and Dr. Sanders were both in the aunt's apartment?" asked Notting.

"Correct," said Marino. "Actually, one of the most nerve-racking times happened when the doc rang the bell. I thought the assailant was waiting on the other side of the door for me. I walked ever so slowly and softly, leaning over from beside the door to look through the peep hole. I was relieved to see the doc. I let down my guard. The doc said a man was coming. I yanked him inside, put him up against the wall, hustled to the opposite wall."

"So what are you thinking at this point? What are you feeling?" asked Notting.

"I didn't think the gunman saw me. I figured I'd have surprise on my side. I felt confident."

"You say all this as if there's a *but*," said Notting.

"You nailed that, doc," said Marino. "For some reason I forgot about the machine pistol. And I wasn't ready for the surreal experience of a machine pistol with a silencer."

"In what way?"

"I trained my gun on the door," said Marino. "Then with no sound, the hallway wall erupted in a wavy line—small quiet explosions beginning inches in front of the doc, then coming through the door and closing in on me. The only noise came from the china and glassware breaking to my left. I dropped to the floor, anticipating the rounds coming my way."

"What are you feeling?" asked Notting.

"I lost my concentration, my confidence," said Marino. "I heard the sounds of changing magazines, the first round being chambered. He pulverized the deadbolt. The door exploded open. He stepped in, turning toward the doc. I squeezed off two shots. He dropped."

"And what are you feeling?"

"Scared. Scared shitless. I heard a shout. I hadn't heard any shots, but of course the shooter had a silencer. I thought sure the doc was dead. As it turned out, so did the doc. Kept checking his chest for bullet holes. Poor guy."

"No, professor," said Julia. "Damn lucky guy. Lucky you were there." Julia grabbed his hand in both of hers.

"Damn, Tony," said Tagger. "I can just see those rounds marching right up to you, and there's nowhere to hide."

"Now you've had a little distance on this, any observations?" Notting said.

"Good thing I didn't have to run like these two," said Marino, patting his stomach. "I'd never have made it."

Notting smiled and gestured for him to continue.

"Jesus, Mary, and Joseph," said Marino. "I thank God

I'm alive. I can't think of anything I'd do differently. But I know the doc and I were only inches from being dead. Like you, Lieutenant."

Julia touched her side, as she looked at Marino. Tears streamed down her cheeks.

Willingham hugged Tagger's arm. "Inches," she whispered. "Just like you and that car bomb last April."

"And then there was Saturday afternoon, Lieutenant," Notting said, turning to Julia. "In your driveway?"

"You need to have that little dog here," said Tagger. "He's the lieutenant's guard dog."

"That's right," said Julia. "He saved my life twice."

"I haven't heard about this," said Notting.

"It's every bit as crazy as the spidey sense," said Marino. "I think he's got it, too."

"A few months ago Parsley—that's his name," Julia said, "was under my car keeping out of the rain. I squatted down to coax him out. That's when I saw the pipe bomb. The two of us got out of there just in time. Last Saturday was a little different. I had Parsley in my arms when he unexpectedly took off running and barking. When I went after him I heard the motorcycle he was barking at, dove to the ground with my weapon out. When the rider moved his gun in my direction, I fired."

"All right," said Notting. "Up to now I think I was holding it together pretty well. But bombs, dogs, and another motorcycle?"

"It's never dull around the lieutenant," said Tagger.

"You can say that again," said Marino. "We keep trying to get her to wear a red Superwoman cape."

"So, tell us how you were feeling," said Notting.

"I ran the full gamut of feelings," Julia said. "I drove home from the doctor's office exhausted, worried about my family, feeling guilty for putting them in danger, the whole nine. I heard Parsley coming to greet me, and that made me happy. I was laughing when he ran away. "Fear hit me when I heard the motorcycle, followed immediately by anger. That last feeling clarified my mind. I had one thought—defend myself."

"And when the time came to pull the trigger?" Notting said.

"No equivocation," said Julia. "He aimed that machine pistol in my direction. I fired."

"We're glad you did," said Tagger.

"Another incredibly close call," said Notting. "One way to look at these narrow escapes is to call it *luck*. Luck that might not be there next time. But, I prefer to think those lifesaving inches and seconds came your way because of your instincts, your training, commitment to action, and your unselfishness. You not only saved the lives of the people involved, but you undoubtedly saved the lives of countless others who would have been in the line of fire had these men not been stopped."

# A New Client

"I have news, sidi," said Fahad. "The battle was difficult. Without the helicopters, we never would have gotten near Vargas. Many men died on both sides. Fortunately for us, fewer died on our side. Your men fought bravely."

"Never mind all of that," said the Judge. "Is Vargas alive?"

"No, sidi. The bunker busting missiles killed everyone inside his compound—including his wife and children."

"You find anyone who knew why Vargas would come after me?"

"No, sidi. No one was left alive. No records survived the bomb, no computers, no letters."

"Damn it!"

"It looks like Delgado will be taking over all the Conrios cartel's territory and operations."

"Maybe they'll need to launder some money."

"I made him that offer."

"And?"

"He said he'd want to know more about how things worked, and what it would cost him. Said he'd be calling you."

"This could be a good thing. The Bacarza cartel is almost as big as Conrios. This could double the cartel investment."

"One more thing, sidi. When we were in Venezuela, I assigned men to keep tabs on Akilah."

"What did they find?"

"They couldn't find her. And the money you wired to her account had been transferred to a bank in Zurich. All except fifty dollars, gone." Fahad watched the Judge's face as it turned from anger to calm.

"I would have expected nothing less," said the Judge, smiling.

## Chapter 69

# Special Delivery II

*Tuesday afternoon, New York FBI office…*

"Whatchagot, Angelini?" said Masterson.

"I've been staked out in a foreclosed home down the street from my assigned brownstone. Everything's been boringly quiet. Only person I've seen is the mail carrier."

"I hope this ain't a social call, Angelini."

"Sorry, sir. Thirty minutes later a USPS van pulls up and the driver carries a package up the steps. The driver knocks on the door, but no one answers. He sets the package by the door and drives off."

"And you're wondering if there might be something interesting in that package?"

"Yes, sir."

"Not bad, Angelini. I'll make a few calls. If all goes well, another USPS van will pull up shortly and a mail carrier will collect said package."

***

"Okay. Real careful," said the disguised FBI agent, passing the package to a man in the back of the USPS van. "Our jobs may depend on it. In fact, take a few pictures of the taping to make sure we duplicate it later."

A man wearing rubber gloves slit the packing tape with an exacto knife. The package had been postmarked in Gavle,

Sweden—the Gevalia Kaffe Company. Two twelve-ounce packages of coffee nestled safely within their cardboard forms. He took a bag and gently began to separate the glued top. The strong aroma of freshly ground coffee filled the van. He poured the coffee into a container, inspected the bag. The first one contained two sealed plastic bags—one protecting a wad of hundred dollar bills, the other holding scores of round powder-blue pills. The second coffee bag held one sealed plastic bag protecting a cell phone.

***

*Wednesday…* Masterson telephoned Davenport.

"Anita. This is Lawrence. You seeing all this about the Conrios cartel's compound being overrun?"

"Our people are saying Jose Delgado's Bacarzo cartel attacked their compound with the help of the Judge."

"Payback."

"Indeed."

"How you think the Judge's going to interpret the collapse of Vargas's businesses in the US? It has to be a surprise."

"Maybe he'll just see it as a coincidence, or maybe he'll assume Delgado blew the whistle on him."

"Maybe," Masterson said. "It may not matter. We're looking at a major political feeding frenzy. Washington hasn't had much to crow about in the last several years. The energy around this huge cartel bust is going to suck up everything remotely related. No way we can sit on the Judge's money laundering investigation. In fact, once the media gets through second guessing us, the Attorney General will probably be hung out to dry for not taking action sooner."

"No doubt," Davenport said. "Me too."

"I'll visit you in prison."

"Thanks. Say, any progress on the leak? Not that it seems all that important now."

"Funny you should ask."

"You're kidding. You found him?…Her?"

"This is where I get to stretch it out," Masterson said, smiling. "The clue is something you see every day. Well, six out of seven. We found the answer in another government agency. Yup. When it absolutely, positively has to be there within three weeks or so, who do you call?"

"What? The post office?"

"Regularly scheduled deliveries of coffee, from Sweden."

"You're kidding," said Davenport. "They put burn phones in shipments of coffee? I don't believe it. Those packages would never make it through all the screening procedures. Coffee hasn't been a medium for smugglers since *Beverly Hills Cop*."

"Agreed," said Masterson. "We picked up a USPS special delivery driver. We searched his place. Found Gevalia coffee bags filled with different drugs, burn phones, and varying amounts of money. Turns out he'd pull Gevalia packages at the post office, substitute his prepared bags, then make the delivery. A perfect cover for a regularly scheduled drop. And he had several clients."

"I've had Gevalia coffee, and not too long ago…in somebody's conference room…I remember the logo on the coffee maker," Davenport said." "I just can't place where."

"Be happy to trade one secret for another."

***

"Lawrence," said Julia. "Good to hear from you. I have so many questions."

"Answer one of mine first," said Masterson.

"Sure."

"We've never found out why you and your family were included on the hit list."

"I can answer that one. Just learned myself, Monday.

Turns out the Conrios cartel contracted with a local P.I. to take all those pictures they sent out on the hit men's Androids. The man who took the pictures had a vendetta against me because I arrested his brother, now doing twenty years. He saw an opportunity to let the cartel take care of me and mine."

"I know this has to be true, it's too far-fetched to be made up."

"There's another piece to this story, making it even more bizarre. Suffice it to say the head of our Organized Crime Unit was also a relative of the prisoner. He knew I'd been slipped into the contract hit list, but never said or did anything to intervene."

"Nothing like being stabbed in the back by one of your own."

"Okay," she said. Fill in some blanks for me."

"Sure. Remember our big meeting of the alphabet department heads?"

"Yes."

"Somebody leaked confidential information from that meeting to Vargas, the head of the Conrios cartel. He, in turn, ordered the contract hits."

"Who leaked it?"

"The last person you'd expect, Aaron Collins, head of Homeland's Immigration and Customs Enforcement—ICE, in the alphabet world."

"My God."

"Turns out he had back surgery a few years ago and got hooked on oxycodone. He's been addicted for some time. Bribing government officials and law enforcement officers is a specialty of the cartels. Collins turned quickly. He's been keeping the cartel informed as to changes in the screening and inspection routines at the border. The cartel kept their trucks away from the border whenever inspections were to be increased or reinforced, and ran them through when things got more relaxed. On top of that, he diverted agents away from key drug routes and stash houses."

"The information must have had something special for him to order the contract hits?"

"The operation is still classified. Suffice to say the CIA figured out a way to confiscate the cartel's laundered money. Vargas believed an American banker was responsible, but he didn't know which one. So he ordered contracts on the whole group. Turns out Vargas also tried to take out the man who organized his money laundering. They had a small war. Vargas was killed, all his records destroyed. So, I'd say with Vargas dead, and your Memphis guys put away, you and your family are in the clear."

"You don't know what a relief this is," Julia said. "Thank you so much."

"My pleasure, Lieutenant. There's one more piece of intel I picked up. That warning email you received from Special Agent Cornell?"

"What about it?"

"I need to back into this one slowly. This intel is classified at the highest level. I had a hard time getting it. I hope you can live with a little ambiguity?"

"You know me. Probably not."

"That's what I thought. You're just like me. Well, here's what I can tell you. The email did in fact come from Special Agent Cornell's account, but Cornell didn't send it. The author of the email must remain anonymous to avoid the wrath of far more bad guys than just one little ole cartel leader. The email was intended to save your life and the lives of your family. And it obviously did. Indeed, it ultimately resulted in saving the lives of scores of people, and shutting down the Conrios cartel's operation here in the states."

"I don't know what to say. I'm so grateful, and yet I'm desperate to know."

"Someday you'll know, I have no doubt," said Masterson. "Just not now."

"So, I have a real guardian angel," Julia said. "We owe this angel our lives. Okay, I won't pursue a name. I promise."

## Chapter 70

# My Friend

*Saturday afternoon, Union Station…the conference call.* Teresa and Marino sat at different desks, telephones in hand.

"The camp counselor's name is Ms. Murphy," Teresa said. "She's been working with kids with Asperger's Syndrome for seventeen years, and she's been impressed with Jarvis's progress. We'll be on a super conference call, probably in another five minutes. They've found these kinds of calls work better when the parents are present. So, there'll be the two of us here and four on their end—Jarvis, Ms. Murphy, my brother Raif, and, of course, Alisya."

"It's been a few months since I've seen Jarvis," said Marino. "I'm trying to remember what to say and what not to say."

"Well, you remember the only conversation you had with him was when he went off about the New Madrid fault."

"Yeah, that was an experience. I just listened while he carried on and on in his one-way conversation, pontificating on every minute detail, covering more than three thousand years of history about the fault."

"And you remember your teacher friend's booklet—ask short specific questions, and be ready to wait for his reply. It might take a while. Raif said the counselors have been practicing with him on how to use the phone. I bet he's a whole lot better than when you talked to him a few months ago from California."

"Ms. Johnson, Sergeant Marino," said Murphy. "Are you there?"

"Yes," said Teresa. "We're both here."

"We'll be on a speaker phone with Jarvis and his parents. We've found this works well for our kids…go ahead, Jarvis. Say hello."

Jarvis fidgeted with his hands and began rocking back and forth.

"Hello, Jarvis. This is Sergeant Marino."

No response.

"He's smiling, Tony," said Raif.

"Jarvis?" said Murphy. "Say hello to Sergeant Marino, like we practiced."

"Hello, Sergeant Marino," said Jarvis, still rocking.

"Hi there, pal," said Marino. "Did you get the Road Atlas?"

"He can't see you nodding your head," said Murphy. "Answer his question."

"Yeah," Jarvis said.

"Which state had the best expressways?"

"No expressways."

"What does the Atlas call the roads?"

"Interstates and highways."

"That's right. So, which state had the best interstates and highways?"

"Arkansas."

"What makes Arkansas's the best?"

"No potholes."

Everyone laughed.

"I heard your father got lost and you told him which way to go."

"Yeah."

"What did you tell him?"

"I told him he was going the wrong way. Then he swore. Then he went faster. Then he pounded on the steering wheel…"

Raif hid his head, and Alisya kept laughing and gave him a gentle push.

"Okay, Jarvis. I get it," said Marino. "Did you tell him an interstate he should take?"

"No."

Marino's brain shifted into overdrive. What am I missing? he thought. Oh, if he didn't need to change interstates… "Did you tell him a direction he should go?"

"Yes."

"Which direction?"

"To Minnesota."

***

"Really, Tony, you were terrific," said Raif. "You have a gift. Thank you so much."

"Yes," said Alisya, grabbing the cell. "You can't know how much this means to Jarvis…how much it means to us. The counselors work all summer getting the kids to identify friends. Jarvis listed you as his friend from day one.

"Except for his discourse on the New Madrid fault, this is the most I've ever heard him talk," said Marino.

"It's more than that, Tony," said Alisya. It's the beginnings of an actual conversation. And it was done on the phone with his friend. It's a small miracle."

Chapter 71

# Pay It Back

*She's okay…my baby's okay.* Susan Determan finished the morning dishes and checked the mail. Sorting through the letters she found one postmarked New York City, the name *Slappy* printed by itself for the return address. She sat down, goose bumps covered her body. Slappy was the nickname she gave a gifted child in her second grade class some twenty-five years ago. She took a personal interest in the girl—arranging placement in the upper grades to challenge her ability levels, reporting her sexual abuse to child protective services, following her through multiple foster home placements, helping secure a full scholarship for her in a prestigious private boarding high school, and serving as her legal foster parent while she attended that school.

Her hands shook as she sliced open the envelope with a paring knife.

*Dear Momma Sue,*

*I apologize for not contacting you until now. My life has not been my own of late. I owe you so much. You have never wavered in your love for me, encouraging, supporting, even forgiving me. I was a child who never should have survived, but thanks to you I did. I was an adolescent who never should have had the opportunities I had, but thanks to you I did. I was a young adult who had no business having a successful career, but thanks to you I did. And for reasons unknown to me, I recently survived yet another terrible Chapter in my life, in large part thanks to things I learned from you.*

*It has been a long time coming, but I believe I am finally beginning to grow up, to mature, to forgive, to see life differently by seeing others in it. I want to give back.*

*I deposited ten million dollars in your bank account. Enclosed in this envelope is the name and phone number of an exceptional financial attorney who is waiting to hear from you. He has drawn up papers which will keep your money safe from crooks, unworthy relatives, and Uncle Sam. The money is yours, no strings attached. However, if you decide to donate any of it, your attorney will draw up those papers as well. And if you do that I would only ask that you consider supporting programs to help children who went through things I did, indeed, things that both of us experienced as kids.*

*I will keep in touch, but for now I must remain apart.*

*All my love,*

*Slappy*


Determan read the letter again through her tears, a third time, then a fourth. My little girl's alive, she thought. My little girl's become a woman, a mature woman. Dare I hope? Yes, darling Charleze, this money will go to help sexually abused children.

## Chapter 72

# Waving Hands In The Clouds

*The Haven…a mini-recital.* Julia and Mark sat on the new sofa in Aunt Louise's apartment. The coffee table and chairs had been moved aside. Louise, Beth, and Dell stood in the living room, Louise in the middle, two steps in front of her friends. Delicate Asian music played softly from an iPod.

"Ready?" Louise said.

"Ready," said Beth.

"Me too," said Dell.

They began to move slowly, gracefully, in lockstep. Every once in a while Louise quietly called out a movement.

"Wave hands in the clouds, to the right," Louise said.

"It doesn't look like they're waving anywhere near the clouds to me," Julia whispered.

"I think they look pretty good, especially for Tai Chi beginners," said Mark. "They're staying right together."

"I thought Tai Chi was like Kung Fu," Julia said. "Are they going to break any boards?"

"Historically, it was a martial art form," Mark said. "These are the movements practiced by Chinese armies for thousands of years. Of course, they put a lot more power in their movements. They were designed for combat."

"Really?"

"I'm thinking waving hands in the clouds is like the Karate

Kid's *wax on-wax off.*"

"Oh, I see it."

"I just had a thought," Mark said.

"Here's a penny."

"Today is preparing us for watching all those dance recit-als and such, if we ever have kids."

Julia's mouth fell open.

"All right, you two," said Louise. "You're supposed to be watching us."

"We are," said Mark, applauding. "You three are terrific. Julia, take some pictures."

# FACTS

**Charlie Munger:** In May 2013, the 89 year-old Vice Chairman and right hand man of Warren Buffet at Berkshire Hathaway was quoted as saying "You can't trust bankers to control themselves." Note: Berkshire Hathaway maintains bank stocks in their portfolio.

**Bernard Madoff:** In 2009 Madoff plead guilty to eleven federal felonies related to a massive Ponzi scheme involving an estimated $50 billion. Madoff, chairman of Bernard L. Madoff Investment Securities from 1960 until his arrest in December 2008, said he began the Ponzi scheme in the early 1990s, but federal investigators believed the fraud began in the 1970s. He is currently serving a 150-year prison sentence. Note: In 2009 SEC Inspector General David Kotz reported to the U.S. Senate Committee on Banking, Housing and Urban Affairs that an SEC examination in 1992 revealed concerns of possible fraud, followed by six significant formal complaints filed with the SEC. In 2004 and 2005 two parallel investigations were conducted. Both identified red flags, but no subsequent investigations were recommended. Kotz did not find evidence of criminal wrongdoing on the part of SEC personnel.

**R. Allen Stanford:** In 2009 the SEC charged Stanford with multiple violations of US securities laws for a massive Ponzi scheme and fraud involving $8 billion. Companies under Stanford's control were also alleged to have engaged in bribery, money laundering, and political manipulation. Stanford Financial Group of Companies maintained offices in Houston, Memphis, and Tupelo, MS. His Stanford International Bank was based in the Caribbean. He is currently serving a 110-year prison sentence. Note: In 2010 Securities and Exchange Commission (SEC) Inspector General David Kotz reported to the Senate Committee on Banking, Housing and Urban Affairs that the SEC office in Fort Worth suspected a Ponzi scheme or similar fraud when reviewing Stanford's activities in 1997, 1998, 2002 and 2004. Kotz alleged the head of enforcement for the SEC's Fort Worth office worked to prevent meaningful investigations and, after leaving the SEC, performed legal work for Stanford in defense of the investigation by the same SEC enforcement group he formerly managed.

**Morgan Keegan**: In 2010 the Securities and Exchange Commission (SEC) filed a federal civil suit alleging Memphis-based Morgan Keegan, its mutual fund manager, and others defrauded investors by inflating the value of risky subprime securities. Investors nationwide lost an estimated $1.5 billion. The alleged fraud occurred from 2006 to 2008. Morgan Keegan reportedly set aside $200 million to resolve the regulatory issues. Eight former mutual fund directors from Memphis and Birmingham, admitted to no wrongdoing, but agreed not to break securities laws in the future as they settled with the SEC in 2013, with no jail time.

**Wachovia bank**: In 2010, following four years of investigation, the Drug Enforcement Administration (DEA) charged the United States' fourth largest bank with processing proceeds of illicit activity and willfully failing to establish an anti-money laundering program. As part of an agreement, Wachovia forfeited $110 million to the US and paid an additional $50 million fine to the US Treasury, but no jail time. Wachovia was purchased by Wells Fargo and Company.

**HSBC** (British-based Hong Kong and Shanghai Bank Corporation): In 2012, Europe's largest bank, through its numerous global subsidiaries, including those in the USA, was found to have laundered money for drug cartels, terrorists, sanctioned countries including Iran, and a Saudi bank linked to al-Qaida. The subsidiaries reportedly transported billions of dollars of cash, cleared what were identified as *suspicious travelers' checks* worth billions, and allowed Mexican drug lords to launder money through Cayman Islands accounts. The US Justice Department agreed to a settlement of $1.9 billion, without jail time.

**Liberty Reserve**: In 2013, this Costa Rican bank was shut down following charges it laundered more than $6 billion for the criminal underworld. The bank provided digital currency in exchange for real money, without proof of identity. The Liberty Reserve website offered what prosecutors called *PayPal for criminals,* saying it allowed users to transfer money without leaving a trace. The system allegedly was designed to move money earned from credit card fraud, online Ponzi schemes, child pornography, and other crimes without being detected by law enforcement. The bank had about one million users worldwide, including some 200,000 people in the US. The investigation is ongoing.

**Mexican cartels**: Mexico's drug-related violence has claimed an estimated 50,000 lives from December 2006 through December 2012, including 17,000 deaths in 2011.

A 2009 report from the US Department of Justice called Mexican drug-trafficking organizations "the greatest organized crime threat to the United States." Note: In 2013 Jose Martinez, a Mexican cartel hitman, confessed to murdering more than 30 people over the past 7 years within the United States, from Florida to California.

**ICIJ**: In April 2013, the International Consortium of Investigative Journalists released its report *Secrecy For Sale: Inside The Global Offshore Money Maze*. Eighty-six journalists from 46 countries contributed to this global investigation of 120,000 offshore companies and trusts, representing 130,000 clients and agents from 170 countries. The report has been the subject of a G-20 summit, concerned with lost tax revenue and bankruptcy for entire countries, as well as the subsidizing of a range of international crime and terrorism.

**Legal Framework**: US statutes have covered money laundering for decades. The Bank Secrecy Act of 1970 required businesses to maintain records related to criminal, tax, and regulatory matters. The Money Laundering Control Act of 1986 criminalized money laundering. The USA Patriot Act of 2001, in part, amended the Bank Secrecy Act requiring financial institutions to establish proactive anti-money laundering programs, as monitored by the Financial Crimes Enforcement Network (FinCEN).

**Financial Action Task Force on Money Laundering (FATF)**: The G-7 Summit, concerned with the loss of revenue to governments of its member nations and the growing subsidy of international crime, authorized the formation of the FATF at its 1989 meeting in Paris, France. Currently, the FATF consists of representatives of thirty-four member nations.